VAETRA UNVEILED

BOOK ONE OF THE
VAETRA CHRONICLES

DANIEL R

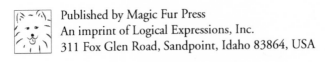
Published by Magic Fur Press
An imprint of Logical Expressions, Inc.
311 Fox Glen Road, Sandpoint, Idaho 83864, USA

This is a work of fiction. All names, characters, places, and events are either the product of the author's imagination or are used fictitiously. Any resemblance to actual persons, living or dead, business organizations, events, or locales is purely coincidental.

VAETRA UNVEILED

ISBN: 978-1-61038-007-2 (paperback)
      978-1-61038-009-6 (hardback)
      978-1-61038-008-9 (EPUB)

For my wife Susan.
Your patience gives me determination,
your support gives me courage,
and your love sustains me.

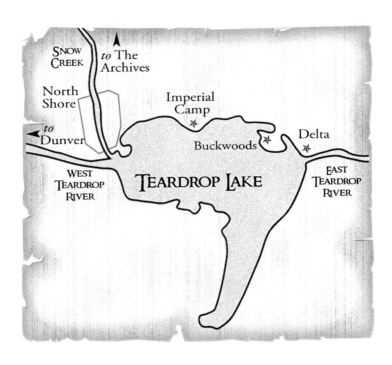

CHAPTER 1

The folded piece of parchment was sealed with a tiny dot of red wax. It had my name on it: *Jaylan Forester*. I peeled the note open and read the words scrawled inside. *Need help. Meet at inn at dusk. Can pay.*

I looked up at Captain Borlan Koster. His deep brown eyes were watching my green ones as he leaned over his desk, bracing his sturdy dark frame with his fists on the stained surface. His stance would be intimidating to people who didn't know him, but Borlan had been my friend and my boss for more than a year. We stood in the sparsely furnished entry area at the Northshore town chapter of Raven Company, next to the front desk where Borlan met with clients.

"Who dropped this off?" I asked.

Borlan shrugged. "I didn't see. I just heard the front door open and shut. The note was on the front desk when I came downstairs. What's it about?"

I shook my head, turning the note over in my hand and scowling. "No idea. The note just says to meet at the inn later." I handed it to Borlan.

He grinned as he read the note. "I like the 'can pay' part," he said, handing it back to me. The dark skin of his scarred hand contrasted sharply with the light, freckled skin of mine. We were physical opposites; he was tall, dark, and bulky with short-cropped black hair, while I was lean, pale, average in height, and wore my long red hair tied behind my back. When people saw us walking together, they often did a double-take.

I slipped the note into my pocket. "We'll see. If the coin is worth the work, I won't turn it down. Whoever it is must know something about me and what I do here."

Borlan nodded. "Or knows someone who does."

Raven Company mostly employed mercenary soldiers who worked as guards for hire. I did that kind of work when necessary, but my skills and background made me more valuable to Borlan as a problem solver. I was better than most people at finding things that were lost and digging out the truth when it was hidden. If the person who wrote the note just needed a bodyguard, Borlan would have been the logical addressee, and any Raven Company man could have done the job.

"I guess I'll find out at dusk," I said. "Any other prospects?" Business had been slow lately. The regular contracts for bodyguards and caravan guards were disappointingly thin at the moment, and we'd had none of the commissions that took advantage of my skills.

Borlan pursed his lips and shook his head. "If something comes up, you'll be the first to know. Finding work for you would be good for all of us." He'd be happy because my contracts were some of the most lucrative, and Raven Company got a cut of whatever I made on a job. "We did get work for two men, and I assigned Kefer and Peltor to it. They're escorting a wagon from Delta to Plains End. Small job, but it's something."

"Good to hear," I said. "Maybe this will turn into something good too," I added, patting the pocket with the note. "Well, I'd better get back to the inn. Dusk is only an hour or two away, and Dela needs me to help her with something. I'll let you know how the meeting goes." I raised my hand in farewell and headed toward the door.

"That girl will have you married and settled down as an innkeeper before the year is out," Borlan said with a laugh.

"Let's see if we can get me some more work here so that isn't necessary," I said wryly over my shoulder as I opened the door to leave.

"Which, being an innkeeper or getting married?" Borlan teased.

I closed the door behind me without answering him. "Either," I said to myself after the door had closed completely.

∼

I was glad for my thick woolen shirt as I headed back to the Snow Creek Inn. A breeze stirred the budding branches of the birch in front of the Raven Company building, adding to the late afternoon chill. The previous night's rain had slowed to a light, misty drizzle for most of the day. The sun was just above the mountain peaks to the west, but it was barely visible as a bright spot in the clouds.

I crossed the street, dodging horses and nodding to townspeople on their final errands of the day. I was thankful the streets had dried enough to firm up before the recent storm arrived. Just two weeks ago, the streets had been rivers of rutted mud and half-frozen puddles.

A customer went into the bakery as I passed, and the delicious aromas escaping the open door made me salivate. But I wasn't tempted to stop. One of the nice things about living at the inn was that fresh bread was always available.

Across the way, Burl the blacksmith was cleaning up as he prepared to close his shop. I waved to him when he looked up, and he tentatively waved back. Apparently, I still had more work to do to restore my reputation around town.

As I walked, I pondered what this new job might be about. Why the mystery? Most Raven Company clients just walked into the office and told us what they wanted. Someone obviously did not want to be seen talking with us. Well, with *me* actually.

I shook my head and chastised myself for the directions my thoughts were going. I'd learn more soon, and any speculation before then would just be making up stories. I seriously hoped it was a job I could take. I wasn't cut out to be a full-time innkeeper, even if my share of the income from the inn did cover my basic needs.

Dela disagreed with that assessment, of course. She was the eighteen-year-old daughter of my late partner, Griz, and now she and her mother, Luma, ran the inn. Dela had recently decided that our pairing was meant to be, since I was single and already invested in the business. In her eyes, we would make a perfect couple.

She didn't understand that the life of an innkeeper wasn't enough for me.

I had originally invested money in the inn three years ago to help out my friend Griz when he decided to buy and renovate the venerable building. At that time, I was the recently-promoted Captain of the Imperial Guard here in Northshore. I had plenty of cash and not much to do with it.

But then everything had changed. I scowled at the memory, and a little boy who was walking the opposite direction with his mother clutched her hand tightly and hugged closer to her when he saw the look on my face. His mother glared at me as she passed, and I shrugged my shoulders in mute apology.

A little over a year ago, I had discovered that Belomy Trask, the local tax collector and brother of Northshore Governor Marrin Trask, was running what amounted to an extortion scheme. His job was to collect the Imperial and local taxes. But he collected more than the mandated amounts and filled his own purse with the surcharge. Merchants who refused to pay the extra coin experienced an unusual amount of misfortune in their business or family.

Before I could build enough evidence to prosecute Trask, I found myself accused of masterminding the crime. It seemed that no one wanted me to investigate, not even the victims. Rakerus, my second-in-command and the man who eventually replaced me as Captain, was allowed to prove that no such crime had taken place. I was exonerated, and the true conspirators smugly let me walk away.

But Belomy Trask made sure that my career in the Guard was over. According to him, I had falsely accused a respected family and had proven myself unworthy of my responsibilities. The years I had invested in that career were wasted. Well, almost.

I turned onto Cedar Street and passed the Stone Tonic Shop. I scowled at the front door as I walked by. Caslin Stone, the proprietor, had been one of the townspeople who had warned me not to pursue the investigation. He had testified along with a few other shopkeepers that no crime had been committed, thus helping to exonerate me, but also sealing my fate with the Imperial Guard.

Down the road ahead of me, I could see the sign for the Snow Creek Inn swinging slowly on its chains above the front door. The inn represented my salvation to a degree. It was there I had holed up after being expelled from the Guard. My apartment was attached to the north side of the building, and it had given me plenty of room to sulk.

Griz and Luma had given me time to recover and offered me a more active role in operating the inn. Meanwhile, Dela defended me in arguments with townspeople who sneered at my failure. She argued with such confidence and maturity that I was shocked to realize that she was no longer my friend's gawky little girl; she had grown into a strong and attractive woman.

Initially feeling betrayed by the town I loved, I was grateful for Dela's friendship and attention. I should have realized that her feelings ran much deeper than mine, and that the eight-year difference in our ages didn't matter to her. I should have set her straight when I first recognized that her feelings were becoming romantic, but even now I couldn't bring myself to break her heart when she had worked so hard to heal mine.

For a while, the distraction of helping out at the inn had been welcome, but doing the work of a stable boy and barkeep eventually left me restless and miserable. That's when my friend Rakerus suggested I consider going to work with Raven Company.

I was resistant at first. As Captain of the Imperial Guard, I was used to thinking of Raven Company as a potential source of trouble. I had doubts about the ethics of a band of mercenaries, although truthfully, they had never given me reason to distrust them.

But then one day last spring, a well-dressed merchant arrived at the inn and paid for a room. When I took his horse, his attitude toward me was so condescending that I nearly punched him right there in front of the stable. That was when I knew I had to do something else with my life, and I needed to do it quickly.

I went to the Raven Company offices the next morning and talked with Borlan about working with them. We both knew of each other, and after some cautious conversational circling and testing, we realized we had a lot in common. Over the months and the jobs that followed, we became good friends.

I sighed as I approached the inn. Mercenary work paid well, and it was challenging in a satisfying way, but it wasn't steady. I thought once again of the note in my pocket. Maybe the dry spell was finally easing up.

～

I opened the door to the inn, and as I entered the serving room, mouth-watering food aromas enveloped me. The kitchen staff was busy preparing for the evening meal, and my stomach growled in anticipation.

Weak afternoon light filtered through the front windows, barely fighting back the darkness of the room. The regular patrons seemed to prefer the gloom, as they were all huddled at the tables furthest from the door or were hunched over stools at the bar along the back wall. Oil lanterns hung along the overhead beams softly lit their quiet conversations.

Dela looked up from wiping down the bar and called to me. "Where have you been? I still need you to get those potatoes and chives for Mother's soup tomorrow."

Dela is one of those women who dominates the room. Her tall, full-figured build caught the eye of most men, while her green eyes and full-lipped smile charmed them. She moved with confidence and purpose and brooked no foolery from the patrons. Men who had the temerity to pinch her butt as she walked by usually found themselves led out the front door by their ear with the admonition not to return until they had learned some manners.

One of the men at the bar looked over at me and chuckled. I rolled my eyes.

"I told you I'd take care of it, and I will. I just need to pick up the list you made," I said.

"Where were you anyway?" she asked. "You're going to run out of daylight."

"I was at Raven Company. I have a lead on a new contract and needed to meet with Borlan."

She frowned and looked down at the counter, scrubbing a little more vigorously. "Things are busy here, and I need your help. Can't you put off your contracts for a while?"

"It doesn't work like that," I said patiently. "I'm either in or I'm out. Raven Company needs men they can rely on to take contracts when they are available." I knew my mistake as soon as I spoke.

She stopped cleaning the counter and threw the cloth into a tub of water with a splash. "*I* need you to be reliable too! Spring business is picking up, and it's too much for just Mother and me." She came around the counter, wiping her hands on her apron, and stood in front of me. She put a hand on my arm and spoke more softly. "Besides, I need you. We can't let all the hard work that Father did go to waste. I don't know what would happen to us if the inn were to fail."

I sighed. "You know that running an inn has never been my goal. I invested in the inn so I could have the apartment and help out your father."

She rubbed her hand up and down my arm affectionately. "I know, but you can't return to the Guard, and Raven Company doesn't have enough work. We have plenty to do here."

I knew it was useless to continue the discussion. We'd had more or less the same exchange every day for the past month. The idea of settling down with Dela and becoming an innkeeper had its appeal; it would be the easy path to take. But whenever my thoughts went down that path, I felt like I would be betraying Griz and maybe even Dela. I remembered Dela from when she skipped around with a rag doll in her hand. She was grown now, but I still had trouble seeing her as anything other than a kid sister.

But, unfortunately, she was right. Things were slow at Raven Company, particularly for the investigation work I preferred and that Borlan singled out for me. Meanwhile, business at the inn was on the rise. We were getting more travelers, and the locals were discovering that the kitchen served an excellent meal at a reasonable price.

I wished Griz were still around. Things would have been so much simpler. He would have been thrilled to see the inn beginning to thrive, making all that hard work—the work that essentially killed him—pay off. It wasn't fair that his heart gave out just as he was completing the renovations.

Dela's eyes scanned my face, seeming to read my train of thought. "I know," she said quietly. "If father were still here, things would be different." She looked down at the floor. "He'd take care of the inn, and you could run off on your adventures."

As much as I cared for Dela, and as much as I hoped the inn would grow into the success Griz had envisioned, Dela's subtle manipulations got on my nerves. I needed to leave before I said something I'd regret.

"I'd better get going. Do you have that list?"

Dela looked into my eyes for a moment and saw the unyielding set of my face. She went over to the bar and came back with a slip of parchment that listed the things she wanted me to pick up. I looked over the list and decided I should have plenty of time to take care of it before dusk and get back for my meeting.

I turned and headed out the door without saying another word. I swore to myself that my future would not consist of running errands for Dela.

CHAPTER 2

The young man walked slowly into the inn and hesitated just inside the door. He filled the opening more than most men, and his gaze scanned the room. When his eyes met mine, I gave him a subtle nod.

He wound his way through the tables, looking aside at the other patrons several times. His caution made him conspicuous to anyone who watched him closely, defeating his obvious desire for secrecy.

When he reached my table, he remained standing and looked me over. "Jaylan?" he asked softly. I nodded again.

He swept into the chair next to me with a waft of stale sweat and damp wool. Tiny beads of condensed mist slipped off his cloak to the floor as he settled in. He glanced at me with haunted eyes underscored by dark circles. Those eyes belied the softly bearded face of youth that came with them. He shivered, adjusting to the close warmth of the inn's serving room. Scanning the room once more, he sighed and deflated into a hunch over the table.

He cleared his throat and spoke in a low, hoarse voice. "Thanks for meeting me. I'm Raleb."

"No thanks necessary," I replied. "Although I admit I'm curious. Your message was rather vague." I took a sip of my ale and raised the mug toward Dela as she passed, tilting my head in the direction of the man next to me. She scowled down her nose at him but nodded in acknowledgement.

"Sorry about that. It had to be. It's a sensitive matter," he said as he ran a thin, shaking hand through his dark, wet hair.

"You should take off that wet cloak," I suggested. "You're freezing." Our table was close to the fire, making my choice of seating comfortably warm. His soggy cloak had already started to steam a bit around his shoulders.

He shook his head. "Thanks, but I may need to leave quickly."

It was as I suspected, then. Raleb was a man on the run. Disappointment soured my mood as I realized the odds were high that this job would require me to do something illegal or at least unethical. I'd have to refuse the contract.

"Then I suppose you should tell me what it is you need from me," I prompted with little enthusiasm.

He looked over at me, reading my reticence. "You're right, we shouldn't waste time, but please hear me out." I nodded for him to continue.

"My partner and I were hired to...*retrieve* an item for a client. We succeeded and were on our way back when we were ambushed last night. We got separated, and I escaped. I don't know what happened to my partner or the item he was carrying. I've been trying to find him, but I'm still being hunted."

"By whom?" I asked. He looked up quickly and said nothing as Dela approached with a tankard of ale.

"Thanks, Dela. Please put it on my tab," I told her with a wink as she set the mug on the table.

"Oh, yes sir," she responded sarcastically and quickly moved off to answer the hail of another customer.

Raleb waited until she left and then continued. "I don't *know* who it is," he growled. "They tracked us somehow, and I didn't think it would be a good idea to stop and ask them why." He took a long drink of his ale and closed his eyes with a groan that was almost a sigh.

"Probably wise," I concurred. "So why did you want to meet with me?"

"The man who hired us won't be pleased with failure. But I can't search for Donal, my partner, while I'm trying to evade the hunters. I need help finding him while I work on staying alive."

I interrupted him with a raised hand. "Not to put too fine a point on it, but I can't involve myself with stolen goods."

"Yes, that is your reputation. But you *can* help find a missing person, right? I don't care about the item," he said bitterly.

"Perhaps." I nodded slowly. It seemed unlikely that a thief wouldn't care about the stolen goods, but I sensed no guile in his words. I still didn't like the feel of this contract, but finding a missing person was right in line with the work I normally did for Raven Company.

"I can pay, of course," he said. Below the table, his hand reached inside his cloak. I tensed and eased back from him instantly, and his hand stopped moving. "May I?" he asked with a raised eyebrow.

"Sorry. Automatic reaction," I answered. I relaxed, but remained alert.

"Believe me, I completely understand," he said under his breath as his hand emerged from his cloak with a small leather purse. "It isn't much, but it's most of what I have with me." He offered the purse to me under the table, and I accepted it from him.

I loosened the lacing and quickly peered under the table at the contents of the purse. A satisfying quantity of gold and silver twinkled from within. I looked over at him, both eyebrows raised. "That's plenty. For a couple of weeks anyway. One week if you want me to hire bodyguards for you."

"Thanks, but bodyguards would just draw attention to me. If you haven't found Donal within two weeks, I doubt I'll be around to be disappointed about it." He drank more of his ale and seemed to re-inflate a bit. Something about the way he said the name hinted at a level of respect and affection that went beyond a normal business partnership. I got the impression that Donal was a trusted mentor or perhaps even his father.

"Where did you last see him?" I asked.

"West of here. About a half-day's ride. We were on the main road when a group of four riders stopped us and demanded that we give them the item Donal was carrying." He shook his head. "I don't understand how they knew about it or how they knew we had it. We had no choice but to run and hope we could lose them."

I didn't want to hear any more about "the item." It was definitely the source of my concerns about this contract.

"How do I get back in touch with you?" I asked as I discreetly slipped the purse under my vest, committing myself to the contract despite my misgivings. The amount he had given me compensated for a certain amount of moral discomfort.

"You don't. Meet me behind the big barn north of town, the one that's just this side of the forest, at dusk again in two days time." He took a deep, final swig of his ale and slid his chair back.

I nodded and said, "I know that barn. I'll try to have something useful to tell you by then." I smiled encouragingly. "I don't suppose you need a receipt for this?"

He chuckled once, a fleeting hint of a smile at the corners of his mouth. "I just hope you find him before the others do," he said seriously. "Thanks for taking the job."

"I'll do what I can," I promised.

"In two days then," was his parting response.

He stepped over to Dela for a short, whispered conversation. She nodded and pointed toward the kitchen. Dela's mother stood at the bar near the kitchen door, closely observing their exchange. Anticipating what was wanted, she nodded once and hooked her thumb toward the kitchen door.

Raleb pulled his cloak closed, ducked his head, and slipped quietly through the door to the kitchen, where I knew he would exit the inn through a back door.

My last sip of ale was interrupted by a muffled shout and a clash of arms from behind the inn.

Slamming my mug on the table, I jumped from my seat and rushed through the kitchen. I nearly knocked over Sedora, our aging cook, as she stared nervously at the back door, a knife and a loaf of bread held absently in her hands.

With a mumbled apology I grabbed her by the shoulders to steady her. I then carefully stepped over to the door to listen.

It seemed the scuffle was over. I couldn't hear any more fighting. But I did hear muffled voices, including Raleb's. I eased the door open slowly and peered out into the drifting mist.

⌇

The kitchen door hinges were silent, but the light from the room behind me spilled out to illuminate a strip of ground behind the inn. Raleb was on his knees in the mud. A man was roughly tying Raleb's hands behind his back, while before him stood a woman holding a crossbow to her shoulder, aimed straight at his chest. He hung his head in silent defeat.

Both of Raleb's captors wore studded leather armor, stained dark by the drizzling mist and muddied by travel. The man wore a felt hood that draped limply around his unshaven face.

The woman shifted position to put both Raleb and me in sight and called out, "Either go back inside, or come out with your hands where I can see them."

I removed my hand from the hilt of the dagger in my belt, eased the door open slowly, and stepped out showing her the palms of both hands. Behind me, Sedora closed the door, and the bar thudded into place. Ah well, I couldn't blame her for that.

The door closed off the only source of illumination behind the inn, leaving me facing Raleb and his captors in the gathering darkness. I had just enough light to see their tired faces and edgy movements.

"Who are you, and what business do you have with this man?" the woman demanded, tilting the crossbow toward Raleb while keeping it squarely pointed at me.

"I could ask you the same thing," I responded with some annoyance. I get cranky when someone draws a weapon on me without provocation.

"Well, since I have the crossbow and this man is a known criminal, I think we'll answer my questions first," she retorted. Her partner grunted in agreement as he guided Raleb back to his feet, one hand on Raleb's shoulder, and the other holding the rope that bound the scowling thief's hands.

She was too far away for me to try anything fancy. I'd be a pincushion before I took two steps toward her, and light crossbow or no, getting skewered by a crossbow bolt would be inconvenient.

I was trying to decide how much to tell her when the sound of clattering mail and running boots came toward us from around the side of the inn.

"Imperial Guard! Drop your weapons!" shouted a burly guard as he drew his sword and approached. The second guard also drew his weapon, but stayed back a few steps. He held a flickering torch that glinted off the exposed steel of their swords and dimly lit our little scene.

I knew Jorj Berman, the guardsman who stepped forward. In my time as Captain, he had been a gate guard. It seemed he had managed a promotion to Constable, a job that put him in more direct contact with the townspeople and required more initiative and judgment. Good for him. I didn't recognize the second guard.

The woman's aim never wavered from me, and her eyes only glanced at the guard as he approached. "I'm Agent

Sulana Delano, and this is Agent Daven Prost," she said with a tilt of her head toward the man holding Raleb. "Captain Pollard knows we're here to take this thief into custody."

Captain Pollard would be Rakerus Pollard, my one-time second-in-command and the current Captain of the Imperial Guard. The same man who had convinced me to seek employment at Raven Company.

The guard nodded and sheathed his sword. "The Captain told us about you." Seeing Raleb held securely by Agent Prost, he turned to me. "Good evening, Cap…Mister Forester. How are you involved in this?"

"That's just what I was asking a moment ago," the woman interjected. "It seems a popular question. Suppose you answer it," she said to me.

"Agent, is it?" I said. "Agent of what?"

"Please don't try my patience. Just answer the question," she said tightly.

The arrival and apparent acceptance of the guards reassured me somewhat. I looked at Raleb, but he didn't meet my eyes.

"Fine. This man hired me to locate a lost friend." It was the truth. Not exactly informative, but the truth.

"Yes, I know all about his *lost friend*," she said with an eye roll. "We've been tracking them both for a while now. What do you know about the item they stole?"

"There was no mention of a *stolen* item," I hedged. "He did say that an item of some importance was involved, but he didn't say what it was, and locating it was not part of my task."

Constable Berman interrupted. "Agent Delano, I would appreciate it if you would lower your weapon. I know this man, and if he says he isn't involved in the theft, then he isn't."

Lucky for me, Berman was apparently one of the men who thought I got a raw deal when I was discharged from the Imperial Guard. The guardsmen had been about evenly split between those who were happy to see me go, those who thought I'd been treated unfairly, and those who didn't give a pigeon dropping either way.

She lowered her arms and pointed the crossbow at the ground, which was nice as it made the tickling feeling in my chest go away. It's much easier to have a civil conversation when you aren't worried about an errant muscle spasm sending a bolt through your heart. I lowered my hands slowly to my sides, carefully keeping them away from the front of my vest, which didn't quite conceal the dagger at my waist.

Raleb glanced from the woman to me. "The job still stands, if you'll do it," he blurted with a desperate edge.

I hesitated, and then replied. "That all depends upon our friends here."

"We don't need help, and I don't want you in the way," Agent Delano said curtly. "If you interfere, it will prove that you are in on this and we'll deal with you accordingly."

Agent Prost cleared his throat. "This man is local. He could be useful if he knows the surrounding area well."

"No! This mission is too important to blindly trust someone we know nothing about and who has questionable ties to the very men we are hunting," she replied.

"Look," I said with a little heat, "I never met this man before tonight, I know nothing about this item you seek, and all I was hired to do was locate his friend. I'm still willing to help with that part of it, and I don't give a damn what you do with this item, even if we do run across it."

She narrowed her eyes at me and was silent for a few moments.

She finally pursed her lips and nodded her head once. "Here's the deal," she said, "You stay where I can see you at all times, and you head straight back here if I tell you to leave. As soon as we locate the other man, your job is done, and you return here immediately."

In the dim light, she probably couldn't see the color rise into my face as she spoke. I'm much more accustomed to giving orders than receiving them, and being treated like some kind of criminal or yokel was getting on my nerves. I really wanted to take this woman down a peg, but continuing to be confrontational wouldn't help me or my notorious client.

I bit back the response I wanted to make and answered calmly. "That works for me. When do we start?"

"Right now. Get what you need, and be quick about it," she said as she removed the bolt from her crossbow and eased the tension on the string.

Her partner spoke up again, "Sulana...we've been sleeping in the saddle for two days. I think we could all use a decent night's rest."

She looked up and glared at him as he started to speak. Before he finished, she opened her mouth to interrupt him, but then stopped herself, closed her eyes, and sighed heavily. "I guess you're right," she said, and then she squared her shoulders. "We'll spend the night in town and head out tomorrow morning just before dawn."

She turned to Constable Berman and asked, "Would you be willing to keep this man locked up for us until we can return for him?"

"I'll check with the Captain," he said with a nod, "but I'm sure that won't be a problem." He motioned to his partner to take Raleb into custody. The second guard sheathed his sword, handed his torch to Berman, and approached Agent Prost. The agent handed him the end of the rope that bound Raleb's hands. Raleb stared sullenly at Agent Delano.

After watching the exchange, she turned back to me. "We'll meet you in the serving room of this inn about an hour before dawn tomorrow. Be ready to go, and don't get any ideas about heading out by yourself before then."

Slowly shaking my head in frustration, I mumbled, "Yeah, I got it. I'll be ready."

"Good. As long as we're clear." And with that, she turned and walked off, apparently certain her orders would be obeyed without hesitation.

Her partner looked over at me, raised an eyebrow and snorted in amusement, and then followed quickly in the wake of his commander.

I couldn't help wondering what, exactly, I had gotten myself into.

CHAPTER 3

Agent Sulana Delano stepped out into the chilly twilight of the approaching dawn with Agent Daven Prost at her side. A good night's sleep and a satisfying hot breakfast helped erase the fatigue of two cold wet days in the saddle. She was impatient to continue her search for the remaining thief, but her mind and body appreciated the brief respite.

Sulana and her team had spent the night at the local Sanctuary, a home known to be sorcerer-friendly. Agents Talon Destry and Barek Hunter, the other two members of her team, stayed at the house to prepare for the day's journey. The two men had been keeping watch at the front of the inn the night before and had missed all the excitement.

"Are you sure we have time for this?" Daven asked Sulana as they walked through the mostly deserted streets toward the Governor's Complex.

"I'm not going to take this man Jaylan Forester along with us until I know more about him," she insisted. "Our host at the Sanctuary knew little, other than that he lost his place as Captain of the local Imperial Guard detachment last year." She looked over at him. "You don't need to come you know. I don't think I'm in any particular danger on the streets of Northshore."

Daven blushed a bit, but shook his head emphatically. "I'd be doing a poor job of my duties to let you walk off into the dark alone."

Sulana was a Sword Sorceress, and the only member of her team skilled in sorcery. Daven's primary job was to protect her while she conjured. He was, in effect, a bodyguard. She sometimes thought he took his responsibilities a little too literally.

Sulana rolled her eyes and held up her hands in surrender. "Fine. Then let me do *my* job. I'm responsible for this team, and I take my job seriously too."

Daven smiled and said, "Yes, ma'am," dipping his head toward her in a slight bow as they continued walking.

Sulana scoffed and turned her attention to the Governor's Complex ahead of them.

Every province in the Tanes Empire had a capital city, and every capital city, including Northshore, had a Governor's Complex. The complex was like a town within a town. It was gated and surrounded by its own wall. Within the wall were the Governor's home, a barracks for a troop of the Imperial Guard, a prison, a commissary, an infirmary, and a large stable.

The gates to the complex stood open, and two guards stood at ease just inside the opening. One guard covered a yawn, but both men straightened up when they saw Sulana and Daven approaching. The guards each wore a maroon tabard over their armor, the rampant eagle emblem on the front proclaiming them to be Imperial Guards. The guard on the right was a big, red-bearded man who quickly assessed the approaching strangers and addressed Daven.

"How can I help you this morning?" he asked.

Sulana, unimpressed with the guard's conclusion of who was in charge, stepped forward and answered. "We're here to see Captain Pollard."

The man looked her up and down and grinned. "Then I suggest you come back later. Like at noon."

Sulana shook her head. "I'm Agent Sulana Delano. The Captain knows I'm here in Northshore and has agreed to help. I need information from him, and it can't wait. We need to leave shortly."

The guard narrowed his eyes at her and thought for a moment. "Yeah, I heard about you. I'll let you pass, but you'll have to convince the Captain's secretary that it's urgent." He stepped back and swept his hand aside in invitation.

"Let me worry about that," Sulana said as she stepped quickly through the gate and headed toward the Captain's office.

～

Inside the captain's office, the secretary wrung his hands. The fussy little man looked like an insufficiently stuffed scarecrow with his belted tunic draping loosely over his thin frame. "Agent Delano, you don't understand. Captain Pollard is late to bed and late to rise. If I wake him now, we'll all be paying for it the rest of the day."

Sulana folded her arms. "He can go back to sleep after we leave. I just need a moment of his time, and it's very important. Please wake him now."

The secretary sighed deeply and hung his head. Then he took a deep breath, gathered himself, and exited the room through the door to the inner chamber.

A moment later, Sulana and Daven both jumped at a roar of rage from the other room. They couldn't hear exactly what was said, but the sentiment was clear.

The secretary scuttled out of the back room and closed the door carefully behind him. He glanced over at Sulana with an injured look and positioned himself in the back corner of the room away from the door he'd just exited. "The captain will be with you in a moment. I hope for your sake that it really is important," he said with a shaking voice.

They heard a few bumps and grumbling from the other room, and then the door opened. Captain Pollard straightened his shirt and ran a hand through his sleep-mussed hair as he stepped into the room. He glared at his visitors.

"What could possibly be so important that it has to be dealt with before the first light of dawn?" he shouted. The secretary cringed in his corner, but echoed his master's glare at the interlopers.

Sulana replied calmly. "We're leaving at dawn and I need to know something before we go. It's important to my mission."

He motioned his hand in a circle, encouraging her to continue. "Well, out with it then. What do you need to know?"

"I need to ask you about Jaylan Forester," she replied.

The captain's brow knitted in confusion. "How is he involved?" He looked over at his secretary for enlightenment, but the secretary shook his head and shrugged his shoulders.

"It seems our thief hired Mister Forester to help him find the missing partner," Sulana answered.

The captain stared at Sulana for a moment and considered her words. Then he spoke slowly and carefully. "That seems a bit unusual, but it fits with Jaylan's work for Raven Company. I still don't see what you need from me."

"I need to know if Forester is reliable. I understand he used to work with you, and I want your opinion as to whether or not involving him in my mission puts it at risk. If I take him on the search for the missing partner, would he be a help or a hindrance?"

The captain looked thoughtful as he went over to his desk and sat heavily in the chair behind it. He folded his hands behind his head and responded. "Jaylan is sharp. A little too sharp, and a little too enthusiastic. He annoyed the wrong people and paid for it with his career. But he's an honest man and I would still trust him with my life. Is that good enough for you?" The captain finished with a huge yawn that his large fist barely covered.

Sulana smiled. "Yes, Captain, that's exactly what I needed to know."

Captain Pollard pushed himself out of his chair and headed toward the door to his chamber. "Good. Go away then. Good luck on your mission."

As the captain left the room, Sulana spoke loudly at his retreating back. "Thank you sir, I appreciate your taking the time to see me." The last two words were cut off by the slamming of the chamber door.

Sulana turned to the secretary. "Thank you for your help as well. We'll be on our way now."

The secretary made shooing motions with his hands. "Yes, yes. Please go now. I'll have to prepare a special breakfast for the captain when he rises again and hope that helps him forget this little interruption."

Sulana and Daven both laughed and let the secretary usher them out of the captain's office.

CHAPTER 4

I sat at my favorite table in the serving room the next morning, hands cupped around a steaming mug of coffee, a rare and expensive indulgence for me. I held the mug up in a brief salute to Dela, who had just brewed it for me. She smiled and left the serving room carrying a tray of dirty dishes.

Coffee beans traveled by caravan all the way from Xelapai, a land far to the south, across a route that was fraught with bandits and dangerous wilderness creatures. The Snow Creek Inn rarely had an opportunity to purchase the beans, but while we had them, the rich and stimulating drink they produced attracted some of the area's more affluent residents.

I blew on the hot brew and took a sip, thinking about the day before me. I wasn't sure what to expect, and I frowned as I thought back to last night's confrontation with the Agents of Whatever.

I needed more information. Running off on a hunt with people I knew nothing about added a level of risk that made me uncomfortable—thus the need for a bolstering coffee. I nodded to myself as I concluded that I needed to get some things straight before we headed out, aggressive agent notwithstanding.

As if on cue, the serving room door opened and Agent Delano walked in.

She spotted me immediately and headed my way, three men trailing behind her. The pale morning light reflecting in through the door and the windows showed me details that I couldn't see during our encounter last night behind the inn. Sulana had shoulder-length blonde hair and blue eyes. Her face had strong, simple features that summed up to be cute, verging on pretty. Her stride was even and unhurried, and she calmly surveyed the room as she walked over to my table.

As the four agents came forward, the entire serving room fell silent. The three men with Agent Delano scanned the other occupants thoroughly as they walked confidently through the room behind her. The comfortable way the agents wore their weapons and armor declared them to be competent and dangerous men. Most of the patrons dropped their curious stare and poked at their food or turned to their table companions when one of the agents met their eyes.

I swallowed the last of my coffee, cringing as it burned down my throat but unwilling to leave any of the rare elixir behind. I stood as Agent Delano approached my table. "Would you like to have something to eat or drink before we go?" I asked, gesturing at the seat across from me.

She smiled back at me and answered. "No thanks, we've eaten already."

The smile transformed her face. Shallow dimples framed her mouth and her gaze softened. I blinked and nearly fell back into my chair. Was this the same woman who had leveled a crossbow at my heart a few short hours ago?

"Allow me to introduce my team," she said, gesturing at the three men behind her. Two of them stepped forward to stand beside her, while the third remained just behind, his height giving him a clear view over her head. Standing closer to her this morning, I realized that she couldn't be much more than five feet tall. On her left stood the man I had met briefly last night. He nodded once in greeting as I met his eyes.

"This is Daven," she said gesturing at the man I'd already met. She put her right hand on the shoulder of the man on her right and added, "and this is Talon, my second in command." She hooked her thumb over her shoulder, "and the tall one is Barek, who always seems to have my back," she said with a short laugh. "And I'm Sulana," she finished.

Daven was a bit taller and thinner than I am. He had blonde hair and blue eyes like Sulana, and I guessed them both to be in their early twenties. I wondered briefly if they could be related, but saw no other similarities in their features. Talon was about my height and the oldest of the team, perhaps in his mid forties, with black hair graying at the temples and intent grey eyes.

Barek loomed over all of them, standing at least six-and-a-half feet tall with a broad chest and shoulders. He was probably in his early thirties, and his size was explained by his slanted eyes, brown skin, and long, beaded locks of brown hair. Barek was a Winterman, from the Borealis Tribes that lived to the north. Sulana looked almost like a child standing in front of him; the top of her head didn't even come to his shoulders.

"Gentlemen, this is Jaylan, the man who will accompany us on our hunt today," she said with a wave of her hand.

"If you don't mind my saying so, you seem a bit more friendly today," I said cautiously.

"Finally getting a little sleep has something to do with that, but I've also had the chance to do some checking up on you," she said. "Captain Pollard was kind enough to see me this morning and answer a few questions about you."

I imagined Rakerus' reaction to being awakened before dawn. "Oh, *that* must have made you popular with him," I said with a laugh.

"He doesn't seem to be much of a morning person, does he?" she said with a smirk. "But after some initial swearing, he was willing to share his confidence in your integrity and capability."

"I'll have to thank him for that," I replied. "This trip will be a lot less tense if we aren't at each other's throats the whole time."

"Yes, well, sorry about our misunderstanding last night. This mission is important, and I can't take any chances. I hope you understand," she said with a tilt of her head.

I shrugged. "Sure. But I'd feel a lot better if I knew a little more about *you*. For starters, I understand that you are official agents of some kind." She nodded as I paused. "But I still don't know who you represent."

She glanced quickly around the room, taking in a couple of the inn's customers who were having their breakfast. Her gaze lingered on the bar area, and I looked over to see that Dela had returned to the room and was watching us closely from behind the bar as she unloaded a few bottles of wine.

Leaning toward me conspiratorially, Agent Delano spoke quietly. "How about we talk about that on the move? I'll answer what questions I can once we are on our way. Would that be acceptable?"

I nodded. "Alright, I can live with that." I grabbed my cloak and slipped it on.

A bottle of wine slammed to the counter and looked over to see Dela glaring at me. I patted my coin purse in an attempt to communicate that this was about the contract. Her glare changed to a frown and then her lips drew into a thin line as she went back to rustling behind the bar. She didn't look up again.

"Is that your wife?" Agent Delano whispered as we turned to go.

"Uh, no," I answered under my breath. "Let's just go."

The spring days were getting warmer, but the mornings still had a biting chill of frost to them. The sturdy linen shirt and pants I wore under my hardened leather armor would be fine after the sun had a chance to warm things up a bit. Until then, my cloak would keep off the chill and still allow me quick access to the short sword I had strapped to my waist and the dagger attached to my belt.

Agent Delano noted my outfit and equipment as I settled my cloak on my shoulders and nodded approvingly. "Let's go," she said, and turned to lead the five of us out into the early morning light.

～

I walked into the stable, shivering briefly as I adjusted to the cold morning air. Patches, my reliable horse, nickered softly in greeting and came over to the rail of his stall, snorting steam from his nostrils. Patches had pinto coloring, with brown on his neck, shoulders, and hind quarters. He had white splashed haphazardly across his face, sides and tummy. The name Patches came from two small white "knee patches" on his front legs.

I rubbed his face and gave him a chunk of carrot I'd filched from the kitchen earlier. He munched contentedly as I saddled him up. When saddled, much of his white was covered, except for the knee patches and his underside. It amused me how everyone we met while riding instantly understood the reason for his name.

Our fellow travelers were mounted and waiting for me when Patches and I ambled over to them. Agent Delano gave me a nod, turned her horse, and urged it into a trot without a word.

A few folks hurried out of our way as we rode through the nearly empty streets, but most of the town was blanketed with the peaceful stillness of early morning. Only the bakery seemed fully awake; the rich smell of baking dough wafted out across the road in a thin cloud of steam that floated out of the open front door. We passed through the town's west gate and continued riding west on Riverview Road.

Riverview Road followed the Teardrop River to the west, passing by or through small villages along the way. Eventually the road split, angling across the river and south toward Plains End as South Riverview Road and continuing west toward Silver Falls as North Riverview Road. The entire northern route was flanked by tall conifers and followed along the river at the base of steep mountain slopes and cliffs. The view often opened up to a spectacular panoramic scene of the wide river flowing through the valley. I always looked forward to traveling the north fork of the road as we would today.

The sun angled steeply through the trees from behind us, casting our long shadows to the front and side. Where the sunlight struck the needles of frosty trees along the road, a wisp of mist rose like a tiny puff of smoke. We rode through pockets of warming air perfumed with the sharp odor of pine. I took a deep, satisfied breath, thankful for the change to relatively clear weather, a rarity this early in spring.

Small mounds of snow clustered in the most shaded areas under the trees, but the road was clear. Our horses clopped along firmly on frozen mud that would later thaw and probably become an impediment on our return journey. Unseen squirrels chattered at us as we passed, and an occasional blue jay swooped by with a harsh scolding caw.

Patches and I trailed the other riders. I was just thinking about moving up to ride alongside Agent Delano so I could repeat my question about her employer when she broke into a full gallop. "Let's put a little distance behind us," she shouted over her shoulder before she leaned forward in her saddle and thundered off.

Our horses needed no urging to follow her. They were all a little frisky this morning and seemed more than willing to stretch their legs. The other agents and I charged down the road after her, our cloaks flapping in the breeze of our passage.

We covered the first few miles quickly and then Agent Delano slowed her horse to a walk. "That's a good start. Let's rest the horses a bit," she said as she pulled her pretty tan appaloosa back and alongside Patches.

"You said you had questions. I can only tell you so much," she warned me, "but I'll answer what I can."

"Thanks," I said. "Where are we headed?"

"We lost the trail of the other thief in the woods off the road west of here. We were following his tracks, but they became confusing and finally seemed to disappear. Barek is a good tracker, and it's unusual for someone to completely lose him like that," she said.

I had an uncomfortable thought and grimaced. "About how far west?"

"About as far again as we've already traveled, beyond that little village west of here," she answered. She looked over at me and cocked her head. "Is there something I should know?"

I thought for a moment about what she had described. The little village Sulana referred to was named Dunver. I decided that an experienced tracker losing the trail west of the village was no coincidence. "There's an old healer living back in that area," I said, "and she has some skill with Wards."

Agent Delano sat back in her saddle thoughtfully. "Well, that would explain a lot," she murmured, "but not everything. What do you know about these Wards," she asked.

"Not much, really. She keeps a Ward around her cottage that deflects unwanted visitors, which includes just about everyone. A few years ago, I helped her lay in wood for winter, and she gave me something that let me go through with no problem."

"Do you still have the means to go through the Ward?" she asked.

"No. She gave me a trinket to carry that let me pass. I gave it back to her when I was finished."

Agent Delano nodded. "What can you tell me about her?"

"Well, she's getting to be fairly old now. I don't know how much longer she'll be able to live back up there all by herself.

She used to travel around to the nearby towns, healing folk for trade and the occasional coin. She had a strict rule that people needed to call for her when they wanted help, but one day someone brought a sick child up to her home instead. Her husband caught the illness and never recovered. She became reclusive after her husband died."

Agent Delano listened to my story and then grimaced. "Wonderful. An angry healer with warding skills."

"Oh, she's not so bad now," I reassured her. "She seems to know when someone really needs her help. A friend of mine fractured an arm badly, and she came out to treat him when it started going septic. That was the autumn I helped with her firewood in thanks. However, she does still have a strict policy against visitors to her home, and the Wards ensure it's never ignored again."

We rode in silence for a few moments. Our swift ride through the cold morning air had given me a chill, so the sun warming my back was welcome.

I finally turned to her. "So, *Agent* Delano, how is it that you are in the business of tracking down thieves?"

"Finally getting back to that, are you?" She looked at me intently, her blue eyes locked on mine. "This isn't something I'd like widely known," she confided, "but we are agents of the Archives."

I was stunned for a moment, unable to respond at first with more than "Huh. Really? Wow." Agent Delano laughed at my feeble response.

I didn't know much about the Archives. Just that it was a refuge and a school for sorcerers. Their members tended to move secretly, and in all my years of working with the

Imperial Guard, I'd never run across any Archives agents. Not that I knew of, anyway.

An unpleasant thought entered my head. I narrowed my eyes at her and spoke hesitantly. "Uh...you aren't going to have to kill me now or something, are you?"

She laughed again. "No, don't worry. We aren't murderers. Believe me, I wouldn't have told you, except Captain Pollard vouched for you, and you are going to see some things on this trip that would require some kind of explanation. Sometimes the truth is the simplest explanation," she added with a shrug.

"Well, thanks for telling me," I replied. "How do our thieves fit into all this?"

She thought for a moment, obviously deciding how much she was willing to tell me. "They stole a dangerous artifact from one of our people who was holding it for safe-keeping. My team was deployed to intercept them and get it back."

"How were you able to find them?" I asked with surprise.

"Well...that's one of the odd things you'll see on this trip," she responded cryptically.

I pushed my curiosity aside. Getting answers is often about the timing of the question. She'd apparently said as much as she would on the subject, for now at least.

"Okay. How about the Wards? Do you have a way to get past them?" I asked.

"Wards are most effective when they are unexpected," she answered. "Now that I know what we are dealing with, I think we can push through, depending upon how she formed the Ward."

"There's more than one way?" I asked. I knew almost nothing about the workings of magic. Most of the populace distrusted magic and its practitioners. I had encountered those who used magic enough times to learn to respect it and them, but I had never indulged my curiosity about the subject. Showing an interest in magic was...unpopular.

"Yes. Some Wards are like a bubble," she said. "They are strong around the edges of the effect, but drop to almost nothing inside the affected area. Others are radiant, like light given off by a lantern. They are strongest at their center and the effect eventually trails off to nothing over a distance."

"You seem to know a lot about this. Are you a sorceress?" I asked her quietly. I was used to speaking of magic in hushed tones, and I wasn't sure she would be comfortable admitting that she could use it.

She waved my caution aside, "I have some ability with magic, or vaetra as we call it. I've studied it, but my skills are limited. For me it's just a tool that helps me get my job done, rather than a vocation in itself."

Her comment surprised me. I had never considered that there might be a middle ground. It seemed to me that everyone who had the ability to use magic focused on developing their skill to the exclusion of just about everything else.

"Is there a difference between magic and this 'vaetra' you mentioned?" I asked.

She snorted. "There is to us, but most people don't understand the distinction. Magic is what the man on the street corner does when he pulls a coin from behind your ear. It's just slight-of-hand tricks. Vaetra is a living force that only a sorcerer can transform into a physical effect. To call a sorcerer a 'magician' is an insult."

We both fell silent when we heard the jingle of harnesses and rattle of wagon wheels approaching. The wagon appeared through the trees around a curve in the road with the driver urging his pair of draft horses to pick up their speed. The wagon was heavily loaded with hay.

"Make way, please," he shouted out to us as he approached. "Need to stay in the middle of the road."

The five of us eased our horses to the sides of the road so the wagon could pass between us. "You're running a bit late," I called to him as he got closer.

"Don't I know it!" he replied. "If I don't get this load to Northshore before the road thaws, I'll be up to my hubs in mud," he added as he bounced by.

"Safe journey!" I called after him. He just raised a hand and waved it in acknowledgement, and was nearly unseated when the wagon hit a particularly large rock in the roadway.

Barek snorted and shook his head. "Won't do him much good if he breaks a wheel," he muttered. The rest of us laughed our agreement and continued on our way.

Rounding the curve in the road, we found ourselves at the edge of Dunver.

~

We rode slowly through the village of Dunver. The village proper wasn't much more than a small collection of thatched wood huts and a tiny shop with sundries. The day was far enough along that a few villagers were wandering around taking care of their various duties. They glanced over at us as we passed, occasionally waving or offering a greeting. A man carrying an armload of wood came around the side of one of the huts and stopped short at the site of the giant Winterman in our midst, but he continued on his way when he saw no sign of aggression from our group. A couple of dogs barked at us, but two young children yelled at them and hurried forward to chase the dogs back to their homes.

We were an imposing group. Five well-armed travelers on horseback tend to cause alarm, but most of the villagers looked more curious than concerned. Dunver straddled Riverview Road, the primary western route to Northshore, so the residents routinely saw a wide variety of travelers.

At the far side of the village square where the road continued out of Dunver to the west, Agent Delano spotted a well with a watering trough alongside it. She angled her horse over to the trough. A teenaged boy was busily filling a couple of large buckets from the smaller one that came up from the well.

"Would it be all right if we watered our horses?" she asked the boy.

He sized us up quickly. "Five coppers, ma'am, and you'll have to draw the water yourself."

The sum was outrageous, but Agent Delano didn't blink an eye. She responded flatly. "One copper and I won't have you arrested for attempted theft."

The boy smiled apologetically and shrugged as if to say it was worth a try. "How about two coppers and I'll draw the water for you?"

Agent Delano nodded her head in assent and dismounted to hand the boy the coins. The rest of us followed suit, glad for the opportunity to stretch our legs.

The boy filled the trough with water, and Agent Delano's horse drank first. The horses were not terribly thirsty because we had been riding through the cold morning, but they were ready for a little refreshment after the run we gave them.

I had been through Dunver on many occasions before, so I didn't feel compelled to give our surroundings more than a cursory glance. My attention went to my companions instead.

While Agent Delano worked the water transaction, Barek looked around briefly, took the reins from Talon and Daven, and waited to bring the horses to the trough with relaxed confidence. Talon took up a position just outside our cluster of horses and people, continuously scanning the edges of town. Daven stayed very close to Agent Delano's side and kept a close eye on every movement of the villagers. I nodded to myself in appreciation of the agents' teamwork and professionalism.

We could have saved ourselves the copper and just watered the horses from one of the many streams we'd pass along our journey, but I suspected that Agent Delano was using the coin to buy more than water. The villagers would remember her and appreciate the fact that she had contributed to their meager livelihood. One never knew when that kind of goodwill might come in handy.

The boy offered to top off our waterskins as well. Barek and I accepted, and then we mounted back up.

We left Dunver behind and continued east down Riverview Road. If Agent Delano's team had lost the thief where I was thinking they did, we didn't have far to go.

CHAPTER 5

Beyond Dunver, the road narrowed and wound its way along a steep hillside and through thick forest down toward the north bank of Teardrop River. Barek dropped behind a few paces and Talon took point position. Daven stayed alongside Sulana and I rode just in front of the two of them.

Before long, the forest opened up and gave us a broad view of the river valley. An osprey glided high over the river, watching for an unsuspecting fish, and an enormous bald eagle glared at us from atop a tall snag. The wide green river flowed to the west with hardly a ripple on its smooth surface.

We came to a fork in the road. The left fork eased down to the river's edge and ended at the planks of the short dock at the Dunver Ferry. Crossing the river on the ferry would take us onto South Riverview Road and through the Valley of Veils, which got its name from the veils of mist that frequently blanketed the area. Eventually, that direction would lead south to Plains End at the western border of Lakewoods Province.

The right fork became North Riverview Road, which continued along the north shore of the river. Talon continued down the right fork as he waved at the ferryman, who had emerged from his dockside hut at the sound of our approaching horses. The ferryman returned the wave and went back inside.

Sulana picked up her pace to ride alongside me. "There's something I've been wondering," she said.

"What's that?"

"Why did you agree to take this job for someone you knew was a criminal?" she asked. "The captain made it sound like you usually operate alongside the law."

"That's true. Normally, I would not have agreed to work for him," I confirmed. She looked over at me and waited for me to continue. I shrugged. "If he had asked me to help him retrieve the item, I'd have said no. But he asked me to help him find his partner."

Sulana thought about that for a moment, a skeptical frown appearing on her face. "Isn't that just semantics? I mean, find the man, find the item. Or so we hope."

"I understand what you're saying. But it wasn't so much what he asked, it was the way he asked it," I explained.

"What do you mean?" she asked.

"He seemed afraid of what would happen if he failed to deliver the item to their employer, but he wasn't angry about the lost payment. What I saw was desperation and hope related to finding his partner and frustration at being prevented from doing it himself."

"That does seem unusual," Sulana muttered.

"When I got the note to meet with him, I was hoping for the best, but expected I'd have to tell him to go away. Instead, I found myself wanting to help him find his partner," I concluded.

"Well, either way, he'll have to answer for his theft," she said with an edge to her voice. "I'm just glad to hear you weren't planning to help them escape."

I chuckled and shook my head. "No, I may no longer be in the Guard, but I often work closely with them. On the other hand, the private work I do for hire sometimes does require a certain degree of...discretion."

"I think I understand that," she mused. "But it seems like a fine line to walk."

"You don't know the half of it," I said with a sigh.

When taking contracts, I refused work that would force me to break the law, but the reasons for why clients went to Raven Company instead of the Imperial Guard were many. In some cases, the Guard didn't have the resources or motivation to investigate a matter to the client's satisfaction, so the client would come to us for the help they needed. In other situations, the client specifically wanted to avoid involving the Guard. Those cases always had to be handled carefully.

Sulana looked ahead and pointed to a track—little more than a trail really—that led off the road to the north. "That's our turn," she said.

My suspicions were confirmed. "So, you followed the other man up that trail and lost him?" I asked.

"Yes. Is this the way to the home of that healer you mentioned?"

"It is," I said. I wondered if old Meghan could be in danger. Her Wards were good at keeping people away, but if the thief was able to get through them somehow, he could be holed up in her home. I frowned as I realized that this search could end in a hostage standoff.

Sulana was watching my face and seemed to read my mind. "You're concerned for the healer, aren't you?" she asked. I nodded, and she continued, "Well, let's see what we can find out first. It's possible the thief circled the Wards and escaped into the mountains."

Barek cleared his throat behind us and I looked back. He was scowling and shaking his shaggy head. The beads at the ends of his locks clicked together as if to emphasize his disagreement with her statement.

Sulana laughed. "Don't worry Barek, I'm not insulting your tracking skills. We just don't know what resources these thieves had available to them." Barek shrugged, his face noncommittal.

"Man of few words," I commented to Sulana.

"He's no chatterbox," she agreed.

"Can we get on with this?" Barek said.

Talon chuckled and led the way up the trail. The rest of us followed, shifting into single file.

The trail was just large enough for two horses to walk side-by-side, but by staying in the center, a rider was less likely to be struck by the encroaching tree branches. The local flora was quick to take advantage of any bit of light that managed to penetrate the tree canopy, which meant the trails needed to be cleared back every two or three years. This one was overdue.

We followed the deeply shadowed trail into the forested foothills, pulling our cloaks a little tighter around us to fend off the late-morning chill that persisted within the understory. We passed through a couple of clearings and reveled in the sudden expanse of deep blue sky and the warmth of the sun.

Along the way, Barek moved up to point position and Talon replaced him at the rear of the party. We passed a couple of offshoot trails, which I knew led to other cabins in the area, but Barek was convinced that our quarry had continued on.

At one of the trail intersections, we heard a branch crack above us in the trees. We all looked up, but the thick foliage made it impossible to see very far into the network of branches. Our hands went to our weapons, but there were no more sounds. The horses bunched together as we stopped.

Two of the horses shifted and whinnied as they caught the scent of something. Patches and the other horses raised their heads and perked their ears forward as they sniffed the air as well.

I looked up at the trees along the intersection, my eyes searching the bark just below the lowest branches. I finally found what I was looking for: a series of small gouges just under the lowest branches of one corner tree. "Everyone hold here for a moment," I said.

"What is it?" Sulana asked, reaching for her crossbow.

I held up my hand to stop her. "Try not to make any threatening moves. I know who it is and we're in no danger."

Daven seemed unconvinced. He edged his horse closer to Sulana's and kept his hand ready on his sword.

"Well then who is it," Sulana asked more insistently. "Why are we stopping?"

"This section of forest is home to a band of arbolenx," I answered.

"Arbolenx? What makes you think they'll talk to us? And how could they help us anyway?" she asked, shifting nervously in her saddle and peering up into the dense canopy.

Arbolenx are large intelligent felines that inhabit forests and make their homes in the tree canopy. They are capable of human speech, but rarely interact with humans. I could attest that this band was less reclusive than most.

"Not much happens around here that they don't see," I responded. "That branch snap was an invitation to speak. If they didn't want us to know they were here, we'd have never seen or heard a thing that would have betrayed their presence," I said as I dismounted from my horse.

I walked a few paces away from the others and stood near the tree that had been marked. I tilted my head back and made a show of sniffing the air. "I smell you, Ru-Rahl" I said aloud.

I glanced back at the others, who were looking at each other in confusion and over at me as if I'd lost my mind. They could smell nothing, of course, and neither could I really. I suppressed a smirk, thinking how the ritual words sounded insulting to a human. However, I knew that to an arbolenx, it was a greeting of respect.

There was a light rustling of branches, and I barely had time to register a blur of motion down the trunk of the tree as an arbolenx appeared on the ground in front of me. He settled back on his hind legs and regarded me with his deep green eyes, his pupils shrinking to slits as they adjusted to the brighter light on the ground.

As I told Sulana, we never would have been aware of their presence if they hadn't wished it. Arbolenx have natural camouflage magic, which is why Ru-Rahl seemed to blur as he descended the tree trunk. He was showing off. There could be a dozen more of his band up in the branches, and as long as they held still, we'd probably never spot them.

He glanced disdainfully over at the group of riders, who were watching with cautious interest and trying to calm their horses. Only Patches stood without agitation, since he had met Ru-Rahl several times before. The other horses shied at the sudden appearance of the predator, and Barek's big roan stallion nodded his head and pawed the ground.

Ru-Rahl was an exceptionally large and handsome example of his kind. Sitting, his head came up to my waist, and his fur was deep brown with faint black stripes along his shoulders and hips. He wore a back-pack, which left his paws (better described as sharply-clawed hands) free for climbing. Long black tufts of fur twitched nervously on the tips of his ears. Short, stiff black whiskers trembled on his cheeks as his nostrils took in the scents of the humans and animals before him.

Satisfied that no violence was imminent, he tilted his head back and sniffed the air emphatically as I had done. "I smell you, Zhalan. Wath seeg?"

I was certain that Ru-Rahl knew exactly why we were there, but since I was the one seeking help, it was only polite that I ask for it. Besides, when bargaining with arbolenx, one party must name the favor and the other must name the price.

"A man passed through here last night on horseback, probably moving swiftly. These riders attempted to follow him, but lost the trail," I added, gesturing toward the others. "I would like to know if you have information that can help us find him."

Ru-Rahl considered my request for a moment and glanced significantly at the others again. He wanted to make sure I understood that bringing armed riders to this meeting would increase the price of my favor. "One ravith," he stated.

One rabbit. The price was high by arbolenx standards, but worth it if he had anything at all useful to tell us.

I nodded my head. "Agreed."

"Gounthed," he replied, which meant he had "counted" the rabbit toward my debt to him. Arbolenx speech avoids hard consonant sounds, like "t" and "k" because they resemble spitting, which in the feline world indicates fear or aggression.

"Human smell of vlud," Ru-Rahl finally volunteered.

"He smelled of blood?" I asked, and Ru-Rahl nodded once. "Did he continue up the trail on his horse?"

Ru-Rahl nodded again. "Inthu fear. No follow."

Into the fear, where Ru-Rahl's gang would not follow. He must have been referring to the Ward. "The fear didn't turn him away?"

Ru-Rahl shook his head negative, the claws on his front hands extending reflexively as he considered what he'd seen.

So the Ward hadn't affected the man on the horse. He must have had some kind of magical protection. Or perhaps his injury was so severe that he was delirious with pain. I wasn't sure if that would make a difference, though.

"Thank you, Ru-Rahl. The bargain is fair."

Ru-Rahl nodded once again, and in a single motion, leaped onto the trunk of the tree where his strong claws held him suspended. He looked over his shoulder at me and said, "Good hunthing Zhalan."

"Good hunting Ru-Rahl," I replied.

With two powerful strokes of his hind legs, Ru-Rahl disappeared up the tree and into the branches overhead. I walked back to the others.

I could feel Sulana's stare while I mounted Patches and gathered my reins. "I'm impressed," she said. "What did we learn? I didn't quite catch all of that."

I sat a little straighter in my saddle, pleased with having finally done something to impress this woman, and a little surprised to discover that it mattered to me. "We learned that our thief was injured when he came through here last night. We also learned that he went into the Ward, not around it, as you suspected." I said the last to Barek with a nod, and he gave a grim "I told you so" smile in return.

Sulana looked down the trail, thinking about what we'd learned. "I'm concerned that he was able to move through the Ward," she finally said. "That may imply he has sorcery at his disposal."

As we got our horses moving down the trail again, Daven asked, "So, do we need to come up with a rabbit for your friend?"

I smiled at him and said "Ah, you understood that part?"

He shrugged. "Wasn't hard."

I shook my head. "No, Ru-Rahl still owes me several rabbits and squirrels. He'll deduct the price of today's bargain from that tally. I'm not sure how much credit I still have with him, but I have no doubt that he knows exactly."

"How'd you get to be on such good terms with an arbolenx?" Sulana asked.

"The healer we're on the way to see introduced me to them. This band has lived near humans for a long time and even trades with the people of Dunver occasionally. I got into the habit of leaving rabbits and squirrels for them when I travel through here. Ru-Rahl appreciates it, but I think it annoys him that I keep increasing his debt to me. I'm sure that's why he let me know he was around. He probably recognized you and knew we might need to know what he'd seen. It also gave him an opportunity to reduce his debt."

"You're a man of surprising talents, 'Zhalan,'" Sulana teased.

Daven looked over his shoulder at me and frowned, but didn't say anything. I understood that his job was to protect Sulana, but his attitude toward me was puzzling. Eventually, I was going to have to figure out the nature of the relationship between those two.

~

At last, we reached a small clearing where I suggested we stop. "This spot is just outside the Ward's influence," I informed Sulana. She looked around the clearing and nodded her agreement. I was curious to find out what she intended to do about getting through the Ward.

The clearing was at a confluence of trails. One trail continued to the northwest deeper into the mountains. A second narrower trail left the clearing toward the northeast. I mentioned that the second trail would take us to the healer's cottage, and Barek confirmed that was the way they had gone the previous night.

A stream flowed out of the trees and created a small pool at the western edge of the clearing. The water burbled as it tumbled down the last few rocks into the pond, the steady flow indicating that the water would be fresh if we decided to let the horses drink. The ground was covered with grass that would grow to shoulder height in summer, but it was just getting started. The horses lowered their heads to tear at the tender new blades.

Sulana dismounted and walked a few paces away from the group. Daven slid down from his horse to stand nearby. Talon and Barek stayed mounted, watching the paths leading into and out of the clearing.

I watched from my saddle as Sulana took out a leather pouch and removed a small glass rod attached to a chain. I dismounted and joined her and Daven to get a better look.

The glass rod was about the size of Sulana's smallest finger. It was clear with rounded ends, and had a twist to it with a swirl of blue along its length. The sun sparkled off the glass and lit up the blue swirl, which appeared to form lettering of some kind. "Pretty," I commented.

"Yes. Pretty and functional," she said with a distant tone. The chain attached to the glass rod had a ring on the other end. Sulana slipped the ring over her middle finger and let the glass rod dangle.

"What does it do?" I asked.

"It seeks," she replied, and held up her other hand to stop my next question. "Hold on for a moment while I concentrate on making it work."

She said something quietly and stared at the glass rod. I knew when she activated it, because it gave off a high-pitched tone. But it continued to just dangle and turn on the end of the chain. Sulana frowned and stared at it a bit longer. The rod continued to dangle and turn. It didn't seem to be reacting to her efforts in the way she wanted.

While Sulana worked, Daven stepped a little closer to me and watched me carefully. He seemed relaxed, but had one hand casually resting on his sword pommel. I wondered why he would suddenly perceive me as a threat of some kind, so I resisted the urge to step closer to Sulana for a better look at what she was doing.

She finally growled something in frustration and the rod went silent. She slid the ring off of her finger. "This is very strange," she said. "It's still not working."

"What is it supposed to do?" I asked.

"It is *supposed* to point the way to the item the thieves stole," she replied, stuffing the rod back into the pouch and putting it away.

"Didn't the noise mean it was working?"

Sulana stopped abruptly and stared intently at me. "You *heard* it?"

Her reaction surprised me. Uncertainty crept into my voice. "It started whining when you dangled it and spoke to it. Don't you hear it when you use it?" I looked at each of the others. "Doesn't everyone hear it?" But Daven, Talon, and Barek shook their heads, staring at me with unreadable expressions.

"I don't hear it. I see it," Sulana answered. "It glows a bit when activated and brightens when it finds what it seeks." She looked at me thoughtfully, her head tilted in an appraising manner.

This was news to me. I had assumed that everyone heard sorcery when it was used nearby and that most chose to ignore it, as they did with virtually everything else related to sorcery. This was the first time in my life that I had encountered someone who was willing to speak about sorcery openly.

"But what does it mean?" I asked Sulana.

"It means you are a Sensitive," she answered. "You're sensitive to vaetric manifestations." I looked at her in confusion. She clarified, "The workings of sorcery. Some people hear manifestations, some see them, and others smell them. A rare few even feel them as vibrations."

Then she shook her head and strode over to her horse to remount. "Well, let's go find this Ward and see what we're dealing with."

I felt as confused as ever, but this was obviously not the time to pursue the matter further. Daven and I followed Sulana's lead and got back on our horses as well. Thinking about Daven's behavior while Sulana had been using the device, I turned to him and asked, "Why the sudden protectiveness earlier?"

He narrowed his eyes at me and said, "Sulana is somewhat vulnerable while working that device. And sorcery can cause unpredictable reactions in nearby observers."

I nodded and responded, "I've seen that first hand. On the occasions when magic has been worked nearby, I've seen grown men shudder in fear or tremble with rage. It's no wonder sorcerers seldom take to the field with our soldiers. They might be run through by their own men."

"Exactly," Sulana broke in. "But I gather you don't have those reactions?"

"No. Being around sorcery has never bothered me, although you have to be careful who hears you say that. I normally pretend to be holding my reactions in check like everyone else."

Sulana gave me another appraising look, but said nothing. She turned her horse and moved toward the trail to the healer's home. We left the clearing and entered the forest in single file again. Barek continued to lead.

After about five minutes of riding, I started to feel uncomfortable, like I was being watched by unseen and malevolent eyes. As the feeling quickly grew, I knew we must be entering the Ward.

My sense of unease increased. The sound of something large crashing through the forest came from just ahead and to our right. I scanned the area, but the vegetation showed no sign of disturbance. I couldn't tell what was making the noise, but it seemed larger than a bear. If it was a mountain troll, we'd have a hard time trying to fight it on this narrow trail. I had a strong desire to return to the clearing where there was room to maneuver.

We continued forward, and a threatening roar arose from the forest all around us. It started as a low rumble and steadily increased in volume as we advanced. I looked around and my senses screamed that we were on the wrong trail, although intellectually, I knew that wasn't true. My instincts told me that we should go back to the clearing and take another path; that all this danger was for nothing. I felt that every step we took forward was moving us farther away from the man we were trying to find. My rational mind struggled to maintain focus, but I was rapidly losing the battle against the emotional turmoil and instinctive urges imposed by the Ward.

Suddenly, the overwhelming sense of danger and futility faded, and I found myself back in the small clearing where we'd stopped earlier. Sulana's team was there as well. We were all looking around trying to get our bearings. I was relieved to be out of the Ward, but disturbed by the fact that I couldn't remember making the decision to turn around.

"That's a strong Ward," Sulana stated with a bemused smile. "Definitely a bubble."

I remembered how she had said earlier that a Ward could be like a bubble or a lantern. She seemed to have decided that Meghan's Ward was a bubble, so most of its force was along the outside edge. "How do we get through it?" I asked.

"It will be harder than I thought, but I'm sure we can do it," she said confidently. "I don't have anything that can negate the Ward, but I have a device that should shield us from the worst of it. We just need to penetrate the edge of the bubble." She leaned back in her saddle and reached into one of her saddle bags. After a bit of rummaging, she pulled out a leather case the size of a large book. She untied the flap and folded the case open to reveal a series of small pockets. She extracted a glass disk from one of the pockets. The disk was about the size and shape of a good skipping stone, and it had purple spots in it. She slipped the disk into a more convenient belt pocket and returned the case to her saddlebag.

"Okay, here's the plan," she said, looking around at us. "When we first start to feel uncomfortable again, I'll activate the Veil." She patted the pocket that held the device, and continued, "then, we'll run the horses through the Ward. Concentrate only on following the horse in front of you. Barek," she said turning to him, "I want you to focus on nothing other than following the trail." Barek nodded his understanding.

"We should get through the Ward quickly, and once we're on the other side, we'll be fine," she assured us.

We headed back up the trail toward the Ward. Moving this direction still felt wrong to me, which hinted at the power of the Ward and its residual effect on my mind. As soon as the sensation of malevolence started to rise again, Sulana palmed the Veil and called out, "Okay, let's go!" We all kicked our horses into a gallop.

I focused on Sulana's back and concentrated on thinking only of staying close to her. It was difficult. The roaring sound and the crashing noises started up again. This time the crashing was heading through the forest directly toward us. We were going to be ambushed and have to fight our way out. Meanwhile, the thief was getting away in the other direction!

Before the sense of panic fully took hold of me, it suddenly eased off. The forest seemed to blur a little and the crashing noise sounded less threatening. It was more like something was pacing us alongside the trail. Sulana's Veil gave off a low-pitched hum, and whatever it was doing helped me push aside the sense of going the wrong way. I remembered that I needed to just keep moving and follow her. The competing spells of the Ward and the Veil gave our charge a slow-motion, almost dreamlike, feeling.

As before, the Ward's effects suddenly dropped from my mind. I shook my head to clear it and looked up to see Sulana returning the Veil to her case. She turned to me and smiled. "That worked nicely," she said. All I could do was nod.

I looked around to find that we were at the edge of a large clearing. The trail we came in on disappeared into the forest behind us. The healer's familiar squat cottage sat atop a long rise before us, backed up against the trees on the opposite side of the clearing. Smoke curled out of the chimney and faded into the sky. It all seemed so incongruently peaceful after our wild ride down the trail.

That's when I noticed the horse quietly cropping grass at the side of the cabin. It wore a stained saddle and a set of saddle bags. The reins trailed to the ground, giving the horse the freedom to wander as it wished.

What concerned me was that Meghan didn't own a horse.

~

Barek started to ride forward. "Wait," I told him. He stopped to look at me questioningly. I pointed up the hill. "That's not the healer's horse."

Barek leaned out of his saddle and looked at the ground for a moment. He turned to Sulana and said "These tracks match the ones we were following yesterday."

"Good. I think we finally found our thief," Sulana said. She narrowed her eyes and observed the cabin carefully. "He may use the healer as a hostage. We'll have to do this carefully." She swung down from her saddle and armed her crossbow.

The cabin's windows were shuttered, which wasn't a surprise given that the morning air was still cool. I figured that if we circled around the base of the hill and approached the cabin from the side, we would be able to get close and still have cover. Sulana apparently had the same thought.

Her expression was serious and her voice determined as she gave us her orders. "Stay with the horses," she said to me. "Talon, you and Barek approach from the left. Daven and I will go right." Everyone nodded their understanding.

I was reluctant to stay behind. I didn't want Meghan to get hurt, but I knew I was still just along for the ride on this mission. I would have to trust that Sulana's team would do what they could to protect Meghan. Still, I itched to sneak forward with the others.

Ducking low and staying near the tree line, both teams quickly moved toward the cabin. They didn't even make it half way before the front door opened. Talon and Barek melted back into the trees, while Sulana and Daven hit the dirt. Sulana aimed her crossbow at the open doorway.

Meghan stepped out of the cabin with her hands held up and her palms facing us so we could see that she was unarmed. She wore a long tan linen dress with the sleeves rolled up above her elbows. The front of her dress was covered by a white apron that was stained with blood, and her long grey hair was tightly restrained behind her. Her clear voice called out to us, "You can come forward. The man you seek is in no condition to fight you."

Sulana stared at Meghan for a moment. There was no way to tell if she was telling the truth or if the thief stood right behind her with a knife at her back.

Meghan stepped forward a few paces and added, "If you want to see him before he dies, you'd best hurry up."

Sulana turned to Daven and said something. He shrugged, and they both rose to their feet. Sulana kept her crossbow aimed at the open doorway and Daven drew his sword. "Please step away from the doorway, ma'am," Sulana called out.

Meghan stepped to the side of the doorway as Sulana and Daven approached. Talon and Barek emerged from the trees and quickly loped up to the cabin. They both moved stealthily around to the back with their swords drawn.

From my position at the bottom of the hill, I could see Meghan sigh and cross her arms. I was certain then that she was telling the truth, but I understood that Sulana's team couldn't take any chances.

Sulana stayed back several paces from the doorway with her crossbow aimed straight into the opening. It was hard to see inside the cabin because outside it was brightly sunny, and the shuttered windows put the interior into heavy shadow. Daven ran to the far side of the door and waited there.

Sulana nodded her head, and Daven ducked low and slipped into the cabin. A few moments later, Daven appeared at the doorway and waved Sulana in. He had sheathed his sword. Sulana called out that the way was clear and walked in. Meghan slowly followed them into her home.

I took that as my cue to move forward with the horses. I left them to graze along with the thief's horse and walked up to the cabin doorway just as Talon and Barek moved into guard positions at the front and side of the cabin.

The healer's cabin was small but well made. It had a course of river stone along the bottom quarter of the outside wall, and the rest was constructed of log. The cabin had a cedar shingle roof, and many of the shingles were covered with a light green coating of moss. A few along the edge of the roof were broken off or showing signs of rot. The whole roof would need to be replaced soon.

I stepped through the doorway and into the cabin where the odor of healing herbs hung thick in the air. I stood just inside the threshold for a few seconds while my eyes adjusted to the darkness of the candle-lit interior. Daven stood with his back to the fireplace, warming his hands behind him. "In there," he said, tilting his head toward an open doorway to the bedroom beyond.

I passed a wall of shelves that was filled with numerous jars and pots containing the herbs and concoctions of Meghan's trade. I stopped just inside the doorway to the small bedroom. Inside the room, Sulana was leaning over an unconscious man who was bandaged across the chest. Bright red blood soaked through the bandage. I'd seen enough battle wounds to know that this man wouldn't be around long.

"Last night, I was surprised to hear a horse wander up to my home, and when I went out to investigate, this man fell out of the saddle at my feet without saying a word," Meghan explained to Sulana. "I was able to rouse him enough to walk him inside. He had a bolt through his chest," she said, looking at the crossbow in Sulana's hand and raising an eyebrow. "Your handiwork, I suppose?"

Sulana nodded. "Yes, but I didn't realize I'd hit him. Last night's darkness and rain hid the fact that he was bleeding." She lightly touched the man's shoulder. His eyelids fluttered briefly, but he didn't open them. His breathing was shallow and rattling. "I wish you hadn't run," she spoke softly to him.

The man on the bed shivered and Meghan pulled a blanket up over his chest and arms. "I did what I could, but his wound is beyond my skill. He's lost a lot of blood and the bolt punctured his lung," she said.

So this was Donal, the man I was hired to find. I didn't look forward to telling Raleb about his partner's current condition. Especially since his condition would probably get a lot worse real soon. Donal was much older than Raleb. His thinning hair was turning grey and he had the roundness of someone who more often gave orders than exercised them. His face had the pallor of extreme pain and his brow was beaded with perspiration. Every breath was labored.

Sulana turned to Meghan. "Where are this man's belongings? He and his partner are wanted men. They stole something of value that my team was sent to recover."

Meghan narrowed her eyes at Sulana and answered with irritation in her voice, "I believe I know what you are looking for, but I don't know why it would be worth taking this man's life."

Sulana's face flushed and she looked down at the man with a frown. She sighed and looked up at Meghan. "Just let me see what he had with him, please." Meghan stared at Sulana a moment more, nodded once, and started out of the room.

I stepped aside to let Meghan and Sulana pass, and I followed them back out into the main room. After we passed him, Daven moved away from the fireplace and over to the doorway to keep an eye on the comatose thief.

Meghan crossed the room to a shelf, upon which sat an odd-looking box. Peering at it more carefully, I realized that the box looked odd because it seemed to be made completely of stone. The healer turned a clasp on the front and opened the lid. She reached inside and removed something. When she turned around, she was holding a small gold ring that was set with what looked like a ruby. The red gem sparkled in the candlelight as she held it out to Sulana. "Is this what you are looking for?"

"Yes!" Sulana said as she quickly but carefully took the ring from Meghan. "Thank you."

Surprised by the simplicity of *the item*, I blurted, "That's it? All this excitement over a ring?"

"Don't be foolish," Sulana said. "This is no ordinary ring." She narrowed her eyes. "Assuming this is the *right* ring," she added with concern, glancing at Meghan. "Well, there's one way to find out," she said, and she slipped the ring onto her finger. Sulana walked over to the fireplace and muttered something I couldn't hear.

Instantly, a slow pulsing sound came from Sulana's direction. She raised her arm, the hand with the ring extended in a fist. She slowly turned in a circle, and the pulsing sound picked up in speed. She lowered her arm. "This is it," she said with relief, and pulled the ring from her hand.

Meghan had watched with interest as Sulana completed her little performance. She nodded to herself as Sulana put the ring into a leather pouch and stuffed it into a pocket under her leather breastplate. "I suspected it was enchanted. May I know what it does?"

Sulana shook her head. "I appreciate your safeguarding it, but I'm under orders to divulge as little as possible about our mission and this artifact," she said apologetically.

"I understand," Meghan sighed, and then she added with a grimace, "The work of the Archives is always *important* and *secret*."

"So you know something about who we are?" Sulana asked, narrowing her eyes at the old woman.

Meghan spread her hands and shrugged slightly, "Who else but the Archives would send an armed team lead by a Sword Sorceress to retrieve a vaetric artifact?"

Meghan's familiarity with the Archives surprised me, but I guess it shouldn't have. The Ward had to have come from somewhere. And I suspected that some of her healing talent involved more than just knowledge of herbs. She had never said anything about sorcery or the Archives during the time

I had helped her. But then again, she would have had no reason to speak of such things with me.

Sulana chuckled once and said "I see you *do* know something about us." She looked over at the bedroom doorway and turned thoughtful. "Our thief is in no shape to travel, and I doubt we can wake him to question him, at least not without killing him in the process."

Daven appeared in the doorway. "Not a problem. He's already dead."

Meghan rushed into the room to see her patient. I turned to Sulana and asked, "Sword Sorceress?"

"Later," she promised dismissively. She made no move to follow Meghan into the room.

Meghan returned to the main room with a look of sad disappointment. "Your man is right I'm afraid. He's gone."

Sulana considered the new circumstances. "That both simplifies and complicates our mission. I had hoped to get information from the man."

"Shooting him was probably not the best way to accomplish that," Meghan said sourly.

Sulana's eyes flashed. "You're right, but when the thieves split and ran, they left me little choice. It was getting dark and I couldn't let them escape into the woods. A man fleeing on a horse presents few non-fatal target options."

Meghan glared back at Sulana and took a deep breath. She seemed about to argue the point, but stopped herself. "Well, there's nothing to be done for it now," she said instead.

Sulana lowered her voice. "I'm sorry he's dead. I shouldn't have shot at him, but at the time, it seemed like the only way to end the chase."

We all stood awkwardly for a moment. Daven stepped up behind Sulana to place a comforting hand on her shoulder. Meghan looked into Sulana's eyes and seemed to accept what she saw there. She nodded her head once and folded her arms.

Sulana walked over to take a closer look at the stone box. "This is a lovely piece of work. How did you acquire it?"

"It was a gift from my husband," Meghan said quietly but with pride in her voice. "He loved to work with stone, and that box was the last thing he gave me before he died."

Sulana turned to Meghan and asked, "Did you know it would hide the ring?"

Meghan looked up sharply at Sulana. "No I did not," she replied. "What do you mean by *hide?*"

"I have a Seeker that is tuned to the ring. But while the ring was in the box, the Seeker was unable to find it," Sulana said, watching Meghan's reaction closely.

"How delightful!" Meghan clapped her hands together and smiled. She moved over to the box and caressed the lid, a wistful look on her face. "My Jon protects me even now," she muttered.

Sulana glanced toward the front door. "We should get going. We'll take the body with us along with anything he had with him." She reached under her cloak and pulled out a purse. "I can pay you for your care of him. If he had a purse, I'd like to take that with me along with its contents."

Meghan held up a hand. "I don't want your money. The knowledge you have given me about my precious box is worth enough to me. But there is one other thing I would ask of you." Sulana motioned her to continue. "I would like to see for myself how the box defeats the Seeker."

Sulana considered her request and shrugged. "I'd like to see that proven myself."

She took the ruby ring out and handed it to Meghan, who placed it back inside the box. She then produced the Seeker and went through the same routine I'd seen in the clearing. She placed the chain ring on her finger and dangled the Seeker. This time, I was close enough to distinctly hear her say, "Seek." Once again, it emitted a faint, high-pitched tone. The Seeker rotated once on its chain, but nothing else happened. She then said "stop," and the Seeker fell silent.

Sulana removed the Seeker's chain from her finger and looked closely at the device. "I suppose it may have just stopped working for some reason. We'll see."

Meghan retrieved the ruby ring from the box and passed it to Sulana. Sulana looked back and forth between the two objects in her hands, and then up at me. A mischievous smile appeared on her face, and she carefully handed the Seeker to me. "Here, you try it. Just please don't drop it."

I accepted the Seeker from her and held it away from me as if it were a live snake. "What do I do?" I asked uncertainly.

"Just put that ring at the end of the chain on a finger and dangle the Seeker like I did." She said.

Confused by the rapid turn of events, I did what she asked without questioning it. I put the Seeker's ring on my finger and dangled it as she had. Nothing happened. "Now what?" I asked.

"You have to tell it what to do," she explained. "The Seeker does all the work. Just tell it to seek."

I stared at the Seeker and said "seek," as I had heard Sulana do. But nothing happened. "It's not working," I said.

"Think about what you want it to do. Its purpose is to find this ring. Think about that and ask it to seek again," she instructed as she stepped a few paces away toward the fireplace.

I stared at the Seeker again and thought about the ruby ring. Find the ring, I thought, but aloud I said, "Seek."

To my surprise, the Seeker made its high-pitched whine again and started to rotate at the end of the chain. If it had not been attached to its ring on my finger, I think I may very well have dropped it. When the colored end pointed toward Sulana and the ruby ring, it stopped rotating and the volume of the whine increased.

In that moment, I felt a disorienting shift inside me. It was like something long dormant had awakened and shaken off the cobwebs of disuse. When the Seeker located the ruby ring, a tingling sensation of power flowed through my mind. The feeling was dizzying, as if I had drunk a bit too much wine.

I heard a gasp, and I looked over at Meghan. She was staring at me like I had sprouted antlers; her mouth had literally fallen open. I looked at Sulana to find that she was grinning triumphantly at me for some reason. Then I looked over at Daven, but he just rolled his eyes and shook his head.

"I thought so!" Sulana cried.

"What?" I asked a little too loudly over the Seeker's whine.

"Just proving a theory," Sulana said with satisfaction.

"How do I turn it off?" I asked.

"Just think about making it stop seeking the ring and say *stop*," she replied.

I did as she suggested and the Seeker fell silent once again. A sense of relief washed over me as the dizzy feeling went away. I removed the Seeker's ring and held the device out to Sulana. She took it back from me with an amused smirk.

Meghan had regained her composure and was considering me now with interest. She looked at Sulana. "I never imagined he was a Sensitive," she commented.

"Oh, he's more than that," Sulana said. "He's a Channeler."

"So I see," Meghan murmured, looking back at me appraisingly.

It was frustrating to feel left out of a conversation about me while I was standing right there. I gestured at the Seeker. "Would someone care to explain what just happened here?"

"You made the Seeker work," Sulana replied in a matter-of-fact tone. She seemed to be enjoying my discomfort and confusion.

"So what?"

"So, it means that not only are you sensitive to vaetra, you can also channel vaetra. I don't understand how you couldn't be aware of that."

Meghan interrupted. "You grew up among sorcerers, did you not?" she asked Sulana. Sulana nodded in reply. "Out here among the mundane, one is taught at an early age to fear and avoid sorcery. Showing an interest in it or fraternizing with those who practice it can have unpleasant consequences."

Sulana turned her attention back to me. "So you never tried to find out why you could hear manifestations? You never wondered if you could do more?"

I shook my head and shrugged my shoulders. "When would I have done that? Every time I've been in the presence of magic, sorry, *sorcery*, I've been with people who were suspicious of it, afraid of it, or hostile to it."

I looked at Meghan. "I gather that people who cannot sense vaetra are the *mundane?*" She nodded.

I looked back at the Seeker in Sulana's hand. "Anyway, I figured the sound sorcery makes is one of the things that unnerves people about it. And nobody wants to talk about it, so I had no idea that others don't hear it too."

"That's incredible!" Sulana exclaimed with a laugh. "I wonder how many other Channelers are out there who have no idea of what they can do?"

Meghan frowned. "Probably not many. Sensitivity often runs in families, and those families are often more accepting of sorcery, although they keep quiet about it. Many even test their children for the ability to channel and apprentice them to a sorcerer when it's practical."

Sulana nodded. "Yes, that's how we get most of the initiates at the Archives. A parent brings them to us for training. I never realized just how unusual that was."

"So what do I do now?" I asked, more than a little uncomfortable with my new status as a *Channeler*, and whatever that might imply.

"Nothing," said Sulana. "Unless you want to do something about it. You can just go back to your life and pretend all this never happened. Or you can travel to the Archives and learn how to use your gift. It's up to you."

It was too much to think about right then. I had a life. It had its frustrations, but I was busy enough already just trying to get back on my feet. The idea of running off to become a sorcerer held little appeal. I knew nothing about that world, and wasn't sure I wanted to.

Then again, operating the Seeker, even without realizing what I was doing, had been...interesting. No, more than that. In spite of it being a bit scary and disorienting, it had been *exciting* to make the Seeker work.

CHAPTER 6

Talon and Barek bundled up the dead thief in the blood-stained sheet he was lying on, and took him outside to be tied across his horse. It was an ignoble end to an ignoble life. The horse shied and sidled away when it scented the blood on its former master, so Talon held the reins and calmed the animal while Barek secured the corpse.

Meanwhile, Sulana negotiated with Meghan for a few samples of healing herbs and tonics that the healer was willing to sell. The two of them seemed to have settled into an unsteady truce, although I suspected Meghan was charging a premium, which Sulana accepted without haggling. Sulana seemed to have mastered the art of human relations through commerce.

I stood away from the others. My eyes wandered unfocused over their activities while I grappled with my first sorcery experience and tried to decide what I was going to do about it. Part of me longed to understand and explore the sensation that the Seeker had stirred within me, but I'd been taught to fear and avoid sorcery all of my life.

When I was seven years old, my mother took me home after a visit with a group of her women friends. Night had fallen, and the dark buildings lining the street loomed over us. Our lantern did little to fend off the darkness, and my little hand gripped hers tightly. We turned a street corner and saw an eerie red light moving down the street toward us. My mother stopped short and pulled me closer, her hold on my hand tightening so much that I squirmed with pain. As the light got closer, I could see it was bobbing at the top of a walking staff being carried by a man in a long, black, hooded cloak. Most of his face was hidden by his hood, but I saw him nod to my mother as he passed us. A small globe at the top of his staff gave off a high-pitched sound in addition to more light than a lantern could possibly produce. I stared in fascination as he passed, watching him continue down the street in a radiant halo of crimson luminosity.

My mother started walking again, pulling me along as fast as we could go. I tried to ask her about the man and his glowing staff, but she shushed me. She then told me something that has never left my mind. "You just stay away from people like that. Trafficking in magic will only bring you grief."

As I grew older, I learned that sorcerers had once tried to rule the world and that their rule had resulted in widespread death and destruction. After the Wizard Wars were over and the sorcerers were defeated, the Sorcery Accords ensured that sorcerers would never again hold dominion over mundane affairs. But now even centuries later, fear and distrust ran strong, and everyone believed that given the opportunity, sorcerers would try to rule again.

The idea that I might have the ability to work with magic, or "vaetra" as Sulana called it, made me feel a little ashamed and dirty. I even felt a little nauseous, but I couldn't tell if that was because of my concerns about this new discovery or because of a reaction to channeling.

Besides, the very idea of dropping everything and going off to the Archives for training was ridiculous. I had responsibilities at the Snow Creek Inn and issues to work out with Dela. I didn't want to miss opportunities with Raven Company either. If work came in, I had to be there to take it.

Nevertheless, I found myself drawn to the idea of spending more time with Sulana. I liked being near her. What that meant for my relationship with Dela was uncertain and probably not good.

Daven leaned on the outside wall of the cottage with his arms folded and watched me in bemusement as I paced back and forth considering my future. I finally stopped pacing and sighed.

"What have you decided?" Daven asked me. His tone was casual, but his words had an edge to them that hinted at more than a passing interest in my response. His gaze didn't waver from me as he waited for me to answer.

"Nothing," I finally said. "My life is complicated enough already without adding sorcery to the mix. As disturbing as the revelation is, I don't see how I can do anything about it right now."

Daven nodded, his lips pressed into a serious line. "I don't blame you. It's a lot to take in all at once. You've lived your life so far just fine without sorcery, so what's the point of changing that now? Even if you did decide to pursue it, you'd be starting pretty late in life and you'd have a lot of catching up to do."

I agreed with him completely, but for some reason, hearing it from him rankled a bit. "I'm a fast learner, so I think I could pick it up quickly, but you're right. Now isn't the time."

As the last words came out of my mouth, Sulana emerged from the healer's cottage with an armful of bottles and pouches. She headed over to her horse to add them to her saddle bags. As she walked by me she said, "It's up to you, of course. But I wouldn't waste your gift or the opportunity to develop it lightly. It could be a tremendous help to you in your work with Raven Company."

I considered her point. "That might be nice in the end, but I'd have to abandon my responsibilities for however long while I developed those skills."

Sulana finished lacing up her saddle bags and turned back to me. "Every goal has a price. It's up to you to decide if the price is worth achieving the goal."

I snorted. "How very philosophical of you. But from where I'm standing, the decision is far from easy."

"Life-changing decisions are never easy. I just think you should know what you may be giving up. I can probably answer the questions you must have about sorcery so you can make an informed decision."

Daven rolled his eyes and grunted. He walked off to where Barek and Talon were finishing their grisly task. Sulana watched him walk away and waited until he was out of earshot before turning back to me.

She lowered her voice and continued. "If you went to the Archives for training, it wouldn't take long to find out if you had a knack for sorcery and if you liked it. Within a month or so, you'd know if you wanted to continue. If you didn't think it could improve your life, you could just leave."

My eyes widened. "A month!" I exclaimed. "If I told Dela I was running off for a month, she'd sneak into my room and slit my throat in my sleep."

Sulana shrugged. "It would take at least a month just to learn the basics. If you decided to continue, it would take a year or more to become proficient. What did you expect?"

I smirked. "Well, that pretty much settles it. There's no way I can abandon my responsibilities for a year or more to learn skills I may never need to use. As Daven said, I've been doing fine without sorcery up to now." Okay, maybe I wasn't doing particularly fine at the moment, but I was working on it.

Sulana looked disappointed, which made me want to reach out and touch her arm, but I had nothing encouraging to say to her. She shrugged again. "Suit yourself. But the work you do for Raven Company isn't that different from what I do for the Archives. I'm certain sorcery would be a big help to you."

She looked over toward the horses and saw that the others were preparing to leave. "Well, we'd better get going," she said, and then she turned and walked away.

I wanted to stop her. To tell her something, anything, that would make her smile at me again. Every step she took away from me was a nail being hammered into the coffin of a possible future that might include her.

A future with Sulana held possibilities. And dangers. And complexity. My heart sank with the recognition that a significant opportunity had just passed, and I'd chosen to let it go.

~

Our return trip to Northshore was a somber procession. As expected, the road had thawed to mud in the morning sun and we had to move carefully. The horses occasionally hit a soft spot and slipped a bit, but overall the footing was not as treacherous as it would have been even a week before.

We all seemed lost in our own thoughts. I was busy wrestling with my conflicting feelings about sorcery and feeling anxious about the idea that Sulana would soon be on her way to finish her quest for the Archives. Sulana occasionally stole a glance over her shoulder in my direction and seemed about to say something, but each time she looked away quickly when she caught my eye. Talon and Barek plodded along and looked bored. Barek trailed the group, leading the horse that carried the dead thief.

Daven was the only one who appeared to be in relatively good spirits. He rode up alongside Sulana and tried to engage her in conversation a few times, but he gave up after getting a few monosyllabic responses from her.

The sun was now high in the sky and the morning had progressed from chilly to warm. We had removed our cloaks, and the sun on my hands and face was relaxing. But the warmth didn't lift my mood as much as it normally would.

We finally arrived at Northshore in the early afternoon. The guards at the west gate watched curiously as we passed, but they didn't try to engage us in conversation. Their job wasn't to inspect traffic as much as it was to watch for good reasons to close the gateway. If a threat appeared outside of town or a manhunt began on the inside, these two seemingly listless men would be swift to slam and bar the heavy gates.

One of the men nodded to me as we passed, mouthing my name. I acknowledged him with a nod of my own and continued on my way. That man had once been under my command, but now I was just another citizen.

We rode carefully through town, slowed by townspeople crossing the roadway and wagons heading to and from the town gate. Heads swiveled to watch us pass every step of the way to the Governor's Complex. Sulana took the lead as we approached the gate to the complex and the guards on station there. One of the guards stepped forward to get a closer look at the mud-splattered corpse draped over the horse that Barek led.

"We need to deliver this thief into custody and question the other man we captured yesterday," Sulana said to the guard who remained at the gate.

The young guard, whose name I knew was Zak, craned his neck to look over at the dead thief. "Doesn't look like we'll get much trouble from him," he said with a grin. "I gather he *resisted?*"

Sulana responded with clipped words. "It was an accident, actually." Even from behind her, I could see the color rise on her slender neck.

"An accident," nodded Zak with a knowing grin that was starting to annoy me. "I understand completely."

Sulana glared at him, but didn't respond to his needling. "May we pass now?" she asked.

"Be my guest," Zak said, as he stood aside to give our horses clear passage through the narrow gate. "Take the corpse to the infirmary for inspection and the horse to the stable for impound," he ordered in a more serious tone as we passed. He pointed unnecessarily at the infirmary, which was clearly identified by the large red circle above its door.

Sulana nodded her understanding and mumbled a thank you in his direction.

As I went by, he shouted up to me. "Hey Jaylan! How did you get mixed up with this crowd?"

In spite of my serious state of mind, I chuckled at his jocularity. "It's a long story, Zak. Buy me a drink sometime and I'll tell it to you."

"It's a deal. Good luck!" he said with a grin and a wave.

We brought the corpse over to the infirmary. A healer wearing a long grey smock and white skullcap came out to take a look. He asked Talon and Barek to move the body inside.

I waited outside and watched the normal afternoon bustle around the Governor's Complex. Guards crossed the courtyard on their various errands. The clang, clang of a smith's hammer rang out from the open doors to the stable and echoed off the front of the Governor's Residence. A young herald skipped down the steps of the residence, ran across the courtyard, and out through the gates to the town beyond, clutching a message tube in his hand.

I knew better than to think there was any particular urgency to his mission. The heralds were usually older teenage boys who were excited and proud of their chance to serve the Governor. They ran like that everywhere. The Governor encouraged them to treat every task as if it were a matter of life and death. One never knew when it really would be.

Sulana interrupted my musings. "Well, you've completed your bargain with Raleb. Do you want me to break the news to him? There's no sense you hanging around and wasting more time on this."

I looked at her closely, thinking maybe she was either goading me or trying to get rid of me, but she seemed sincere. "No, I should tell him myself. That's the least I can do for the amount of money he paid me, especially considering how it turned out."

She nodded. "I understand. I'll let you go in first and speak to him before I question him. He was apparently the junior partner, so I'm not sure how much I'll get from him anyway."

"Thanks. I think I'll head over there now," I said, turning my horse toward the prison.

"We'll catch up to you after we're done here," she said, gesturing toward the open door of the infirmary.

The guardroom at the prison was occupied by a single guard. The man looked up from his old wooden desk, which was little more than a small table really, as I closed the door behind me. "What can I do for you?" he asked stiffly.

The man knew me, of course. Most of the guards did. But he was apparently one of the crowd who had never forgiven me for getting myself mixed up in the scandal that had cost me my job. Or maybe he just hadn't liked working under me.

"I'm here to see the thief you are holding for Agent Delano. He's also a client of mine, and I need to pass on some information."

"A client?" he asked sharply, "Then perhaps you'd better leave your weapons here." He pointed to an empty weapons rack along the wall next to his desk. "Do you need to enter the cell?"

"No. I don't need to enter the cell. I just need to talk to him." Relieving me of my weapons was unnecessary, particularly since I didn't need to enter the cell, but there wasn't much point arguing about it with him. I unsheathed my sword and dagger and placed them on the rack.

"That it?" he asked.

"Yes," I answered, exasperation evident in my tone.

For a moment I thought he might frisk me, but he seemed to be satisfied with his control over the situation and grabbed a key from a nail on the wall beside him as he stood. He unlocked the door to the cell block, let me pass, and closed the door behind us. He stayed back at the door and said "third on the left."

I walked down to Raleb's cell, thankful that the guard had chosen to remain behind. The cells had stone walls and heavy, wooden doors with a foot-square, barred grate in the top half. The grate wouldn't make for the most intimate conversation, but I'd be able to impart what I'd learned.

Raleb had heard us enter and came over to the door to see what was happening. His eyes lit up when he saw me, but when he saw my expression, his face fell and he looked down at the floor. "It's bad news then."

"Yes, I'm sorry. We found Donal, but he was wounded in the ambush and didn't make it, in spite of a healer's care."

Raleb turned away from the door. He seemed to curl in on himself, and his shoulders heaved once. Then he straightened and took a few deep breaths. "Well, you earned your payment," he said hoarsely, and wiped his nose with a loud sniff. He turned back to me, his watery eyes giving testimony to his grief.

"Are you sure?" I asked gently. "It barely took a day and you paid me enough for two weeks."

He glared at me and said "Yeah, I'm sure. What would I do with the money in here anyway?" he waved his arms around and looked at the walls of his cell. Then he calmed again. "Sorry...it's not your fault. You did what I asked, so you earned the money."

I moved closer to the door and spoke more quietly so the guard would be less likely to overhear. "He was more than just your partner wasn't he?" I asked Raleb.

Raleb sighed and looked at me through the grate with watery eyes. "Yes, he was. My parents died from an illness when I was little. Donal took me in off the streets and shared his home. I'd have probably been found dead in an alley somewhere if not for him."

"So he was like a father to you," I concluded.

Raleb nodded and looked down. "He may not have set the best example, but he was all I had."

The guard was leaning against the door with his arms folded, watching our exchange. Then he heard noises coming from the guard room and opened the cell block door to see what was going on. He turned back to me and said, "You done? I have more people waiting." The implication was that he wasn't going to leave me in the cell block alone, which was fine. I didn't have anything more to tell Raleb.

"I need to go. I'm sorry about what happened to Donal and I hope things get better for you," I said.

"Yeah, sure. Thanks," he mumbled. I turned and walked back toward the guard.

Back in the guard room, Sulana and her shadow Daven had arrived. As I buckled my sword belt and stowed my dagger, Sulana came over to me. "How'd he take it?" she asked.

"Not well. The two of them were close," I said.

"Well, they chose a dangerous line of work. It was bound to catch up with them eventually," she said a little defensively.

I nodded back at her. "If they had just handed over the ring instead of running, you probably wouldn't even have detained them."

"Probably not," she affirmed.

I wasn't sure what else to say. This was probably the last time I'd see Sulana, but I couldn't think of a good way to say goodbye. The silence stretched between us.

Daven looked back and forth between us a couple of times and then spoke up. "Are we leaving the thief here after questioning? Or do you plan to take him with us?"

I took Daven's words as my cue to leave. They had a job to do, and mine was done. "Well, it was good working with you," I said lamely and held my hand out to Daven with a smile.

He smiled back at me and shook my hand. "You too."

I turned to Sulana and looked deeply into the blue eyes I was certain would haunt my thoughts for some time to come. "Good luck with your mission," I said, and held my hand out to her as well.

She shook my hand slowly. "Thanks for your help. And good luck with the inn and your Raven Company work."

We stopped shaking hands, but left them clasped together for a moment. We slowly let them drop apart. "Thanks," I said, and turned to go.

I opened the door to the courtyard and stopped. I half-turned back to them. "If you are ever in the area again, please come by the inn and look me up." My glance included both of them, but I think Daven knew who I was really inviting.

Sulana just nodded. Daven stepped a little closer to Sulana, waved at me, and said, "Okay, bye."

CHAPTER 7

Sulana watched Jaylan leave the room and close the door behind him. She wished he would reconsider the idea of exploring his skills with sorcery. It seemed like such a waste for him to let them lie dormant. There were so few sorcerers as it was. She shook her head with a reminder to herself that it was his decision to make.

Sulana turned to the prison guard. "We're here to question the thief we captured yesterday."

The guard looked them both over and nodded. "Right this way."

The guard led them into the cell block and down to Raleb's cell. He shouted through the grate, "Prisoner, back away from the door and get down on your knees." He watched while Raleb complied and then unlocked the heavy cell door. Keeping a close eye on Raleb, the guard let Sulana and Daven into the cell.

Sulana heard the guard close the door behind her, but focused her attention on Raleb. "You can sit," she said to him.

Raleb got off his knees and sat on his sleeping mat. Daven took a position between Raleb and Sulana, but out of their line of conversation. He pulled his dagger and kept it at the ready. Raleb looked up at him sullenly and then glared at Sulana.

"You're the one who killed Donal, aren't you?" he asked.

Sulana grimaced and looked down. "I'm sorry about what happened," she said. "I never meant to kill him. I just needed to get the ring back." She looked into Raleb's eyes. "You shouldn't have run."

Raleb snorted and shook his head. "Of course we ran! We had no idea who you were. You jumped us out of nowhere, and our customers don't appreciate it if we hand over our cargo at the first sign of trouble."

"Watch your tone," said Daven and he took a step toward Raleb. Raleb just raised his chin and sneered at Daven, daring him to do his worst.

Sulana waved Daven back. "Actually, it's your customer I wanted to ask about."

Raleb sighed and looked down at his hands. "Donal handled the negotiations, so there's not much I can tell you."

"Do you know who hired you to steal the ring?"

"I never heard his name. Donal seemed to think he was some kind of sorcerer," Raleb answered.

Sulana's eyes narrowed, and she leaned toward Raleb. "Are you sure of that?"

Raleb looked up at her. "No, I'm not sure. Like I said, Donal handled the negotiations."

"Okay, right." Sulana thought for a moment. "Where were you supposed to deliver it?" she asked.

"Some village near Delta," he answered. "Donal said something about it being on a peninsula, but never said the name."

Daven glanced over at Sulana. "Well, that should narrow things down quite a bit," he said.

Her eyes brightened, and she nodded at him. "I think it does. If memory serves, there's only one peninsula near Delta, and I doubt there's more than one village on it." She turned back to Raleb. "How did you know what to steal and where to find it?"

"Donal had a description of the ring, but he didn't know exactly where it would be hidden. Turns out it wasn't hidden at all. It was in a black lacquered box on a dresser, practically the first place I looked. I was in and out in about two minutes."

Daven chuckled, and Sulana smiled as well. "We'll have to tell the sorcerer who owns it to be more careful with it in the future," she said. "Thank you for cooperating."

Raleb shrugged in response. He looked back and forth between Sulana and Daven, his glance lingering on the drawn dagger with a doubtful frown. "What are you going to do with me now?" he asked.

Sulana's tone became serious. "You caused a lot of trouble, but we recovered the ring. We'll leave you in the hands of the local authorities. What the Governor decides to do with you is up to him. Unless you have a criminal history here in the Lakewoods Province, I doubt the punishment will be too severe."

Raleb nodded his understanding and shifted uncomfortably on his pallet. He then asked, "I'd like to know something. How did you know where to ambush us? Was it the ring? I know there's sorcery involved."

Sulana hesitated. She wouldn't normally divulge the kind of information he was asking about, but he had already guessed half of it, and she felt bad about what happened to Donal. She finally nodded. "Yes, I have a way to track the ring." Daven looked over at her with raised eyebrows, surprised she had answered honestly.

Raleb waited for her to continue, but shrugged when he saw that was all she was willing to tell him. "Thought it was something like that. I knew that contract would be trouble the day we took it, but the money was too good for Donal to pass up. And he's the one who used to tell *me* that money was no good if you were too dead to spend it."

Sulana stepped back to the cell door and rapped on it a couple of times to let the guard know they were ready to leave. The guard must have been standing outside the entire time because the door opened almost immediately.

Sulana turned back to Raleb and said, "I'm sorry about your partner and I hope you can find something better to do with your life, once you've served your time."

Raleb looked back at her with a grim expression. "Believe me, I've been trying to do that for a long time."

Sulana and Daven left the room, Daven sheathing his dagger as he did so. The guard stared openly at Sulana when they emerged, then shuddered and locked the cell door behind them. Sulana assumed he had heard the part about her being able to track the ring with sorcery.

Back in the guard room, Sulana turned to the guard as he hung the prison door key back on the wall. "What will his sentence be?" she asked.

The guard shrugged. "Probably a couple months of hard labor, since the merchandise was recovered and he's been cooperative with your investigation."

Sulana nodded and thanked him for his help. She and Daven went back outside where Talon and Barek waited with the horses. She climbed into her saddle and checked around for nearby listeners. Satisfied their conversation was not being overheard, she spoke quietly to the others. "We have a problem."

Barek responded, "What? We have the ring. We caught the thieves. Mission accomplished."

"The thieves were hired," Talon interjected.

"Exactly," Sulana said. "By a sorcerer." She let that sink in. "This was no random theft. The thieves were hired specifically to retrieve the ring. That means this sorcerer knows what it is and what it can do."

Barek asked, "Why does that matter? He didn't get the ring."

Sulana shook her head at Barek's single-mindedness. The mission had been to retrieve the ring, and they had done that. As far as Barek was concerned, the mission was a success and returning to the Archives was the only task remaining.

"Not this time, but he may try again," Talon concluded.

Sulana nodded at Talon. "That's what I'm thinking too. We need to find out what he's up to. We can start with the village that was going to be the delivery spot. We need to go now before this sorcerer figures out we've intercepted the ring and disappears."

Talon held up his hand. "Hold on there, Sulana. That investigation is way outside our mission objectives. Our mission was to retrieve the ring and return it to the Archives. Confronting some unknown sorcerer of unknown skill could jeopardize everything we've just accomplished."

Barek nodded with a satisfied smile on his face. "Yes. Finish this mission first. Then maybe we go after the sorcerer."

Seeing that Talon and Barek were resolute on the issue, she looked at Daven, who shrugged his shoulders and looked down. "What they say makes sense, Sulana, but you're in charge."

Sulana was anxious to get to the bottom of the theft, but knew that Talon was right. Although she was in charge of this mission, his experience and perspective were not to be taken lightly. It was the reason he had been chosen to be her second in command. He was more a mentor than underling. Normally, he would be the one in charge of this group, but she had earned this chance to prove her leadership, and she was thankful for his respectful support.

Sulana exhaled harshly in frustration. "Delaying the investigation may mean we lose our chance to catch up with the ringleader, but you're right. We have no idea what we're up against, and it wouldn't hurt to have stronger sorcery on our side."

Talon nodded at her, encouraging her line of thought. Barek continued to smile, and Daven watched her face, waiting for her decision.

Sulana narrowed her eyes in thought for a moment, and then took a deep breath. "Fine. Back to the Archives then." She turned her horse toward the gate and rode out of the Governor's Complex. The others followed in her wake.

CHAPTER 8

The morning following my journey to the healer's cottage, I was determined to stop thinking about sorcery, channeling, and a certain pair of blue eyes. I threw myself into one of the Snow Creek Inn's remaining restoration tasks for a distraction.

I went to the stable, observed the current state of the stalls, and shook my head. They had been poorly constructed to begin with, and now the hinges were either crumbling into piles of rust flakes or pulling free of the gate's rotting wood. Half of the gates were held in place by loops of thin rope, which made it difficult to open and close the flimsy things.

The week before, I had been trying to close one of the ruined gates when it caught on the stable floor and sprang back to whack me in the forehead. I was so angry that I literally tore the gate off its hinges and threw it across the stall where it shattered against the stable wall into a pile of cracked boards and splinters. The two horses in the nearby stalls whinnied and ran in circles, kicking out and nearly crashing free in their distress. I'd had to speak soothingly to them for a while before they finally calmed down.

I stared at the gateless stall, ashamed that I had put off repairing it for so long.

Griz had completed most of the renovations on the inn building itself, but he had saved the outbuildings for last—a "last" that never arrived. I had been slowly working on finishing the repairs myself, in between helping Dela and her mother with the daily operations of the inn and my occasional Raven Company contracts.

As I surveyed the challenge awaiting me, I consoled myself with the knowledge that this week was much better than last week. Thanks to Raleb, I had plenty of money for the wood that was needed to rebuild the gates and stalls. The new boards stacked in a pile at the back of the stable would get me through the day, but I'd have to pick up some more wood soon.

I decided to replace the stall I had damaged in anger first. I settled into the satisfying work of demolishing the old stall and constructing the new one. I turned the new gate hinges I had purchased that morning over in my hands, admiring their craftsmanship and smooth movement. Burl the blacksmith did good work. These new hinges would outlast the old ones tenfold.

I had just finished hanging the gate and was testing how well it opened and shut when the light from the stable door dimmed. I turned to see a young man enter the stable wearing a black tabard, trimmed in grey, with the Raven Company crest over the left breast. He stepped around the old boards I had discarded when I demolished the old stall.

"Nice job, Mister Forester," he said with a smile.

It was Meldon, Raven Company's most recent recruit. Meldon was a lanky lad of about twenty years of age, with brown hair and eyes, and a face that made the girls smile and blush at him as he walked past. His fighting skills were coming along nicely on Borlan's steady training regimen, and he had proven to be a good bowman.

"Thanks, Meldon. What's up?"

"Borlan sent me over. He'd like to see you as soon as you have a moment. He has a lead on a contract for you." Meldon walked around me to inspect my handiwork. "Let me know if you want help with this," he said. "Things are slow at Raven Company and I could use a little extra work."

I thought about that for a minute. "Do you think you could take it on unsupervised, or would you need me to show you what to do?"

Meldon perked up, seeing that I was seriously considering his suggestion. "Oh, I have experience. I used to help my older brothers on my father's farm all the time. After a while, they trusted me to take on some of the repair jobs myself."

I scratched my chin and mulled over the idea of hiring him. If his help didn't come at too high a price, I could handle my responsibilities for the inn and make more on the Raven Company contract than I'd spend paying him to get this work done. That train of thought raised a question.

"Why didn't Borlan give *you* the contract?" I asked him.

Meldon shrugged and hesitated before answering. "Well, he said it was the kind of work you're best at...and he didn't think I was ready to do the job by myself," he finished with a disappointed sigh.

Meldon had only been with Raven Company for a couple of months, and his inexperience limited the kind of work Borlan was willing to entrust to him. In the short time I'd known him, Meldon seemed eager and conscientious, but he was also reticent to engage in any kind of confrontation. That quality was the true source of Borlan's concerns about his potential effectiveness as a guard.

"Tell you what. I think we can make this work for both of us. I'll see what Borlan has, and if it works out, I'll hire you to take over for me here while I attend to the contract. How does that sound?"

"That'd be great, Mister Forester!" he said with vigorous nodding of his head and a wide grin.

I laughed and slapped him across his back. "Call me Jaylan. Now, let's go see what Borlan has for me."

As we walked out of the stable, I briefly considered changing out of my work clothes and telling Dela I'd be gone for a few minutes, but there seemed little point of doing either. I wasn't going to be meeting a client, so the clothes didn't matter, and telling Dela I was headed over to the Raven Company offices would just lead to another argument. I decided to save the argument for later, after I knew whether or not Borlan's contract would be worth it.

~

Borlan looked up from his lunch as Meldon and I walked into the front door of Raven Company. He wiped his mouth and glared. "I told you there was no rush!" he shouted at Meldon. He turned to me and spoke apologetically. "He didn't tell you to drop everything and run over here, did he?"

Meldon looked at me helplessly. I shook my head and chuckled. "Don't get yourself worked up, Borlan. I just happened to be at a good stopping point when Meldon showed up."

Borlan looked over at Meldon with chagrin. "Sorry about that, Meldon. Thanks for taking the message."

"Yes, sir. You're welcome sir. Should I go back to straightening up the armory?"

"Yeah, go ahead. Sorry, kid. Wish I had more work for you right now."

"That's alright sir. I'm sure things will pick up soon." Meldon hurried out of the room and headed for the basement door, which led down into the armory and the training area.

"He's a good kid. But I don't think his heart's in this work," Borlan said to me after he heard the door to the basement close.

"He might just need more experience to boost his confidence," I said.

"Maybe. You could take him on this job with you, if you don't mind sharing the fee with him," Borlan suggested.

"That's not a bad idea, but I may have a better use for him," I said.

Borlan looked at me in confusion. "What do you have in mind?"

I waved my hand and dodged his question. "It depends on this contract. What do you have?"

Borlan looked down at a message on his desk, and then back at me. "A teenage boy is missing down near Delta. He and some friends apparently went out into the forest last night. All the rest came back except this boy."

I frowned. "Why doesn't the father just go look for him?"

"The man apparently has more money than he has time to chase after a runaway son," Borlan reasoned. "Lucky for us."

"How much is he willing to pay?" I asked, my interest piqued.

"Five gold crowns. Two up front, three when you deliver the boy to the father." Borlan raised an eyebrow and watched for my reaction.

"That much?" I said in surprise. The sum was more than double what I had anticipated. Then I narrowed my eyes at Borlan. "What aren't you telling me?"

Borlan chuckled and nodded his head. "There is a bit of a catch. He wants the investigation kept quiet. No raising of alarms, no large search parties, and no fuss when the boy is found. He specifically requested that you not wear a Raven Company tabard," he added with a smirk.

Some of the men wore their black Raven Company tabard with pride, but Borlan felt the same way I did about them; we wished they weren't required attire for all official Raven Company postings. Lucky for me, a lot of the work I did required a low profile, so Borlan often exercised the Captain's Discretion clause of the tabard rule that allowed me to leave mine behind. The Customer Request clause was another such exception.

As much as I appreciated the reprieve, I still wondered why the search would be kept a secret. "Did he say why?"

Borlan shook his head. "No. I asked his messenger what he thought, and the man just said his master's wishes were made clear enough in the request and it wasn't his place to question them."

"Huh." I leaned over Borlan's desk and picked up the note. It didn't reveal anything Borlan hadn't already told me, except the client's name. "Are you familiar with this Jergen Overland fellow?"

"He's the owner of Overland Mercantile down in Delta." Borlan answered. "My cousin works for him down there. He never had much good to say about the man. Says he's a slave driver, but a good businessman."

"What do *you* think about this?" I asked him, putting the note back on his desk.

"Sounds like easy money to me," he said with a shrug. "You actually thinking of turning it down?"

"No. I'm just a little wary of people who seem to have more money than decency."

Borlan snorted. "I hear you, but don't worry about it. All you have to do is find this kid, and you'll be five crowns richer. Well, four anyway." Raven Company would get twenty percent for the referral.

I shook off my misgivings, took a deep breath, and nodded in agreement. "You're right. I'll take it."

I thought about the time of day and the fact that a search for a missing person should get started as soon as possible, while the trail is still fresh. "I should probably try to get down there this afternoon. I'll have to ride hard to make it there with any light left in the day."

Borlan nodded. "Right." He looked at me seriously for a moment more, and then lowered his voice. "I said not to worry, but I think this job has an odd odor to it too. Keep your eyes open while you're down there in Delta."

I smiled at Borlan. "I'll do that. I know better than to ignore my instincts on these things, particularly when you share them."

Borlan nodded and leaned back in his chair. "Good." He picked up a hunk of bread from his desk and waved it at me. "Now get out of here so I can finish my lunch."

I chuckled and headed for the basement door. I had some negotiating to do with Meldon before I rode out to see about finding a lost boy.

CHAPTER 9

I rode up to Overland Mercantile in the late afternoon. Patches' lower half was splattered with mud from our hurried journey down to Delta. His namesake knee markings were barely visible through the grime. The horse plodded slowly with his head down as we clopped up to the hitch rail at the front of the store, and he exhaled deeply when I finally dismounted.

Along the side of the building, two men were loading heavy sacks onto a large wagon that was hitched to a four-mule team. I waved in greeting and tied Patches to the railing before heading toward the store entrance.

The Overland Mercantile store was bigger than you would expect for a small town like Delta. The town of Delta was home to only about a hundred people, but the Overlands had taken advantage of their location near the head of East Teardrop River to become a commerce hub for the entire Lakewoods Province, which encompassed the northern-most territory of the Tanes Empire.

The store protruded from the front of a large warehouse. Behind the warehouse, a long dock extended out onto Teardrop Lake. The Overlands owned a small fleet of boats that moved goods across the lake when the weather was right, which shaved time off the long, circuitous land journey.

I opened the solid front door to go inside. The well-oiled hinges made no sound, but a tiny bell positioned above the door tinkled as I entered, cheerfully announcing my presence. Looking around, I could see open barrels with tools sticking out of them and stacks of crates displaying all manner of items. In one corner, a few crates were draped with white cloth, and some of the more exotic and delicate items were arrayed upon them. Lamp light sparkled on a series of glass figurines, which reminded me of Sulana and our strange adventure yesterday.

A tall, middle-aged woman with a friendly smile and intelligent grey eyes glided toward me from behind the counter at the back of the store. Her plain, woolen, shopkeeper's dress could not mask the aristocratic bearing of a woman of means. She glanced in the direction of my stare. "The figurines are made by a local artist. His work is known throughout the area. If you'd like one of them for your sweetheart, I can give you an exceptional bargain."

I pushed distracting memories of vaetric artifacts and a small blonde sorceress to the back of my mind and smiled back at her. "Thank you, but I'm Jaylan Forester, from Raven Company. May I speak to the owner?"

The woman's smile dissolved into a worried frown and she clasped her hands together. "Oh, I'm so glad you were able to come so quickly. I didn't expect to see anyone until tomorrow at the earliest! I'm so worried about Tam that I can hardly concentrate on running the store."

"You're the boy's mother?" I asked.

"Yes! I'm so sorry, Mister Forester. Where are my manners? I'm Greta Overland, but please call me Greta. My husband is Jergen Overland, and Tam is our son. Tam went out with his friends last night and never came home. He's never done this before."

"Try not to worry, Greta, I'm here to help you find him. And please, call me Jaylan. Calling me 'Mister Forester' will have me looking over my shoulder for my father. So, what about the other boys? Did they make it home last night?"

"Yes. My husband went over to the Wright's home last night, and Tam's friend Alain said they had gotten separated in the forest. They assumed Tam had returned home without them." She dropped her gaze to the floor and frowned.

I could tell she wasn't convinced by the boy Alain's story. "You don't believe him? You think he's lying?"

She looked back up at me, her eyes wide. "I don't know what to believe! Those two boys are so close, I can't believe Alain would come home and leave Tam behind."

"Do you know where they went? Or what they were doing?"

She sighed and shook her head. "No, I don't. My husband was the one to speak with Alain and his father, and I'm afraid he can be a bit...intimidating. Particularly when he's angry, and he was certainly angry. It wouldn't surprise me if Alain said as little as possible. He's probably concerned about getting Tam in trouble."

I lowered my voice. "I don't mean to be insensitive, but I can't help but wonder why you hired Raven Company to deal with a missing boy." I watched her face carefully.

She took a deep breath and blew it out. Then she straightened and looked me in the eye. "My husband has a business to run. He can't waste the day traipsing through the forest looking for a rebellious boy." She bowed her head and mumbled, "Even if that boy is his own son."

"I'm sorry, but I had to ask," I said, and she nodded. "I gather Tam and his father were having a disagreement?"

She snorted. "Don't all teenage boys disagree with their father?" She grimaced and went on with a disapproving tone. "But yes, Tam has this fantasy of becoming an Imperial Guard and traveling the Empire. He has little interest in following in his father's footsteps."

I nodded. "I think I understand. Well, I should probably speak to your husband and then see what I can find out from Alain as soon as possible. I may be able to do a little searching today, but I'm afraid Tam may be spending another night in the forest."

She placed her hand on my arm. "Oh, please don't interrupt my husband. I've already told you what he knows. You can report straight to me." She released me and reached into a pocket of her skirt. "I have your fee right here." She opened a small coin purse, extracted two gold crowns, and held them out to me. When I opened my hand to receive them, she pressed the coins into my palm and closed my fingers around them, holding my hand closed with both of hers.

She looked directly into my eyes, with tears beginning to pool in her own. "Please find Tam. This is very unlike him, even if he was angry with his father. I'm worried that something bad has happened."

I patted the top of her hand with my free one and reassured her. "Try not to think like that. We don't really know anything yet." I nodded over my shoulder at the door. "Tam could walk in at any moment."

She looked down, blinked the moisture from her eyes, and released my hand. "I hope you're right. Well, I suppose I shouldn't keep you. Will you be staying the night in Delta?"

I nodded. "I was hoping to. Can you recommend a place to stay?"

She nodded and pointed north. "Yes, go to the Eagle's Rest just up the road. My friend Penny runs it. Tell her I sent you and that I'll take care of the charges. It's a small boarding house, but you'll be comfortable."

I raised my eyebrows in surprise. "Thank you. That's very generous."

She waved my thanks aside. "Penny could use the business. If you like it there, perhaps you could spread a good word for her."

I smiled and chuckled at Greta's irrepressible focus on business. I was sure that the success of Overland Mercantile was not all her husband's doing. "It's a deal," I told her.

～

I left Overland Mercantile feeling much better about my finances and a little better about the contract. I learned that Jergen Overland had directed his wife to manage the search for Tam and to keep it quiet. Greta didn't share all of the details with me, but it seemed that her husband didn't want everyone to know just how wide a rift had developed between him and Tam, and he was convinced that Tam had run away, not just gotten lost. The five crown fee made much more sense if I was going to have to pursue the boy across the province. Jergen still hoped to secure the future of his business, and the confidence of his suppliers and customers, by convincing Tam to take over for him one day.

Before I departed, Greta gave me a description of Tam and told me where I could find Tam's friend Alain. The boy's father was the local wainwright, and Alain worked for him.

Patches perked up his ears and gave a soft nicker when I came out of the shop to collect him. He seemed to have recovered from our hasty trip down here. I patted him on the neck and promised a treat later. The wagon shop was just down the street, so I didn't bother riding. Instead, I led Patches down to a stand of trees next to the shop, and I left him there to graze in the shade.

As I approached the big open doors at the side of the shop, sounds of industrious sawing and hammering greeted me. I inhaled deeply, enjoying the smell of freshly cut wood. The shop had plenty of windows to admit as much natural light as possible. Each pane was dimmed somewhat by a thin layer of sawdust. Inside the shop were two wagons, two large work benches, and a collection of metal tools stored along the back wall. One of the wagons was a well-used buckboard that was getting a wheel repaired. The other wagon was being newly built and was still just a frame on stands at this point.

When I stepped up to the doorway, a stout, clean-shaven man looked up from marking measurements on a new wagon frame and nodded toward me. "Afternoon. What can I do for you?" he asked. A thin young man looked up from his work repairing the broken wheel.

I introduced myself to the older man and told him that the Overlands had hired me to find Tam. I asked if I could speak to Alain for a few minutes. He looked over at the younger man, and his son glanced back at him. The man sighed. "Go ahead, but don't take too long. That wheel won't finish itself."

"Yes, sir." Alain set down the hammer he was using and stepped around his workbench. As he came outside, the late afternoon sun lit his shock of unruly, bright red hair and emphasized the freckles on his face and sawdust-sprinkled arms.

Alain wiped his palms on the heavy apron he was wearing and we shook hands. He waited for me to speak first.

"I spoke with Tam's mother a few minutes ago. She couldn't tell me much, and she's very worried. What can you tell me about what happened last night?" I asked him.

Alain chewed his lower lip and glanced back in the shop at his father before responding. "I'm worried too. We always stick together, so I wasn't sure what to think when Tam didn't return to the clearing with us."

I shook my head and held up a hand. "Let's back up a bit. Tell me what happened last night from the beginning."

He nodded and took a deep breath. "Tam, our friend Jess, and I went out into the forest yesterday evening. We explored a few trails and then headed home. We got separated on the way back, but when that happens, we normally just meet up at the clearing where we started. But this time, Tam never showed up. It was getting late, so we couldn't go back and look for him. We left his belongings in the clearing in case he came back after we left."

Alain's recounting sounded rehearsed and a little hollow. I was fairly certain I wasn't getting the whole story. "Why go out into the forest and explore trails at night? How do you see where you're going?"

His green eyes darted around as he answered me, and he glanced back at his father again. "The moon was nearly full last night, and once your eyes adjust, you'd be amazed what you can see. The forest is different at night. It's beautiful."

That part rang true, if somewhat strange. "So, you boys go hiking at night because it's what? Exciting?"

He finally looked me fully in the eyes. "Oh, yes sir. It's like nothing else. Different animals are awake. The scents are different. The moonlight shining down through the trees is... magical."

I raised my eyebrows at his sudden intensity and nodded. "Okay. If you say so."

I looked up at the sky to judge the sun's position. I had maybe three hours remaining before dark. "Do you have any thoughts about why Tam hasn't returned yet?"

Alain furrowed his brow and shook his head. "No, sir. We've gone out into the forest at night several times and this has never happened before. Tam was always careful about getting back before his father would start to wonder where he was."

"Can you tell me where this clearing is? I'd like to see what I can learn before the day is done."

Some of the tension eased out of his stance, and he nodded. He seemed relieved that our interview was almost over. "Head back on the road toward Northshore. Right after you pass the part along the slough, you'll see a road that goes out onto the peninsula. Do you know where I mean?" He paused, and I nodded for him to continue.

"Take that road until it jogs to the right. You'll see a sign there that points the way to Buckwoods Village. Behind the sign is a trail that will take you into the forest and to the clearing. It isn't far. You should be able to look around and get back by dark."

I nodded my understanding of his instructions. "Thanks, Alain. I'll go see what I can learn."

"Good luck, sir. I hope you find him and bring him home." He looked over his shoulder at his father again. "If that's all, I need to get back to work." He held out his hand.

We shook hands again and I smiled at him. "Thanks again for your help." He nodded and went back into the shop.

I walked over to Patches, gathered his reins, and slowly climbed into the saddle, thinking through what I'd discovered. I had never been to Buckwoods before, but the peninsula it was on certainly narrowed down the area I had to search, assuming Tam was still around there somewhere.

I turned Patches onto the main road and headed out of Delta to see what clues might await me out on the peninsula.

CHAPTER 10

Sulana stared at Talon's back as he led the way up the steep rocky trail. She hated this part. Their horses threaded along the narrow path across an open area created by an old rockslide. She felt like she was perched on the side of the mountain with a looming mass of unstable boulders above her and a hungry cascade of sharp-edged teeth below her. She cringed when her horse kicked a loose stone and sent it skipping and clattering down the face of the jumbled rocks until it disappeared into the trees.

She had to admit the view was spectacular, though. To her right was an incredible vista of trees and mountain peaks for as far as the eye could see. An enormous eagle rode the air currents with hardly a flap, rising in circles higher into the sky. It soared to land on the top of a tall snag where it screeched an echoing cry. Crows flew from tree to tree, cawing at each other and then suddenly swooping over a ridge to the next crease in the mountain.

At least her team was making good time, Sulana thought. They had left Northshore yesterday afternoon after interrogating Raleb, and they had gone as far as they could before nightfall. They made camp in the valley last night, and got up at dawn to head up the trail into the mountains this morning. She expected to reach their destination before nightfall, or at least she hoped they would. These mountains could become unfriendly at night.

Sulana breathed a sigh of relief when the horses left the open scree and entered the trees once again, but she also tensed a little and looked carefully around through the thick trunks that limited her visibility. As they had ascended into the mountains, their journey had become more shadowed by the clouds that gathered around the upper elevations. The clouds were a blessing for their horses as they slogged up the trail, but it made the forest understory seem darker and more sinister.

Daven closed the gap between their horses. "Sulana, you never told us. What does the ring do?" Barek and Talon perked up at his question, and cocked their heads to hear her answer.

She considered his question for a moment. She didn't remember receiving any instructions regarding secrecy among her own team, and these men were all trusted by the Archives. They wouldn't have been sent with her if that weren't the case. As a general rule, information about sorcery was withheld from the mundane, but her team had put their lives on the line for her, and they probably deserved to know why.

Before she could reply, Daven's disappointed voice came from behind her. "Okay, fine. Don't tell us."

"I'll tell you," Sulana chastised. "I was just thinking, that's all."

Talon spoke over his shoulder from his position at the head of the group. "Give her a break, Daven. You know there are some secrets she can't share with us non-sorcerer types."

Before Daven could retort, she shook her head and raised her voice. "That's not the case here, though. The ring is a Portal Key."

"I've heard of those," Talon said. "They let sorcerers travel quickly from one place to another."

Sulana nodded. "Right. Portals are scattered throughout the empire, and a Portal Key allows sorcerers to use them. You enter one portal and come out through another."

"But the portals could be miles apart," Daven concluded.

"Exactly," Sulana responded, "and now we need to know who was trying to get his hands on the Portal Key and why."

"So that's why you wanted to go after the buyer right away," Daven said. "You should have told us about this. Maybe we *should* have gone after him while we had the chance."

Sulana shook her head. "No, Talon was right. If this sorcerer has plans that involve a Portal Key, he probably has the power to back up those plans and possibly the support of other sorcerers. We can't confront someone like that with only my limited abilities."

Talon nodded. "Carrying the Portal Key to someone who has the power to take it away from us would have defeated the purpose of our mission to retrieve it."

"So you said before," Daven retorted. "I don't think I fully understood why until now. This guy could be real trouble. Any idea who it is?"

Sulana shook her head. "No. We don't even know enough to guess. I'm hoping Ebnik or one of the councilors will have some theories. But we may not be the ones to find out. They may send a more experienced team to deal with this."

"After all we've been through? Isn't this *our* mission?" Daven asked.

"Our mission is done when we return the ring," answered Talon.

Barek spoke up for the first time in the conversation. "Yes. We finish this mission first. If we get a new mission to go after the sorcerer, we find him and deal with him."

"Barek's right. One thing at a time," Sulana agreed.

Everyone was silent for a moment. Then Daven asked, "If time is critical and these portals are all over the empire, couldn't you have used the key to get us to the Archives faster?"

Sulana shrugged. "Possibly. But I've never used one before, and I've never seen anyone else use one either, so I'm not sure how it works. I'm not comfortable experimenting with sorcery that makes you disappear from one place and, hopefully, reappear in another."

She raised an eyebrow and looked back at Daven, who shuddered.

Interrupting their conversation, Talon suddenly raised his hand and shushed them. "Listen," he said as he stopped his horse. The line of horses closed up behind him and stopped as well.

Sulana listened, but didn't hear anything at first. Then she did hear something. *Thump, thump, crack.* Her horse's ears twitched and it raised its head, nostrils quivering.

Something large was near them in the forest. Talon heard the crack as well and peered into the trees to locate its source, which seemed to be somewhere off to their right. He slowly drew his sword. "Sulana, I think you'd better ready that crossbow of yours," he said quietly.

She did as he suggested, and spoke just loudly enough for him to hear. "This isn't a good place for a fight. Do you remember there being any defensible positions nearby?"

Talon shook his head. "No. The only nearby open area is the landslide behind us, but that has its own problems." Sulana gulped as she imagined trying to carry on a fight while perched on that narrow path where one misstep would mean a tumble down the face of the mountain. Talon tilted his head forward down the trail. "We may be able to reach a spot where the trail's a little wider, though," he suggested.

Sulana nodded. "Okay, let's try for that. What do you think we heard?"

Talon grinned back at her over his shoulder, a fierce gleam in his eyes. "A troll."

Sulana groaned. Fighting a troll in close quarters was not a good idea. Trolls were all teeth and claws and fury. The best way to fight a troll was from a distance, but that wasn't an option on this section of trail.

Sulana looked behind her at Barek and Daven. "Talon thinks we're being stalked by a troll. We're going to try to reach a wider spot in the trail. Daven, ready your bow. Barek, watch for anything coming up from behind us. It could decide to attack at any time."

Barek slid his broadsword from its sheath with a hiss of steel and a grim smile.

Sulana gave Daven a moment to string his bow, which was not an easy feat on horseback. But he'd had plenty of practice trapping one end of the bow in his stirrup and hauling down the other end to loop the string over it. It wasn't something one did on the move, however.

While Daven readied his bow, Sulana tucked her crossbow under her arm and reached into a small pocket on her belt. She extracted a ring with a silver band and a green stone. She slipped the ring onto her thumb, which was the only finger large enough to wear it securely.

When Daven was ready, he nodded at her and the team started forward. As soon as they moved, Sulana heard a low rumbling growl from behind the trees and more thumping noises. She looked over and caught a brief glimpse of dark brown fur moving between the trunks. Her stomach tightened and her pulse pounded in her neck from the adrenalin that flooded her system.

The troll was enormous. She didn't get a clear view, but even on all fours, it looked like it would come up to her shoulder if she were standing next to it.

She had never encountered a troll before, but they weren't uncommon in these mountains, so she knew a lot about them from the tales of others. Trolls were completely covered in thick dark fur and had a leather-tough hide. They had long forelegs and shorter hind legs, both ending with paws that were lethally clawed.

They tended to run on all fours, but would rear up when they closed to attack. The moment a troll reared up was when it was most vulnerable, but the animal was so close to you when that happened that the opportunity to do something was fleeting. In the next moment, you would be fighting off claws that could shred you to ribbons and a long muzzle filled with sharp teeth that could take you apart in chunks.

It was all Sulana could do not to kick her horse into a panicked run, but she restrained her fear and trotted behind Talon toward a wider part of the trail that thankfully appeared ahead. The thumping noise followed alongside them through the trees, with an occasional snap of a branch or swish of a shrub being shoved aside.

The team had just arrayed themselves in a tiny clearing along the trail when the troll charged. It led with a roaring bellow that instantly froze the horses in place. Prey animals were devastatingly affected by a troll's roar because a troll had the natural vaetric ability to lace the sound with paralyzing fear. The horses could remain frozen for up to two minutes.

The humans were briefly affected as well, but Talon and Barek, who had both faced trolls before, snapped out of it quickly. Sulana channeled a little vaetra into her Nullifier ring and invoked it with a stiff word. Her muscles unclenched, and she turned to Daven, who was still struggling to move. She reached over to touch him and triggered the ring again. Daven jumped and then nodded at her in thanks.

In the meantime, the troll was closing in on the team with an easy loping gait through the trees.

Talon slid from his saddle, his long sword in one hand and his dagger in the other. He was grinning broadly now, the light in his eyes almost manic as he stalked forward in a crouch toward the oncoming troll. The troll saw his movement and shifted its trajectory straight toward him, exactly as Talon had intended. Barek slid from his saddle as well, and moved toward Talon's right, ready to flank the troll as it came in for the attack.

Barek called over to Talon. "It's a big one. Think you'll need help?"

Talon let out a harsh laugh. "Probably not, but if you get bored, feel free to jump in. I shouldn't be selfish about these things."

Sulana put her crossbow to her shoulder and took aim at the beast. The trees were a major hindrance, but she thought she could get off one good shot before the creature reached Talon. Daven lined up his shot as well. As the troll emerged from the last of the trees, they fired.

Daven's shot was good, but it bounced off the creature's thick hide at its shoulder. Sulana's crossbow packed enough punch to penetrate the troll's hide, but the bolt to its left thigh didn't seem to do anything other than make it grunt.

Talon looked like a poor match for the animal. The troll reared up on its back legs as it closed with him and opened its mouth in another roar, revealing canines that looked as long as Sulana's hand. It dwarfed Talon, rising to nearly eight feet in height.

The troll reached for Talon, but the old warrior had no intention of letting the beast envelop him. He thrust with his sword at the troll's soft underside and stepped to his left at the same time. Talon's blow was deflected by a rib, but it scored a bleeding line on the creature's chest. Side-stepping carried Talon clear of the creature's chomping bite, but the troll twisted as it came down and slapped him hard in the side with an enormous front paw.

The slap didn't do any serious harm, but the claws scored a furrow of lines in the leather armor on Talon's chest. The blow thrust him to the side and he crashed to the ground, his sword falling out of his hand as the breath was knocked out of him.

Barek came in from behind as the troll turned toward Talon. He swung his broadsword in a two-handed blow that connected just behind the troll's left shoulder. The force of his attack allowed the blade to slice through the creature's hide and damage the muscles controlling its left foreleg.

The troll flinched and roared over its shoulder at Barek. It leaned down and kicked out with a rear leg, connecting solidly with Barek's chest as the big man raised his sword for another blow. Barek's feet left the ground and he flew backward several paces to land on his back in a short skid. He sat right back up, cursing and shaking his head. Then he climbed back to his feet, squared his shoulders, and narrowed his eyes at the troll as he readied his sword and moved forward in a crouch.

With Barek out of his line of fire, Daven twisted in his saddle and leaned forward to see around Sulana for another shot with his bow. He was still unable to move his horse forward to a better position.

Sulana leaned back to give Daven a clearer view, and he let the arrow fly. This time he got lucky. As the creature turned back toward Talon once again, Daven's arrow thudded into the wound that Barek had just opened in its shoulder. The arrow penetrated deeply, leaving nothing showing but the fletching. The creature coughed and pivoted toward Daven and Sulana with a menacing growl.

Talon had recovered himself and took advantage of the troll's distraction to bury his dagger to the hilt in the softer hide under its right arm. The troll flinched back, tearing the hilt out of Talon's fingers, leaving the dagger in place. The troll screamed so loudly and with such fury that everyone froze for a moment. The troll looked at Talon, its eyes narrowed in hate. It bared its teeth and exhaled a rumbling hiss at him. As it did, flecks of blood colored its teeth.

Talon reached down for his sword, keeping his eyes on the monster in front of him as it gathered to strike again. Meanwhile, Barek approached the creature's back in a crouch.

Sulana thought the battle might be nearly over, and she considered using the ring to release Daven's horse and hers from their immobility. However, the troll wasn't dead yet, and she could feel her horse shivering beneath her, struggling against the fear spell to run away. She wasn't sure she could control her horse in the presence of a live troll, so she decided to leave it be.

Instead, she pulled the silver ring from her finger and returned it to the pouch in her belt. She drew a short jeweled dagger instead, right as the troll made its move.

Talon had just gripped his hand around the hilt of his sword when the troll leaped forward at him. He tried to raise his sword to skewer the beast in its underbelly, but rather than stay back to take another swipe at him, the troll simply crashed into him and pushed him to the ground. Talon's sword waved uselessly from under the creature's bulk.

The troll's forward leap also carried it away from Barek's blow, which barely grazed the creature's back. Barek stumbled forward, nearly losing his grip on his sword.

Sulana shook her head in frustration. The troll had Talon down again. Barek was positioning himself for another attack, but he was barely able to hack through the troll's thick hide with his strongest blows. He might not be able to kill the creature before it killed Talon.

The troll raised itself up off Talon with its right arm, while its left arm dangled uselessly from Barek's first strike. It opened its mouth wide and prepared to bite down on Talon's head. Even with the creature's weight off of him, Talon did not have enough room to bring his sword into play, and for the first time since the battle began, his eyes showed fear rather than glee.

Sulana made a split-second decision. The troll was about to bite down on Talon, but he was otherwise clear of the beast. Barek was bringing his sword back for another blow, but he was still clear as well. She jabbed her dagger toward the troll and shouted a word. The shout was as much to warn Talon and Barek as it was to release her spell at the troll.

At her shout, the gemstone set in the hilt of her dagger flash once, and then a bolt of lightning arced from the tip of the dagger into the troll's upper back. The crack of the lightning bolt in the small clearing was deafening, and Sulana felt the boom of its thunder in her chest. She nearly fell from her horse in a faint as she channeled the vaetra necessary to power the strike.

Daven reached across to Sulana, grabbed her arm, and steadied her. She smiled up weakly at him and nodded her thanks. Then she looked over to see what she had done.

Talon was still on the ground panting. He sat up to regard her with a nod and a weak smile. Barek leaned forward against his sword, also breathing heavily. The troll was rolled up against a tree at the edge of the clearing facing them. Smoke curled up from behind the animal. Its eyes were staring, and its mouth sagged open with bright red drops of blood dripping around its teeth to the ground.

Talon got to his feet with a grunt, and a big grin returned to his face. "Come on, I almost had it," he said to Sulana.

Barek leaned back and laughed loudly. Daven joined in and Sulana chuckled too. Their battle tension eased as they all turned to appraise the troll's carcass.

"What a monster!" Daven commented.

Talon nodded and sheathed his sword. "One of the biggest I've seen. That was a satisfying kill."

Barek grunted. "Except when you are the one who gets killed. You're out of practice."

Talon rubbed his left shoulder where the troll had crashed into him and rotated his arm. "You're right. I need to volunteer for the trail crew again and sharpen my troll-hunting skills."

Sulana rolled her eyes. The Archives "trail crew" were a small group of sorcerers and guardians who repaired the trails each spring and maintained them during the year. Occasionally, a troll would move in and claim an area that the trail went through, as this one apparently had, and they would eventually have to deal with the creature. Trolls were fiercely territorial and not afraid of humans.

She knew Talon had worked the trails for years, relishing every troll encounter. As a child he had seen both of his parents killed in a troll attack just outside their village. Trolls normally avoided human habitations, but once in a while, a female would establish a territory near a village, creating a dangerous situation. Talon had a personal vendetta that would never be satisfied until every troll was dead.

The horses shifted nervously as the troll's spell finally started wearing off. If not for their human caretakers, at least one of them would have been lunch for the troll. Trolls weren't particularly fast; an unencumbered human could usually outrun them. But when they were able to sneak up on their faster prey and use it, their immobilizing roar made up for their lack of speed.

Talon and Barek walked over to their recovering horses to calm them. Talon handed his reins to Sulana and nodded at the dagger in her hand. "Nice dagger. I didn't know you had one of those."

She looked down at the forgotten dagger in her hand and put it away. "I borrowed it from the armory before we left, although I'm barely strong enough to use it. I just hope we don't run into another one of those things," she angled her head toward the troll, "because I couldn't do that again for quite a while."

Talon patted her leg and smiled up at her. "Don't worry. I'm all loosened up now. If we find another troll, I'll take care of it."

He looked over at the troll and pulled his dagger from his belt. "Well, do you want the honors?"

She knew what he was asking. Troll teeth and claws were worth quite a bit of money. It would be a waste to leave them behind. But she was still feeling a little sick from channeling the vaetra necessary for the lightning bolt, and the idea of harvesting the troll made her even more nauseous. "No thanks. You're the one who almost got killed," she said teasingly. "It's all yours."

Talon walked over to the troll, motioning Barek to give him a hand. Barek handed his reins to Daven and followed Talon.

Daven looked over at Sulana. "Do we have time for this?"

Sulana looked up at the sky and the crowns of the surrounding trees, but it was hard to tell how much time they had left until sunset. "I don't want to spoil their fun," she said, looking over to where Talon and Barek were busily hacking away at the troll, "and I think we'll still make it to the Archives before dusk."

"Do you really think the Archives Council will send a different team to find the sorcerer?" he asked her seriously.

Sulana considered his question for a moment. "I hope not. We've come this far and I'd like to see it through to the end. Let's just wait and see what they have to say when we get back."

CHAPTER 11

Patches and I left Delta on the road we came in on, and I urged him into a trot. The scenery was lovely, with steep, forested hillsides to our right and the shore of Teardop Lake to our left. A few intrepid wildflowers were starting to bloom along side of the road. Trillium, with its three large green leaves and delicate, ruffled, white flowers nodded in the breeze. Here and there a pink fairy slipper raised its tiny dragon-like head, watching the rest of the world wake up to springtime.

Ahead of me, the Delta Peninsula interrupted the shoreline and spread out across the lake. Almost an island, the peninsula was connected to the northern shore of the lake by a short strip of land. The eastern edge of the peninsula created a narrow slough that was lined with cat tails and acted as a temporary home to early migrating waterfowl. Ducks and geese waddled to the water and glided away from shore, squawking to their fellows in warning as I approached. Some of the ducks quacked with alarm and flew off; their webbed feet splashed across the surface of the lake and left ripples spreading out behind them as they took to the air.

I reached the peninsula road and turned left onto it. The road went straight for a short distance into the forest, and then turned to the right, just as Alain had described. At the turn, a weathered wooden sign pointed the way to Buckwoods Village.

At first, I didn't see the trail that I was supposed to find. The area alongside and behind the sign was cleared back some, but it wasn't until I coaxed Patches behind the sign that I discovered the trail. It went off at an angle and immediately jogged to the right, which made it difficult to spot from the road. The pathway was narrow but cleared back enough for me to continue riding.

I rode along the trail through dense pine forest, occasionally dodging the branches of spindly young trees that had grown up along the pathway. I let Patches drink from a shallow stream that bubbled across the path and then urged him across. A little farther down the trail Patches slowed to step over a couple of rotting logs, which were covered with moss and partially crushed by previous travelers. At last, I came to the clearing.

The area was perhaps 30 paces across and roughly circular. To my right, a fire ring held ashes and a few chunks of charred wood. To my left, many hoof prints and droppings indicated where horses had been tethered. The trail continued on through the opposite side of the clearing, but it was too overgrown to travel comfortably on horseback. I rode Patches over to the tethering spot, dismounted, and tied him to a convenient stout branch.

This late in the day, the tall trees surrounding the clearing completely shaded it. I could see only a short way into the dense thicket of trees that bordered the clearing. The birds in the area were already starting to quiet down, and the deep shadow hinted at the evening to come. I had no time to waste.

I looked around for Tam's belongings. If they were still here, Tam probably was still in the area as well. If he had come back to get them, he may have truly run away as his father suspected. After a moment's search, I discovered that his things were still at the clearing, half-hidden under a shrub near the fire pit.

I pulled the bundle out to take a closer look, and I was surprised to find a full set of clothes and boots. Why did the boys bring a change of clothes with them? What was Tam wearing now? When I moved the boots aside to see if there was anything else in the hollow under the shrub, something rattled around inside one of them. I carefully tipped the boot up, and a small bottle made from dark glass slid out onto the ground.

I picked up the bottle and turned it around in my hand. It was about as tall as my middle finger and had a small cork stopper. Its painted foil label depicted a howling wolf's head on a full moon backdrop and the single word "Eclipse." I had no idea what it contained, but the craftsmanship of the bottle and quality of the label indicated something expensive. I shook the bottle and discovered that it was still about half full of some kind of liquid.

I popped the cork and held the bottle up to my nose. The liquid smelled like some kind of herbal infusion in oil, and something about it made the hair stand up on the back of my neck. I replaced the cork and slipped the bottle into my pocket. I'd ask Alain about it later; or maybe Tam, if I found him first. Given that the bottle was the only thing left behind with Tam's clothes, I strongly suspected it was related to their activities out here in the woods.

In the meantime, I still had enough light left to take a quick hike farther down the path. Perhaps I'd find some evidence of where Tam might be now.

~

I left Patches at the clearing and followed the path deeper into the forest. I jogged for short bursts and stopped occasionally to inspect the ground or the vegetation when something caught my eye. The trail was springy underfoot from layers of rotting leaves and pine needles, but the packed surface wasn't good for tracking because it held no prints. Faint game trails intersected the path here and there. I ignored these trails because they would require serious bushwhacking to investigate and I didn't have time for that.

I came to another stream crossing the path and finally found something interesting. In the mud on both sides of the stream were clear canine paw prints of at least two different sizes.

I knelt down next to the stream to get a better look. Alain hadn't mentioned bringing any dogs. I'd have to ask him about that later too. They could be wolf prints, but they were a little too big. If wolves had created these prints, the animals were much larger than average. Perhaps the eating was good on the peninsula.

I worried for a moment about Patches being alone back in the clearing, but he was pretty good at fending for himself, and he was tied loosely enough that he could get free if he really needed to do so.

From my position closer to the ground, I could see a smudged print along the edge of the grass line. The impression looked like it could have been made by the first two toes of a human foot, but it was hard to imagine someone walking around on this trail barefoot at this time of year. Besides, each print included a clear punch mark in the mud. It was the kind of mark a claw would make. The forest shadows were growing deeper and it was definitely getting harder to make out details, so I decided that I must be mistaken about the source of the print.

I jogged farther down the trail and came to a fork where I stopped to consider the alternatives. I was more or less going south right now, so the right fork would take me west and the left fork would take me east. The right fork was definitely more traveled, and it seemed to me that Tam would go that way if he got lost somehow, so I decided to take the right fork.

I continued down the trail for a few minutes, but saw nothing worth stopping to inspect. A startled squirrel bounded across the path with his bushy tail held high. The squirrel ran up the trunk of a tree, sat on a branch, and scolded me.

I was just starting to think I should turn around and head back when the forest started to thin, and bright sunlight lit the trail in front of me. It was as if time had slid back a couple of hours and evening had turned back into afternoon. I heard voices and slowed down as I neared the edge of the forest. I stayed back in the shadows of the trees and looked out into an open area beyond the trailhead. I had found Buckwoods Village.

The low sun cast an orange glow upon the small fishing village, which occupies a section of the peninsula's western shore. Long shadows turned most of what I could see into silhouettes. The village had five small huts, a dock, and a few outbuildings. Villagers carrying baskets of fish walked back and forth between a couple of large rowboats and a large covered bench. A couple of men were cleaning the fish at the bench. They seemed happy about the day's haul and were chatting amiably about it.

Then I spotted two men conversing next to a small stone building. They wore leather armor and Raven Company tabards. I knew them both. Kefer and Peltor were supposed to be escorting a wagon from Delta to Plains End, but they apparently didn't get very far. What were they doing in Buckwoods?

Well, there was only one way to find out.

I stepped out of the trees with a confused frown and walked over toward them. As soon as I emerged from the trees, one of the men saw me and straightened. The other looked my way too. They drew their swords in unison and ran toward me.

Surprised by their reaction, I stopped walking and held up my hands to show they were empty. My sword was back with Patches, so all I had was my dagger to defend myself, if it came to that. Kefer and Peltor were competent swordsmen, and I doubted I could make a good showing for myself against both of them with only a dagger.

The two men arrayed themselves in front of me, leaving each other room for a clear strike. Kefer looked closely at me. "Jaylan? What are you doing here?"

Kefer is a few inches taller than I am. He stands a little over six feet and has shoulder-length wavy brown hair and light blue eyes. We were occasional sparring partners and had worked one job together as escort guards. It was not unlike the job he was working now with Peltor. We normally got along fine, which made his current behavior unexpected and strange.

Peltor is another story. He is about my height with long, dark, curly hair and a thin dark mustache. A beak of a nose dominates his narrow face. Peltor's sneering personality and mine come together like oil and water, so that nose has tempted my fist on a number of occasions. He seemed perfectly happy to have me at a disadvantage. With a half-smile, he stared at me intently and shifted his weight back and forth. He was barely able to suppress his desire to engage me.

In spite of having recognized me, neither man had made a move to put away their swords.

I kept my hands up and said, "I was just about to come over and ask you the same thing. Aren't you supposed to be on your way to Plains End?"

The two men looked at each other, and then back to me. Kefer answered, "The driver said he needed to stop here along the way."

I nodded my head in understanding. That made sense. But their swords were still drawn and they were watching my movements carefully, as if I still posed some kind of threat. I realized my own sense of unease was not only because of their obvious anxiety. I was hearing a strange noise as well.

The noise was subtle. It was like a chorus of tones that seemed to be coming from the direction of the village and more strongly from the two Raven Company men. I looked beyond the men toward the people in the village. With a start, I realized that all of the villagers had stopped what they were doing to stare at me. The fading sunlight sparkled off an amulet dangling from a necklace one woman was wearing. Then I noticed that several of the other villagers had similar amulets.

Once again, the hair on the back of my neck began to rise. Strange things were afoot on the Delta Peninsula.

Kefer stepped into my line of sight. "What do you need, Jaylan?"

I looked more closely at Kefer. He wore a thin chain around his neck that disappeared behind his tabard. He could be wearing one of the amulets as well.

I had no idea what was going on with these two, and it wasn't my mystery to solve, so I got back to the business at hand.

"I'm looking for a young boy of about sixteen. He has short brown hair and brown eyes, and his name is Tam. He went missing last night. Have you seen him? Has anyone at the village seen him?"

The men looked at each other again, and both shook their heads. Kefer answered. "No. No one has seen him."

I lifted a hand toward the village. "May I ask some of the villagers?"

Kefer shifted from one foot to the other. "We've been here since yesterday. If a boy had shown up, we'd know about it. Talking to the villagers would be a waste of time."

Well, I certainly didn't need to waste any more time. However, their resistance bothered me, and the rudeness of keeping their blades in their hands was baffling. I squinted against the sun to get a better look at their faces, but their expressions revealed nothing to indicate they might be lying to me.

I frowned at Kefer. I wanted to press him with more questions, but again, it was a mystery for another time. "Fine. I'd better get going then."

They both nodded at me simultaneously. I snorted, thinking that these guys had been spending too much time together.

Kefer sighed and relaxed his stance a little. He angled his head toward the trailhead. "See you around, Jaylan."

I turned and headed back to the trail, looking back over my shoulder once to see that both men were still in the same position watching me go. It seemed like they were protecting the village from me or me from the village, but that didn't make any sense. Maybe they were just unnerved by their unexpected side trip.

Whatever their problem was, it would have to wait. I was quickly running out of light and needed to finish my preliminary search for Tam.

⁓

Putting the strangeness of Buckwoods behind me, I jogged back along the trail to the point where it had forked. I stopped at the fork and stood there for a moment with my hands on my hips. I wasn't sure if I had enough light left to check out the other direction.

The other fork was definitely less traveled than the one that had taken me to Buckwoods, so it was possible it simply dwindled to nothing fairly quickly. That would be good to know. I could save myself from having to return here tomorrow to check it out if that were the case. I made my decision and started down the eastern fork of the trail.

I moved as swiftly as I could, which wasn't very fast at all. I had to dodge too many branches and step around small trees that were taking over the trail. I also found more evidence of wildlife along this trail. I ran across several mounds of moose droppings, which look like a pile of tiny brown eggs. The pellets were disturbingly dark and fresh. I slowed down even more after finding a tuft of dark brown, wiry fur stuck to the end of a broken branch. The last thing I needed was to accidentally charge into the back end of a moose. They take that kind of thing poorly.

The trail opened up along a rocky hillside and I was able to see the dark, shadowed waters of the lake below. I took a moment to admire the view of tall pines in the foreground and the slough I had passed earlier in the background.

While I stood there, I pondered the bizarre encounter at Buckwoods. The sound I had heard from the villagers and the Raven Company men tugged at my mind. I wasn't familiar with any kind of jewelry that made noise. Well, except one: the enchanted ring Sulana had recovered for the Archives. Could everyone in that village be wearing an enchanted necklace? That seemed unlikely. The next time I saw Kefer, I'd have to ask him about it.

The trail didn't seem to end right away after all, and the distant peaks were stained purple by the setting sun, so I decided it was time to go back to the clearing and retrieve Patches. The moon wasn't up yet, and I didn't care much for the idea of wandering around on these trails in the dark, regardless of how much Alain had romanticized it.

I was turning to leave when I saw movement out of the corner of my eye.

About thirty paces away, a boy sat on a rock inspecting the bottom of his foot. At least I thought it was a boy at first glance. But the face that turned and looked over at me was all wrong. Hair covered his pointed ears. Hair also covered his face, which had exaggerated cheekbones that extended his nose forward. A set of fangs glistened behind his lips.

The stubby, rounded fingers that held his foot had claws. His toes were also rounded and had claws. A thin layer of fur-like hair covered his entire body. And he wore no clothing.

My brain couldn't come to grips with what I was seeing. I had expected to find a sixteen-year-old boy. What I found matched Tam's description, but only in a general sense. He did have brown hair; quite a lot of it, in fact. He was about my size except thinner, and he had dark eyes that could have been brown. I couldn't tell for sure from a distance. I believed I was looking at the subject of my search, but what had happened to him?

I intended to call out when I first spotted him, but his appearance had stunned me and my breath caught in my throat. Tam, or whatever it was, leaped to his feet and ran down the trail away from me. His speed was unreal, and he vanished before I could close my gaping mouth and calm my racing heartbeat. He was already gone by the time I found my voice.

"Tam, wait! Your mother sent me to find you," I yelled in the direction he'd gone. But it was too late. He had already disappeared into the forest on the other side of the overlook, leaving a wake of waving branches.

I ran after Tam, excited that I had found him already, but not sure I wanted to catch up to the thing he had become. If I could find him and bring him back safely, regardless of his current condition, this job could turn out to be a very easy five crowns.

If anything, the trail got even worse on the other side of the overlook. I practically swam through a blinding thicket of branches, leaves, and spider webs. I called to Tam a few more times and looked for any indication of where he might have gone, but the trail dissolved into a confusion of narrow game paths.

I stopped to catch my breath and think for a moment. Tam had me at a serious disadvantage. He and friends had been exploring these trails at night, while I had no idea where I was going.

I listened carefully for sounds of movement, but heard nothing. The birds of the forest had quieted except for an owl that hooted nearby, a harbinger of the fast approaching night.

As I stood there considering my situation, a wolf howl split the air around me. The sound sent a shock straight up my spine and then back down through my frazzled nerves to my legs. I turned and ran.

Thinking time was over. The next few minutes were all about motion and emotion. I ran as fast as I could manage back down the trail toward the clearing, expecting something to leap on my back and tear into me at any moment. An image of Patches tied up in the clearing at the mercy of a violent predator put a lump in my throat.

I ignored the branches that whipped into my face and bruised my arms as I ran stumbling down the tight trail. I tripped over an exposed root and landed hard on my knees and elbows, my nose halting only inches from a pile of moose droppings. I sat back on my knees, trying to catch my breath and get my fear under control.

Another howl echoed into the night. Thankfully, it was farther away this time, but it was still too close. I got back to my feet and hurried on. I moved a little more cautiously, limping slightly from a sore knee that had caught the worst of my fall.

I burst into the clearing, panting and stumbling. My sudden appearance startled Patches. He whinnied and ran out of the clearing down the trail we had ridden in on. Hearing wolf howls nearby must have agitated him enough to break free.

I stopped and rested my hands on my knees, breathing hard. I called to Patches, but he was gone. Another howl sounded and Patches whinnied again somewhere down the trail. I whistled for him, and soon heard his hooves thumping slowly back toward me.

I stood calmly and got my breathing back under control while Patches approached. I spoke calmly and soothingly to him, but I didn't move. He walked slowly up to me, with his nostrils flaring and huffing, and pushed me with his nose. I rubbed his face and patted his neck, and then I climbed up into the saddle.

I'd had enough of the Delta Peninsula for one day, and it was clear that I wasn't bringing Tam home tonight. That task would have to wait for tomorrow. With any luck, I'd be able to come up with a plan by then.

By the time Patches and I made it back to Delta, night had fallen. Golden light leaked through the cracks in the shuttered windows of the homes we passed. Only a few townspeople walked the streets carrying lanterns to light their way.

On the way back from the peninsula, I had debated how much to tell Greta about her son. I couldn't be sure that the wolf-boy I found really was Tam, but it seemed unlikely that it could be anyone else. I had to assume that Tam's parents knew nothing about his current condition. If Greta did know, I'd be annoyed with her. Details like "has pointed ears and is covered in fur" would have been good information to have at the start of my search.

The circumstances definitely indicated sorcery. I had heard of sorcerers who could shape change into animals, but if Tam were a sorcerer with that kind of skill, he would be training at the Archives, not living in Delta arguing with his father about becoming an Imperial Guard.

There was another explanation, of course. The small bottle of liquid I'd found at the clearing was an obvious clue. The wolf head on the label took on new meaning if the bottle contained a shape-changing potion. Actually, there was a technical name…a lycanthropy potion. But I had never heard of a situation where a person was only partially changed. I was under the impression that it was all or nothing. Either that impression was wrong, or I happened to encounter the boy in mid-transformation.

I knew I should probably report to Greta immediately, but I wasn't sure where she'd be right then, and I was too sore and tired to hunt her down. I still wasn't sure how much I wanted to tell her anyway. I opted to go straight to the Eagle's Rest and face Greta in the morning.

The small boarding house was a welcome sight. A lantern out front lit a small sign that proclaimed room and board could be had for a fair price. Another lantern on the back of the building gave me adequate light to unsaddle Patches and groom him. I fumbled around in the small, dark stable and found hay as well as some oats for the well-deserved treat I'd promised him. I left him in the small corral chewing contentedly and headed into the Eagle's Rest.

The front door opened into a dining area dominated by a long wooden table with seating for eight. The room was warm and cheerful, with sconces along the walls that provided plenty of light. I breathed deeply and smiled as I inhaled the rich aroma of a hot meal and warm bread. My stomach grumbled loudly in anticipation.

Seated at the table were Greta and another woman who I presumed was her friend Penny. Penny smiled back at me when she saw my initial reaction to her home. "Hello. You must be Jaylan," she said.

She got up and came around the table. She was a short, stocky woman with a round, friendly face and an easy, welcoming smile. Strawberry blond curls framed her face and made her look much younger than the smile lines around her eyes and mouth suggested.

"I'm Penny," she said as she patted the back of a chair. "Come have a seat. You look famished. I'll go get you something to eat right now."

"Thank you. That would be appreciated," I said as she bustled off.

Before sitting, I turned to Greta. "I wasn't sure where to find you at this time of the evening, so I figured I'd just speak with you in the morning."

Greta nodded and searched my face for a hint of what I'd discovered. "Did you find anything?"

I hesitated before answering. I was too tired to come up with a delicate way to explain what I had found, so I decided to tell her the truth, just not all of it. "Yes and no," I hedged. She tilted her head and narrowed her eyes, waiting for me to continue. "I believe I found Tam, but he ran when he saw me and I lost him in the forest."

Greta's face lit up, and she clenched her hands together. "That's wonderful! I'm so glad he isn't lost. Was he hurt?"

"I don't think so. A few scratches maybe, but otherwise he seemed to be holding up just fine." I shook my head. "But I only got a brief glimpse of him before he disappeared. I tried to follow, but it was getting dark, and he knows those woods too well for me to keep up."

She motioned for me to sit down and leaned forward. "I'm just glad you found him already. How will you get him home?"

I sat down as Penny walked back into the room carrying a large bowl of steaming stew and a bread board with a wrapped loaf of fresh bread. She overheard Greta's question as she came in. "You found Tam? Oh Greta, I'm so happy for you!"

Penny set the food down in front of me and my mouth watered instantly. I leaned forward and sniffed deeply with my eyes closed. "This is fantastic," I sighed. "Thank you very much."

Penny grinned and gave me a small curtsey. "My pleasure. I hope you enjoy it." She leaned forward and looked closely at my face. "Oh, you're hurt. Let me get something for those scratches." She hurried back out of the room.

I picked up my spoon, but before I started in on the food, I turned back to Greta. "I do have a plan I'd like to run by you."

Greta sat back and looked relieved. She waved her hand in a shooing motion at me. "Go ahead and start your dinner."

I didn't need a second invitation. The stew was thick and rich with big chunks of potato and meat that was spiced to perfection. Penny definitely knew how to cook. I unwrapped the short loaf of bread and ripped a hunk from it. The crispy crust crackled as it tore and steam rose from the exposed crumb. I dipped the bread into the stew and chewed blissfully.

I stopped eating briefly when Penny returned to dab at my face with a wet cloth and spread a little ointment of some kind on my scratches. Her ministrations stung at first, but after she applied the ointment, the pain from the scratches settled into a deep throb. I thanked her and went back to my food.

The two women watched me with amusement as I gave myself over to the sumptuous meal. I had to admit that the stew was better than the version Dela's mother made, although Luma herself would never hear me say that.

After I had consumed several spoonfuls of stew and the first chunk of bread, I started feeling more relaxed, so I stopped for a moment to continue my conversation with Greta. I decided that before telling her about finding Tam, I'd see if she already knew something about his strange condition. Knowing whether or not she had intentionally misled me earlier would affect how I proceeded.

"Have you noticed anything unusual about Tam's appearance or behavior lately?" I asked, watching Greta's face for a reaction.

The question seemed to take her completely by surprise. "Like what?" she asked.

Well, like an excess of body hair, or maybe a strong desire for his meat cooked rare, I thought to myself. But Greta clearly would have no idea what I was getting at. And since she was paying me a lot of money, she was entitled to know what I'd found.

"When I found Tam, his appearance was a little odd," I said. I was going to have to do better than *that* understatement, but I had trouble thinking of a way to describe what I had seen so it would make sense to her. I finally pulled the potion bottle out of my pocket.

"I think Tam and the other boys may have been experimenting with shape shifting," I said as I set the bottle on the table in front of her.

She picked up the bottle and her lips silently formed the word "eclipse" as she read the label. "I don't understand. What is this? What are you trying to tell me?"

"The boy I found didn't quite look human. I think he was shifting into wolf form." There. I said it. And it sounded stupid.

She barked a short nervous laugh and set the bottle back down near my plate. "You must be kidding. Tam would never do anything like that. He knows better than to mess with sorcery. You must have found someone or something else."

"I hope you're right. But that bottle was in his boot. I found his boots and clothes at the clearing where he and his friends meet," I explained.

"Are you telling me that Tam left his clothes behind? Then what was he wearing?" she asked.

"Fur," I stated with a shrug.

Greta and Penny both stared at me. Penny looked over at Greta, waiting for her to say something first. Greta said nothing for what seemed like a long time, her eyes never leaving my face. She finally drew a deep breath and let it out.

"I'm not sure I believe you. You said yourself it was getting dark. But if you did find Tam, we need to get him home safely."

I nodded. "If I go alone, he may run from me again. I need to bring someone with me that Tam recognizes and trusts. I was planning to take Alain along to the peninsula tomorrow morning, if that's possible."

"I'm sure I can convince Alain's father to let you borrow him for the morning if it will help bring Tam home," she assured me. "I'll stop by and speak to him on my way home tonight."

Greta looked over at the potion bottle in front of me and frowned. "I don't look forward to telling Jergen about this. He'll probably want to go with you tomorrow. I'll try to talk him out of it, but I doubt I'll be successful." She looked up at me. "You should probably be prepared to take both Alain and Jergen with you in the morning." She said it like it was a warning.

"Why does that concern you?" I asked. "Are you worried that your husband will scare Tam off?" I didn't know enough about their family dynamic to understand the nature of her warning. I needed to know what to expect tomorrow.

Greta shook her head. "No, Tam respects his father and usually obeys him. But Jergen can be harsh when his will is challenged." Penny nodded her head in agreement, her eyes wide. "If Tam *has* been experimenting with sorcery, Jergen will be very displeased," Greta concluded.

With a heavy sigh, Greta got up to leave. Penny rose with her and gave her a comforting hug. I stood as well and gave Greta a slight bow in farewell. I slipped the potion bottle back into my pocket.

"Don't worry, Greta. We'll get Tam back for you tomorrow," I promised her before she left, and then sat back down to finish my excellent meal.

CHAPTER 12

After two days of hard riding and far too much excitement, I slept soundly and comfortably at the Eagle's Rest. Penny would definitely be getting that recommendation from me when our guests at the Snow Creek Inn asked about a place to stay in Delta. The bed was better than the one I had at home, and the little bags of dried flowers in a bowl on the dresser gave the room a subtle floral scent. I'd have to tell Dela about that idea.

In fact, I was so comfortable that I slept far longer than I normally do. I didn't wake up until Penny knocked quietly on my door. I sat up in bed quickly, yawned hugely, and looked around at the strange surroundings, slowly remembering where I was and why I was there. Her muffled voice came through the door. "It's nearly dawn sir, and I thought you'd like a bite to eat before you meet with Greta's husband."

I hung my feet off the edge of the bed. "Thank you. I'll be right down," I said in a raised voice.

I dressed quickly and collected my things from the room. I ran down the stairs to the common room and laid my sword and saddle bag next to the door. I walked into the dining room just as Penny was setting a plate of eggs and more of that fabulous bread onto the table. Thanking her for her thoughtfulness, I wasted no time devouring my breakfast.

Penny and I talked while I ate. I asked her about her rates and how many rooms she had available, and we engaged in other inn-keeping chatter. I was just setting down my napkin for the last time and settling back contentedly into my chair when I heard the front door open. I turned my head to see a man walk in.

He wore a richly embroidered leather vest over a carefully-tailored brown shirt. His receding hair and trimmed beard were a medium brown that had gone mostly to grey. Intense grey eyes scanned the room from under bushy eyebrows that were drawn together to match his frown. The big man moved deliberately and without hesitation toward the table.

"Good morning, Jergen," Penny said with a smile.

He nodded at her. "Penny."

I looked over at Penny with a grin. "Perfect timing. Thanks for waking me and for the excellent breakfast." I pushed my chair back from the table and got out my coin purse.

Penny put her hand over mine with a look of concern as I untied the purse string. "There's no need to pay. Greta is taking care of that."

"I know. But I wouldn't feel right enjoying such hospitality without at least showing my appreciation." I set a silver coin down on the table. It was a generous tip, but her care had been well worth it.

"Thank you. You're welcome back any time," she said with a smile as she picked up the coin.

Jergen interrupted us. "You're Jaylan?" he asked.

I turned to him and extended my hand. "Yes, sir. Jaylan Forester of Raven Company."

He took my hand and shook it once. "Jergen Overland. I'll be waiting outside." He turned on his heal and walked back out the door, closing it behind himself with a firm thud.

I turned to Penny with my eyebrows raised in surprise. She gave me a small apologetic smile and shrugged her shoulders. Being friends with Greta, she was probably used to Jergen's gruff demeanor.

I picked up my things, waved goodbye to Penny, and followed Jergen out the door.

I started around the side of the house toward the stable and nearly bumped into Alain as he came forward with Patches all saddled-up and ready to go.

Alain licked his lips nervously as he handed me the reins. "I hope you don't mind. Mister Overland instructed me to get your horse ready for you. Did you have anything else in the stable?"

I looked Patches over and accounted for all of his gear. "No, looks good. Thanks for getting him ready." I attached the saddle bags and my sword sheath to the saddle, checked the cinch, and mounted up.

Jergen and Alain were on their horses waiting for me. Jergen was looking around the town slowly, but not really focusing on anything. Alain was watching me and fiddling with his reins, never once looking over at Jergen.

I said, "Okay, let's go." When I spoke, Alain jumped and Jergen slowly turned his attention to me, rather like an owl rotating its head to consider the worthiness of a mouse. He nodded and then urged his horse into a canter, leading the way out of town. My, what a jovial trip this was going to be.

We were about a quarter mile out of Delta when Jergen slowed down and pulled his horse alongside mine. Alain rode just behind us. Jergen seemed ready to talk, now that there was no one to overhear us.

"My wife says you think you found Tam," he stated.

I nodded and said, "Yes, sir. I can't be sure since I never met Tam, but the boy I found was about the right age and more or less fit your wife's description of him."

"She also said you think there's something wrong with him," he said, looking over at me.

Greta's doubts had worked their way into my mind overnight and I was beginning to question what I'd seen with my own eyes. Such is the nature of memories when you see things you don't expect and have trouble believing. I half-attributed Tam's appearance last evening to the fading light and an overactive imagination on my part.

"I could be mistaken. It was dusk when I found him, and the light was bad. I did find his clothes at the clearing, and it seemed to me that he was either naked or wearing some kind of fur." I shrugged in apology for not being able to give him better information.

Jergen half-turned in his saddle and spoke over his shoulder. "What were you boys up to out there, Alain?"

"Nothing, sir. We just went hiking," he replied.

"Hiking naked? Don't lie to me, boy. Why did Tam leave his clothes behind? Did you have girls out there with you?" Jergen asked with a stern tone.

"No sir! We just went hiking. I don't know why Tam left his clothes in the clearing. He must have taken them off later," Alain answered.

I didn't believe Alain for a minute, and I decided to interject my own question. "Did you boys dress up in animal skins for your hikes? Was it some kind of game where you pretended to be animals or something?"

Alain was silent for a moment, and I looked back at him. He was staring at me and his face had gone white. I guessed my question had hit close to the mark. I figured that if sorcery was not involved, what I'd seen could be explained by Tam wearing some kind of costume.

Alain looked down and finally answered. "No, sir. Nothing like that. We just went hiking."

Jergen harrumphed, but didn't pursue the matter further. I don't think he believed Alain any more than I did, but the boy was sticking to his story for now. We'd see how things went when we found Tam.

I thought about the potion bottle that was still in my pocket. If we didn't get better answers from the two boys later on, I'd surprise them with it and maybe shock them into giving us the truth.

∽

We reached the sign to Buckwoods and entered the trail behind it in single file with Alain taking the lead and Jergen behind him. If we encountered Tam, I wanted him to see his friend and his father before he saw me.

I wondered what we would find when we reached the clearing. Would Tam's clothes still be there? Why did Tam stay in the woods for two nights rather than go home? What was keeping him here? Did it have anything to do with whatever was going on in Buckwoods?

The forest seemed more cheery today. The sky was mostly cloudy, but the sun emerged periodically to stream down through the trees and sparkle on the dew-laden branches. The smell of warming pine needles wafted up from the trail, and fresh pine scents breezed across us as we rode forward. Chickadees flitted from branch to branch ahead of us, chirping happily.

I felt a little foolish about running from what I had seen the night before, but then I reached up and touched one of the still-tender scratches on my face and frowned at the memory of my wild dash through the forest. I wasn't easily spooked. The wolf howls had touched on something primitive within me, and remembering them set my nerves on edge again.

As we neared the clearing, Alain exclaimed, "Tam! Stop! It's me, Alain."

We spread out into the clearing to find Tam, still without clothing. He crouched at the other side of the clearing and edged toward the trail behind him. His eyes were wild as they shifted back and forth among us.

Any doubts about what I'd seen the night before evaporated. Tam's face and ears were still distorted and his entire body was covered with light brown fur. His toes and fingers were stunted and clawed. His brown eyes were wide and his lips were pulled back from his teeth in a snarl that revealed long white canines in both his upper and lower jaw.

Alain dismounted, his face flushed and his eyes wide. Tam took a step back, and *growled* like a dog. There was no other word for the sound he made.

"Tam, what's happened to you? It's me, Alain," he repeated. Tam lifted his head and sniffed the air. He didn't growl again, but he didn't relax his stance either.

I decided that being on foot might make us seem less threatening. Apparently, so did Jergen. We both dismounted and stepped around in front of our horses. I stayed back a couple of steps to let Jergen and Alain handle the conversation with Tam, such as it was.

Jergen looked at the thing Tam had become and then over at Alain. "Are you telling me that this creature is my son? How is that possible?"

When Jergen spoke, Tam took another step back and growled again.

Alain held up his hand. "Wait, Tam! Don't run. We're here to help you." Tam stared at Alain and made a whining sound. Alain's hand dropped back to his side, and he looked over at Jergen. "Yes, it's Tam. Something has happened to him," he confirmed.

I slowly reached into my pocket so as not to disturb Tam, and removed the bottle I'd found in his things. I held up the bottle between my thumb and forefinger. "Does it have anything to do with this?" I asked Alain.

Alain glanced over at me and then looked sharply back when he saw the bottle. His eyes went wide. "Where did you find that?" he asked.

"It was hidden in Tam's boot."

"What is that?" Jergen demanded.

For a moment, Alain looked like he might try to run. He swallowed hard and he glanced at his horse.

"Tell us!" Jergen shouted. Tam growled again and crouched lower.

Alain looked at Tam, and then back at the bottle, which I was still holding up. His shoulders fell and he looked at the ground. "It's a potion. A lycanthropy potion," he said in defeated tone.

"What does it do?" I asked, although I had a pretty good idea already.

Alain looked over at me and waved a hand toward Tam. "It lets us explore the forest at night in wolf form."

Jergen took a step toward Alain. "Wolf form? What are you talking about? Are you telling me that this is what you boys have been up to out here? Fooling with dangerous magic and turning yourselves into wolves?"

Alain cringed at Jergen's tone. "It was harmless. We only did it once in a while, and only for an hour or two at a time. I don't understand why Tam hasn't fully changed back. Nothing like this has ever happened before," he said defensively.

Then Alain took a closer look at the bottle in my hand and stepped over to take it from me. He turned the bottle around, and when he saw the label, he gasped.

Jergen narrowed his eyes at Alain and stepped closer to him. "What is it?" he demanded.

Tam snarled and lurched forward a step when Jergen moved closer to Alain. Jergen noticed the movement and took a hesitant step back.

Alain looked back and forth between Jergen and me. "This is Eclipse. This is one of the strongest lycanthropy potions made."

"So what?" I asked.

Alain shook his head and held up the bottle. "We don't *use* stuff this strong. It would change you for hours. Maybe the entire night. We stick to the weakest potions because they are cheaper and only last a short time. This would cost...I don't know...a fortune." He waggled the bottle in emphasis and felt the remaining liquid slosh around. His face went white and he quietly murmured, "Oh, no," as he stared at the bottle in disbelief. He then looked sharply over at Tam. "Tam, what have you done?"

Jergen stepped forward at that moment and snatched the bottle from Alain's hand and yelled. "A fortune? Tam's wasting my money on magic potions so he can run around the forest in a wolf suit?"

When Jergen grabbed the bottle, Alain held out his hand in desperation and said "Wait!"

But Jergen ignored him and punctuated his tirade by throwing the bottle at the fire ring where it shattered upon the rocks. The last bit of potion dripped slowly down the side of the stone to be absorbed by the ground.

Alain stared at the fire ring in dismay.

Jergen's violent action provoked Tam into motion. He roared and launched himself at his father. Jergen, taken completely by surprise, barely had time to bring up his left arm in defense before Tam crashed into him and knocked him to the ground. Tam grunted in pain when he landed fully on his father. He rolled off with a wheezing sigh and lay there on his back, his father's dagger protruding from his chest.

Alain cried out and threw himself to the ground next to Tam. "Oh, Tam. I'm so sorry. Why didn't you tell us what you were going to do? I could have warned you." He lowered his head to his friend's face and began to sob.

Jergen had the wind knocked out of him when he crashed to the ground. As soon as he caught his breath, he sat up on an elbow and looked down at the creature lying next to him. As we watched, Tam's features melted back into the normal form of a sixteen-year-old boy and his breathing stopped.

"What have I done?" Jergen whispered. He reached over and pulled the dagger from Tam's body and placed his hand over the wound. He laid his head on Tam's chest and said, "Don't worry son, you'll be alright." But listening for a heartbeat was futile. Jergen raised his head from Tam's chest slowly with tears in his eyes.

Jergen got to his feet and picked up the dagger. He stared at the weapon, his son's lifeblood dripping from the edge of the blade. "It…he attacked me. I drew without thinking. I didn't even try to use it; he just fell on the blade," he muttered to himself.

Alain looked up from Tam's body and glared at Jergen. "You shouldn't have destroyed the bottle!" he shouted. "It was our only way to bring him back to himself."

Jergen blinked a couple of times and looked down at Alain. "What are you talking about? This is your doing! You and your magic potions!"

Alain glanced at the dagger in Jergen's hand and swallowed. He looked back up at Jergen and explained. "You're supposed to drink the entire potion, but Tam didn't. He must have thought he'd save some for another time, but I'm sure I told him you can't do that. That's why the potion didn't work right. Our only hope to get him back was to have him drink the rest of it."

Jergen's face went ashen, and he turned his face away from the boys. I thought he might be sick for a moment, but he gathered himself and turned to point the bloody dagger at me. "Not a word of this to anyone," he hissed. Then he pointed the dagger at Alain. "You either."

His eyes darted around and he chewed his lip as he thought for a moment. "I don't think anyone gains anything by knowing the truth about what happened here," he finally said, looking at Alain. The boy looked unhappy about what Jergen was suggesting, but nodded his head and looked back down at Tam. Jergen continued, "Tam got lost and fell. He had the misfortune to fall on a sharp branch. When we found him, he was already dead." Jergen nodded to himself, satisfied with the story he'd concocted.

Alain sighed. "You're right. I'll help."

A real investigation might reveal the truth, but the reality was that there would be no investigation. If someone like Jergen made a statement about how his only son had died, no one would question it; at least not to his face, and not to any kind of authority.

"Can I do anything to help?" I asked Jergen.

Jergen looked over at me as if he'd forgotten I was there. He reached into his pocket, pulled out a small purse, and threw it at me. "You can leave! That's the rest of your payment, as agreed. It should be enough for you to keep your mouth shut, and if it isn't, I know about your past *Captain* Forester, and I can make sure you never find work in this area again."

I caught the thrown purse just before it hit my chest, and I stood gaping at him as he issued his threat. My shock quickly turned to anger and I nearly threw the purse back at him. But I had earned the fee and venting my feelings wasn't worth the loss of three gold crowns.

Instead, I tucked the purse away and said evenly, "There's no need for threats, Mister Overland."

"Just get out of my sight. Now!" he roared, taking a step toward me, bloody dagger still in hand.

My hand went to my own dagger automatically, and I might have drawn it, except that I saw tears streaming down Jergen Overland's cheeks into his beard as he shouted. I knew then that his anger wasn't really directed at me, but that I made a convenient target.

Alain looked up from where he kneeled next to Tam and added his own plea. "Please, Mister Forester. Just go, and let us take care of Tam now."

I nodded to both of them and walked over to Patches. Patches was jittery from Tam's attack on Jergen and the subsequent shouting, and he was milling at the edge of the clearing with the other horses. I patted his neck and spoke soothingly to calm him before I stepped up into the saddle. As we left the clearing, I looked back over my shoulder to see that Jergen Overland was kneeling next to his son, holding the boy's head and shoulders in his lap and weeping silently.

I didn't like the idea of obscuring the truth of what had happened, but I couldn't argue with Jergen's conclusion. The truth would only cause trouble. There would be enough anger and grief over Tam's death as it was. Admitting sorcery was involved would only complicate matters for the Overlands and for Alain. And I knew that Jergen had not intentionally murdered his son. It was all a horribly tragic accident.

But I had reasons of my own to hold back the truth, and nausea churned in my stomach as I considered them. I had heard of lycanthropy potions. I knew almost nothing about them or how they worked because I had carefully avoided anything to do with sorcery my whole life. If I had known anything about potions, I might have realized the implications of the half-full bottle I'd held in my hand only moments before. I might have been able to save Tam the first time I found him. Or at least I could have prevented the disaster I had just witnessed.

In a way, my ignorance of sorcery may very well have cost young Tam his life.

CHAPTER 13

My journey back to Northshore went by in a blur. As I rode, my mind argued in circles, trying to figure out what went wrong and second-guessing what I could have done to stop it. Finally, I would chastise myself for fretting over something that was over and done, and then the same useless mental cycle would start over.

The clink of five gold crowns in my purse would normally be cheering, but today it was no consolation. I had satisfied the Overland contract, but not in a satisfying way. I had found Tam, uncovered the mystery of why he hadn't come home, and reunited him with his family, in a manner of speaking. But just the same, Jergen's final payment felt like a payoff to keep me quiet.

The sun was high in the sky overhead when the walls of Northshore came into view. I was relieved to be nearly home, but I wasn't sure what I was going to tell Borlan when I reported to him.

I waited outside the east gate for a moment while a large wagon rumbled through and rolled away toward Delta, and then I urged Patches through the opening into town. The streets were busy with townspeople. Many of the folks moved with a half-smile on their face, enjoying the unusually nice spring afternoon. I was like a dark cloud crossing their blue sky.

I dismounted in front of the Snow Creek Inn's stable. I wondered how Meldon was coming along with the repairs as I walked Patches through the open stable door. No sounds of hammering or sawing greeted me, so perhaps he'd made better time than expected.

My eyes adjusted quickly to the shadowed barn, and I was surprised to see Meldon sitting next to Dela on a bench. A mostly eaten meat pie rested on a small cloth that was spread between them. Meldon looked up quickly when I came in. "Hi Jaylan," he said, much louder than necessary. I could swear a blush rose to his cheeks.

Dela turned and saw me, and then leaped up from where she was sitting. "Jaylan! You're home!" She ran over to me with a big smile on her face and gave me a hug. I hugged her back with my one free arm. "I was just bringing Meldon some lunch," she explained.

Meldon stood and wiped some crumbs from his shirt and then sidled over to take Patches reins from my hand. "Here, let me take him for you." He led Patches over to the stall I had repaired before I left and started to unsaddle the horse.

Dela looked around the interior of the stable. "So, what do you think?" she asked me.

I surveyed the progress Meldon had made while I was gone. Four of the five stalls were done now. The rotten boards had been replaced and the gates had been repaired. "Nice job, Meldon. You're as good as your word. I see you had to get some more lumber after all."

Meldon poked his head from around Patches to answer. "Yes, sir. I'll probably finish up the job today. Thanks for giving me the work."

"I'm glad I did. Thanks for taking care of this for me."

Dela looked up at me hopefully. "So, are you done with that contract now? Will you be able to stay home for a while?"

I took a deep breath and let it out in a sigh. "Yes, I'm quite done."

Dela's voice grew serious. "Weren't you able to find the boy? Did they pay you?"

"I found the boy and I got paid. But the boy was dead. It was an ugly situation."

Dela hugged me again. "I'm sorry. Come inside and I'll give you something to eat. You'll feel better once you put it behind you."

"I'm sure you're right. Thanks," I said. She released me and left the stable with a quick wave at Meldon.

I walked over to retrieve my saddle bags from where Meldon had laid them. Meldon was brushing out Patches, who had found a bit of hay to chew on. "Keep up the good work. I may have more for you to do in the future," I told him.

Meldon interrupted his brushing for a moment to smile over at me. "Thanks, Jaylan. I'd appreciate that."

I angled my head toward the remains of his lunch over on the bench. "You didn't finish your meat pie. Didn't you enjoy Dela's cooking?"

He glanced over at the bench and went back to brushing Patches. "Oh, yes, she's a very good cook. I just wasn't all that hungry, I guess."

I suppressed a smile. "Uh, huh. She can be distracting."

Meldon froze and looked over at me. I chuckled at his reaction and he blushed again, realizing that I was teasing him. "Thanks again for taking care of Patches for me," I said. I hitched the saddle bags up on my shoulder and left the stable.

I went back to the inn and sat down to a nice meal with Dela. She kept her tone upbeat but gentle during our repast, distracting me from my dark thoughts with talk of our current guests at the inn and the latest town gossip. Her calming voice gradually redirected my thoughts to familiar subjects and helped me slowly let go of the tension that had gripped me since the incident on the Delta Peninsula.

While Dela chattered about the inn's preparations for Planting Day, the upcoming mid-spring celebration, I thought back to what I'd seen in the stable. Meldon seemed to have an interest in Dela, even if she hadn't noticed yet. The lad was reliable and skilled, and much closer to her in age than I was. He didn't really seem to fit in over at Raven Company. I wondered what he thought about the idea of becoming an innkeeper.

～

After my late lunch with Dela, I walked over to Raven Company to close out the Overland contract with Borlan. On my way there, I ruminated on how often I had been running into sorcery lately.

I could count on my two hands the number of times I had been exposed to sorcery in my entire life. And most of those events had happened in the past three days. Since my fateful meeting with the young thief Raleb, I had not only encountered sorcery in multiple forms, but I'd unwittingly performed it. Every one of those encounters had reminded me of when I first started learning swordsmanship. The first time I picked up a sword, I knew nothing about how to properly defend myself or press an attack. I looked forward to things settling down and returning to normal.

Borlan wasn't at his desk when I entered the front office, but the muted clang of sparring came from the basement. I opened the basement door and the clash of swords became louder. Borlan's familiar voice shouted curses at his sparring partner.

The basement sparring room was a bit dank, but its underground placement kept it cool even on the hottest summer days. Weapons racks along the walls held a number of practice weapons and a few battle-ready pieces of equipment. I stopped part-way down the stairs to watch the action without disturbing the competitors, but Borlan saw me standing there.

After a final clang, Borlan stepped back and saluted his opponent. Returning the salute was Captain Rakerus Pollard of the Imperial Guard. Borlan and Rakerus had known each other for years, so it was no surprise to see the captain here. In fact, their friendship was what had originally inspired Rakerus to suggest that I speak with Borlan about getting work at Raven Company after my expulsion from the guard.

Borlan grinned over at me as he placed the dulled practice sword he was using back on the rack. "Back so soon, Jaylan? I expected it to take a while to find the boy. That was a quick five crowns." His grin disappeared when he noticed the troubled look on my face. "What happened?"

"The boy was dead, Borlan." I handed him one of the gold crowns. "It was the least satisfying fee I've ever earned."

"How about the Overlands. How did they take it?"

I hesitated before answering. Borlan was a good friend and I wanted to share the whole story with him. I would probably even trust Rakerus with the truth, but it would put the man in a bad position, since he would technically be expected to follow up, and he might have to go to Delta and investigate the circumstances of the boy's death. I decided to keep it simple.

"Jergen Overland was with me when we found the boy's body. He was upset, but I'm sure his wife will be devastated."

Rakerus had placed his practice sword up on the rack and was buckling on his regular weapon. "That's a shame," he said somberly. "Jergen can be an overbearing ass, but Greta always seemed like a nice woman."

I just nodded, trying to keep my face from revealing anything more than I had already said.

Borlan looked down at the coin I'd placed in his hand and pocketed it. "Sorry to hear about that, Jaylan. I'm almost surprised he paid the entire fee, although I guess you did complete the contract. Just not with the ending they were hoping for."

Borlan gripped my shoulder and steered me toward the "meeting room," which was really just a table in one corner of the basement with a cask of ale strategically placed on a nearby cubby. "Let me buy you an ale. How about you, Rakerus?"

Rakerus shook his head. "No thanks. I need to get back to the office. I'm supposed to meet with Caslin Stone about paroling that young thief."

I turned to Rakerus. "Are you talking about Raleb, the thief those Archives agents captured?"

"Yes. Caslin has offered to give him a labor parole for some reason. I didn't even know such a provision existed until yesterday. Seems risky to me. Caslin has to take responsibility for the young man for the duration of his sentence or lose the parole money he puts forth."

"That is odd. Caslin has never struck me as being particularly charitable," I said.

In fact, Caslin struck me as being a bit of a crook. To my knowledge, he had never engaged in illegal activity, but it was well known that his shop carried more than just tonics and tonic ingredients. According to rumor, magical potions were hidden from sight, but available to any customer willing to ask for them and willing to pay the high price.

I thought it likely that Caslin's shop was the source of Tam's lycanthropy potion. The Overland contract was done, but part of me wanted to go over to Caslin's shop and wrest the truth from him. If he had indeed supplied the lycanthropy potion, he shared a measure of culpability for Tam's death.

"He must be busy if he's willing to parole a thief to get help," I concluded, wondering to myself what the real reason for his generosity might be.

Rakerus nodded. "He does seem to be getting a lot of business lately." Then he gave me a sly grin. "Young ladies are always in need of more love potions, and from what I hear, you may need to start watching what you drink yourself."

I laughed. "Very funny. Dela doesn't need any love potions; she's got force of personality on her side."

Rakerus and Borlan chuckled with me. "Well, I'd better get going. Talk to you both later," Rakerus said, and he headed up the stairs to leave. Borlan and I walked over to the table. I sat down while he poured ale for us.

"It's a bit early in the day, but a five-crown fee is worthy of a toast." He sat my mug down in front of me and took a seat. We raised our mugs and tapped them together. The frothy ale was cool and rich, and we each took a big swig. Borlan tapped his chest with his fist a couple of times and we belched in unison.

"I have something else I want to run by you," he said.

"What's that?"

"Something's wrong with that escort contract I told you about."

My stomach tighted and I sat up in my chair. "Now that you mention it, that's something I wanted to ask you about too."

He glanced at me curiously, but went on. "Either Kefer or Peltor was supposed to check in with me when the shipment came past Northshore, but neither of them did. They should have come through here yesterday at the latest, but I haven't seen either one of them. What do you know about it?"

"I saw Kefer and Peltor at Buckwoods, that little fishing village on the Delta Peninsula. They were acting strangely and claimed that the driver wanted to stop off at the village," I told him.

Borlan's heavy eyebrows drew together. "The client from Plains End didn't mention anything about a stopover, and the driver should know better than to take care of personal business on a run like this. Going to Buckwoods wasn't part of the plan or the fee. You saw them there yesterday?"

I nodded. "They drew their blades and blocked me when I entered the village. They told me the driver wanted to stop there, and they wouldn't let me ask around about the missing boy. They claimed they'd been there since the previous evening, and that no one had seen the boy."

Borlan squinted at me. "They've been there since night before last? What do you mean they wouldn't let you talk to the villagers?"

"It was like they didn't want me to come into the village for some reason. I didn't have time to argue with them about it, so I left. But they kept their blades bare the entire time, and they waited for me to leave."

Borlan's look of confusion turned into a glare. "What are those two playing at? They've got some explaining to do when they get back," he said, slamming his mug to the table. He leaned forward and pointed his finger at me. "I want you to go back down there and find out what's going on. I'm cutting you in on a full share of their fee, and if the whole deal goes bad because of those two, I'll cover it myself."

I looked at Borlan and considered his request. I hadn't told him about the sound I'd heard while at the village and the sorcery that the noise might represent. I didn't plan to tell him either. I didn't know Borlan's feelings on the subject of sorcery, and I didn't want to try explaining how I knew it might be involved. Instead, I focused on concerns he would understand.

"I'm not sure I can take on both of them if they decide to fight me," I said.

Borlan leaned back in his chair, letting his hand drop to the table in surprise. "Why do you think they'd fight you?"

"The whole time I spoke with them, the treated me like I was some kind of threat. If I got forceful with them, I think they'd react badly."

Borlan shook his head. "That doesn't make any sense. They're supposed to guard that shipment, but the point is to get it safely to Plains End. Look, I'd go with you, but I'm needed here." He thought for a moment. "How about taking Meldon with you? I'd hate to put the kid into a fight with Kefer or Peltor, but if you've got some backup, maybe there won't be a fight."

I thought about that. Having sparred with Meldon myself, I knew that he was a fair hand with a sword, but he didn't have the experience of older company members like Kefer and Peltor. Like Borlan, I had difficulty believing there'd be a fight in the first place, but I still got gooseflesh when I thought about my encounter with the men yesterday. I also wasn't too keen on the idea of subjecting Meldon to whatever sorcery might be involved—or subjecting myself to it for that matter. Realistically, there wasn't much choice. Borlan had no one else to turn to right now.

"I suppose you're right. Meldon could use the experience and I could use the backup, as you say."

"Good," Borlan said, slapping his hand on the table. "Just get them back on task. You don't have to accompany them all the way to Plains End, but make sure they understand that they aren't to go on any more side trips."

We both finished our ale and stood up. "I'll see what I can do," I said with a tone of confidence in my voice that I didn't feel.

CHAPTER 14

Agent Sulana Delano paced back and forth in the antechamber to the Archives Council Hall. This morning she had stood before the councilors with Talon at her side. She gave them the facts of her journey with professional detachment, and delivered her conclusions and recommendations with conviction. The stodgy panel of five senior sorcerers who made up the Council interrupted her only a few times with questions. They asked Talon for his impressions on a couple of occasions as well. When Sulana was dismissed, she left with the distinct feeling that the Council wasn't taking the situation seriously enough.

The one exception was a sixth aged sorcerer who was also present for the debriefing. Wizard Ebnik Vlastorus had listened carefully to her report, and he nodded at her conclusions, but he no longer had any official standing within the Council. His presence in the chamber was mainly a courtesy that the Council had extended to him as a respected visiting sorcerer and former council member. He also had an interest in the proceedings, since it was his ring that had been stolen.

The antechamber was a square room with long bench seats along the side walls. An open archway allowed access to the chamber from the main hallway, and the back wall was dominated by large wooden doors that opened into the Council Hall. Maroon tapestries with a simple diamond pattern of white lines woven into them draped the walls above the benches. The tapestries were more for muting noise in the antechamber than for any decorative purpose. Banners hung on either side of the doors, topped with the Symbol of Sorcery and proclaiming the entrance to the Council Hall.

The Symbol of Sorcery represented the four primary elements of spell casting: the Well, the Link, the Focus, and the Incantation. The Well, which served as the source of vaetra, was represented by a large sphere. The Link, which represented the path by which vaetra was channeled, took the form of a thick stem that extended up from where it clutched the top of the sphere. The Focus was a smaller sphere cradled within two curled branches that extended up from of the top of the Link. The curled branches represented the many manifestations of vaetra. On the Link was a single rune that represented the Incantation.

Daven sat on one of the benches. He leaned forward over the floor with a small knife and a block of wood in his hands. He was carefully carving a shape out of the wood while Sulana paced. The shavings fluttered to the floor where they landed in a small pile on a piece of canvas that he had spread at his feet. "Wearing a rut in the floor won't make them decide any faster," he said.

Sulana stopped next to Daven and watched him carve for a moment. "I know, but they called Ebnik back into the hall a while ago now. I thought they were going to give us their decision."

Daven snorted. "You know how they are. Sending out another team will be expensive. They have to be convinced of the need first. I think Talon and Barek had the right idea. Go do something useful while the Council makes up its mind."

"You're still here," she pointed out.

Daven waved his carving and knife. "I can do this anywhere. I just choose to do it here. Besides, I'd like to know what they decide too."

Sulana sighed and sat on the edge of the bench next to him. She looked over at his work, which seemed to be evolving into some kind of animal. "What are you carving?"

"An arbolenx. Now that I've seen one up close, I think I can do it justice."

One of the doors to the Council Hall opened, and Ebnik slipped out, closing the door carefully behind him. Sulana jumped to her feet, and Daven stopped carving to watch the old man approach.

Ebnik's weathered and lined face betrayed nothing as he slowly walked over to Sulana. His long brown robe shifted around his legs as he came forward. The robe was reinforced with leather strips across the shoulders and down the front. Its voluminous sleeves were trimmed with dark brocade that shimmered from the silver threads woven into it. The wizard stopped in front of them, his long-fingered hands folded in front of his waist.

Sulana tilted her head back to look up into Ebnik's severe grey eyes, which softened when he saw the anxious look on her face. Standing so close to him, the thick mane of white hair framing his face and cascading down his shoulders made his lean height even more imposing.

"I'm sorry, Sulana. The council decided not to send your team back out," he apologized.

Sulana's eyes widened in disbelief. "Are you serious? Don't they see this sorcerer as a threat?"

Ebnik motioned her to sit, and he sat next to her as she did so. "We have the ring back, thanks to the good work of your team. We only have a thief's second-hand word that a sorcerer is involved. There's simply no evidence of a conspiracy or any danger to the mundane public."

Sulana winced and shook her head. "Who but a sorcerer would hire thieves to steal that particular ring? And why would he do it if he didn't have plans for it?"

Ebnik waved his hand in a conciliatory gesture. "I agree with you. The situation bears more investigation, but it is a practical matter of evidence. We have nothing strong enough to convince the Council that the cost of sending you out again is justified."

Sulana sat back hard against the bench and pressed the heels of her hands to her temples. She squeezed her eyes closed and then slapped her hands back down and gripped the top of her legs. "They need evidence, but they won't let us go get it. That's just the kind of circular logic I'd expect from councilors with tight purse strings."

Ebnik chuckled and put his hand on her shoulder. She relaxed a bit at his touch. "Don't give up yet. I'm not quite done with them myself. I just need a little time to come up with more information and a more compelling argument."

"But we may not *have* time. We don't know how long the buyer will wait at this village, Buckwoods did you say?

Eventually he'll figure out that the ring isn't coming and he, or she, will suspect we are on to him."

Ebnik nodded as she spoke. "I argued that point myself. In fact, they believe the buyer is already gone by now, so the trip would be wasted even if something is going on. Buckwoods is just a small fishing village, if memory serves. There's no reason for the buyer to remain there for an extended period of time."

"So how are you going to convince them?" she asked with a helpless spread of her hands.

He patted her shoulder and smiled as he stood up. "Leave that to me. If something significant is happening, it will cause ripples. I intend to find a ripple big enough to get the Council's attention. This was no random theft, and the person behind it has been careful to remain at a distance from Archives agents and sorcerers. That level of caution indicates something important at stake...something that doesn't bode well for any of us."

CHAPTER 15

The breakfast crowd at the Snow Creek Inn was light that morning. A young couple who were staying at the inn had come downstairs to the serving room and were yawning over their platters of eggs and cheese. The rest of the tables were empty.

Meldon and I sat at a table across from Dela. We sipped from cups of an herbal tea concoction that Dela had devised herself. Rakerus' joke yesterday afternoon about love potions came to mind, and I hesitated before taking another sip. I looked across at Dela, who was watching me carefully.

"Well, what do you think? Don't you like it?" she asked.

"I do like it. It's the best tea you've made so far," I responded.

She sat back with a satisfied smile and folded her arms. "Thanks. I think it's nice to give the guests something new when they stay with us. What do you think, Meldon?"

Meldon took another sip and made a show of serious contemplation. "I'm not much of an herbal tea drinker, but this is excellent. I give it my highest marks."

Dela smiled and giggled. "Thanks, Meldon. Coming from such an expert, that's high praise indeed."

Dela's face became serious again and she folded her hands on the table. "I understand that things are picking up at Raven Company, but do you have to take *every* contract that comes along?" she asked me.

"Borlan is short-handed right now. Things have been so slow lately that some of his men haven't been renewing their commitments. My commitment isn't up for another two weeks, and Meldon and I are the only available hands right now."

When I joined Raven Company, I had to give Borlan a commitment for a specific period of time. The commitment period was usually from three months to a year. I could do whatever other work I wanted during that time, but if Raven Company business came up, I was supposed to drop what I was doing and take the contract. You could refuse contracts during your commitment if you had a good reason, but doing so was frowned upon, and refusing too often could get you blacklisted from all future Raven Company work.

She frowned. "Do you have to take Meldon with you? Hiring him to help out around here while you are gone has worked out well. With both of you leaving, it will be hard for Mother and me to keep things going."

I looked over at Meldon, who was watching Dela over the rim of his tea cup as he took another sip. "Borlan convinced me yesterday afternoon that I could use the backup. I'm not sure of exactly what kind of situation I'm walking into," I answered.

Dela reached across the table to grip my hand with hers, her brow creased with concern. "That sounds dangerous. Please be careful."

I flipped my hand under hers and quickly squeezed her hand a couple of times before withdrawing mine. "You know I will be. I faced plenty more dangerous situations when I was with the Guard. My Raven Company work has been pretty safe by comparison."

Meldon put his cup down. "I just hope you're wrong about the magic."

I closed my eyes and silently groaned to myself. I had told Meldon about my concerns regarding the possibility of sorcery because I thought it was his right to know what he was getting himself into. I should have told Meldon to leave that little piece of information out of any discussions with Dela.

"Magic? What do you mean? You aren't going out to fight some magician, are you?" Dela's voice pitched higher and louder with every word.

I grimaced and waved her quiet. "Relax. We don't know there's a sorcerer involved. The situation just has some odd aspects that could have a perfectly normal explanation." I didn't believe that myself of course, but I also didn't have proof of any sinister influences.

She huffed and folded her arms again. "Let the magicians take care of themselves. You should stay away from anything that stinks of magic."

Her words summed up the attitude of just about everyone I knew: stay away from the stink of magic, indeed. If only it were that easy, I thought to myself.

"I took the contract, and we're going," I insisted. Dela's face darkened and she blinked a tear that rolled down one cheek. I softened my voice and tried to sound confident. "Don't worry, we should be back by nightfall and I'll have more coin to show for it."

I reached across the table and laid my open hand down for her to take. She looked down at my hand and sniffed. Wiping the tear from her face, she got up from her chair and marched out of the serving room. I slowly drew back my hand and sighed.

I rolled my eyes at Meldon. "Thanks a lot."

He shrugged. "Sorry, Jaylan. I didn't know you wanted to lie to her about that."

"I didn't want to *lie* to her, I just didn't want to worry her unnecessarily," I defended.

He snorted. "Well, *I'm* worried."

I patted him on the back. "You're supposed to worry. Worrying keeps you alive. Now let's go see what's really going on in Buckwoods. If we're lucky, Kefer and Peltor will be back on the road doing their job by now."

Meldon looked at me with one raised eyebrow. "You don't really expect that, do you?"

I swallowed a final gulp of Dela's new tea and got up from the table. "No. I don't."

CHAPTER 16

Sulana awoke from a dreamless sleep and stretched luxuriously before flipping the covers to the other side of the bed. It felt good to sleep in her own room again after nearly a week of hard travel and stressful days. She rolled over in the complete darkness and felt around for the base of the lamp on the nightstand next to her bed. She closed her eyes and channeled vaetra into it. At the top of the lamp, an igniter-crystal sparked the wick into a flame and room filled with a dim golden light. She opened her eyes into a squint, adjusting to the sudden illumination.

She sat up and looked around her small and simple chamber. It wasn't much, but it was hers. Her room was only about twelve feet square, but it contained everything she needed: her bed, the nightstand, a dresser, an old armoire, and a small desk with a chair. The solid stone walls made it difficult to hang decorations, but she did have a beautiful tapestry on one wall that depicted the legend of Horace Gaunt, the first Sword Sorcerer and a founder of the Archives.

The center of the design featured Horace on his horse with his sword raised. Around him were images related to his travels, including a rendition of the Archives Castle in the upper-right corner.

Sulana's mother had given her the tapestry on her 16th birthday, her Day of Adulthood. She treasured it, knowing that her mother had probably spent the better part of a year's earnings to pay for its well-wrought artwork.

She got out of bed and saw that someone had slipped a note under her door. She brought it over to the lamp and discovered that the note was from Ebnik. He wanted her to meet him in the main library at midmorning. She wasn't sure how late she'd slept, so she quickly got dressed, extinguished her lamp, and walked confidently in the dark around the room's obstacles to her chamber door.

Sulana's room was deep underground, so she had no windows from which to judge the time of day. She needed to go out to one of the exterior rooms or find a suntracker along the way.

As she opened her door, a small illuminator on the opposite wall reacted to her presence and instantly lit the hallway with a bright white glow. Illuminators throughout the Archives were small half-spheres of glass, about two inches in diameter, mounted on a circular brass base with a stem that was embedded into the wall just below the ceiling. The glass focusing device drew vaetra from the stone wall through the metal stem and converted it to light when it detected a person nearby. They were extremely helpful in the dark underground hallways that made up the majority of the castle.

Sulana quietly closed the door behind her. There was something about the utter silence of these subterranean passages that made one speak in a hushed voice and tread lightly. Every sound you made seemed muffled and yet intrusive.

The hallway outside her door connected to a much wider main hallway that led to the front of the castle. She knew she'd find a suntracker on the wall where the halls met. She walked to the end of her hallway past two other doors and looked up at the wall across from her. The suntracker's hand-sized disk was placed just above eye level, and the center-mounted indicator was pointing almost directly to the left. The enchantment that drove the suntracker followed the sun's movement in the sky, turning the pointer around the disk to point straight up at midday and straight down at midnight.

Sulana saw that she had apparently slept longer than she thought. It was well past sunrise, but she still had time to grab something to eat before she had to meet with Ebnik. She turned right and strode down the larger passage.

The large double doors of the dining hall were near the end of the main hallway, and both were swung fully open. The dining hall was one of the few rooms in the castle with an exterior wall and natural lighting. A half dozen robed residents were seated on the benches at various tables around the room. Sulana's stomach growled as she walked along the perimeter of the room toward the aromatic kitchen to see what was available.

After a small but satisfying breakfast, she hurried back into the depths of the castle to the main library on one of the lower levels.

The heavy wooden door to the library swung open smoothly on silent hinges as Sulana entered. She immediately spotted Ebnik seated at a carrel, bent over an open tome. The old man looked up when she walked over, and he closed the book he was reading. "Good morning, Sulana," he said as he got up. He took the book over to one of the library shelves and put it back into the gap where it had come from.

"Good morning, Ebnik. What did you want to see me about?"

He turned to face her, his baritone voice carrying a hint of mischief. "I have a treat for you. We're going to see someone who may be able to help us get the evidence we need to convince the Council to let your team go to Buckwoods."

Sulana tilted her head. "Truly? Who would that be?"

He winked at her. "You'll see. Follow me." Ebnik turned and walked deeper into the library.

Sulana hesitated as he walked away. She had expected Ebnik to leave the library the way she came in, not go the opposite direction. She finally put herself in motion and followed Ebnik's flowing robes between the stacks to an old wooden door at the back wall of the library. The door had a glass sigil embedded into the wood. Ebnik placed his hand on the sigil, and Sulana saw it glow briefly through the gaps between his fingers. With a distinct click, the door unlocked and slipped open a few inches.

She didn't hear him say the trigger word for the implement on the door, but that wasn't a surprise. Ebnik was more than just a sorcerer; he was a wizard, which meant he could cast incantations and activate vaetric implements with thought alone. It was a rare gift, and one that appeared only after many years of casting experience. It was just one of the reasons Sulana had tremendous respect for the old sorcerer.

The door opened into a passageway that was too roughly hewn to merit the term hallway. It went straight back, deeper into the mountain than any place she'd been before. No illuminators came to life as they entered. Ebnik picked up a lantern that was resting on an old stool on the other side of the door, and lit it with a brief but intense stare. He gestured for Sulana to close the door behind them, and holding the lantern in front of him, he led the way down the passage.

They didn't have to walk very far. The passage turned to the left about thirty paces down and then went another ten paces or so before they came to a pair of doors. One was at the end of the passage and the other was in the left wall.

The end door opened as they approached, and a shaggy-haired, middle-aged man wearing a simple long brown robe stood framed at its threshold. He nodded his head when he recognized Ebnik and stepped back to let them enter. "Welcome Ebnik. It's been a while." He motioned for them to take a seat on a long padded bench near the door, while he sat in a nearby chair.

"Greetings, Arinot. I hope things are well with you." Ebnik sat the lantern down on a small table near the door. It added significantly to the light on that side of the room.

Sulana looked around and realized the room was lit entirely by candles and one other lantern, which sat atop a dark, wooden desk that was piled with books and papers. She didn't see a single illuminator.

"I'm as well as ever. Who have you brought to see me?" Arinot asked, looking over at Sulana curiously.

Ebnik held both hands out toward Sulana. "May I present Archives Agent Sulana Delano, battle-hardened Sword Sorceress and Trollbane."

Sulana blushed and scowled at Ebnik, then turned apologetically to Arinot. "He's mocking me. I'm a 'Sword Sorceress' with one mission into the mundane world under my belt, and yes, *my team* encountered a troll on the return journey."

Ebnik shook his head insistently and leaned toward Arinot, his voice dropping to a dramatic rumble. "She's being too modest. Right when her most experienced warrior, himself a Trollbane, was about to be gobbled up by a troll of legendary size and power, Sulana slew the creature and saved the warrior's life with one mighty spell."

Arinot's green eyes twinkled as he watched Sulana squirm in her seat at Ebnik's rendition of her story.

When Ebnik finished, Sulana's frown turned to a smile and she laughed. "Ebnik, I think you missed your calling. You should have been a bard."

Ebnik looked down with a sad expression. "Alas, I fear my voice and playing would chase away the crowds before they could hear my stories."

Arinot chuckled. "Well met, Sulana Trollbane. How may I be of service?"

"I brought Sulana with me to see if we might ask a favor of you," Ebnik answered for her.

Arinot's expression grew serious as he looked into Ebnik's eyes. "You have need of...my particular talent?" He looked quickly aside at Sulana.

Ebnik nodded. "I have permission from the Council to let Sulana observe, so you may speak freely."

Sulana looked back and forth between Ebnik and Arinot. "What's this about? Does Arinot have unique implements or incantations we can use?"

Arinot chuckled and shook his head. "No incantations or implements, I'm afraid. I'm no sorcerer."

Sulana's confusion grew and she wasn't sure what to say. Ebnik rescued her from her discomfort.

"Arinot is a Sensitive. Actually, there should be a different word for Arinot's sensitivity, as it is so far beyond anything we normally equate with the term."

"What do you mean?" Sulana asked.

Arinot answered her. "I can hear vaetric manifestations from as far away as the Imperial Capital."

Sulana gasped. "How is that possible? With that kind of range, anything that happened close by would be..."

"Deafening," Arinot finished for her with a nod. He raised his hands, palms up, and looked around the room. "That's why I'm down here in this cave. The thick stone blocks out most manifestation sounds and gives me a measure of peace."

Sulana looked at Arinot for a moment, absorbing the implications of his words. "So, you're a sound Sensitive, just like...someone else I met recently." He nodded again. "Wouldn't you be more comfortable somewhere farther away from the Archives? This place has to be the source of a lot of manifestation noise."

He nodded. "You'd think so, but this really is the best place for me. This hole in the ground protects me well enough, and I have an arrangement with the archives that gives me a comfortable living."

Ebnik spoke up. "Arinot is also a scholar and scribe. He understands more about vaetra than many sorcerers."

Ebnik stood. "But that's not why we're here either. We've come to find out what Arinot can hear for us, not what knowledge he can share." Arinot and Sulana rose to their feet as well.

Arinot grimaced. "To the tower, then?"

"Indeed. To the tower," Ebnik confirmed.

Sulana wasn't sure what they were talking about, but the Archives had only one tower, and she assumed that was where they were headed. Arinot grabbed a lantern and left the room through the door she and Ebnik had entered. He turned to the other door she'd seen at the end of his hallway and opened it to reveal another dark passageway. Arinot led the way, his swaying lantern pushing back the darkness as they moved forward.

This passage was similar to the one that had taken her from the library to Arinot's chamber; it was rough-hewn and possessed no illuminators. Sulana wasn't sure of their direction, but she suspected that this route would allow them to bypass most of the castle's main corridors on their way to the tower.

A short distance down the corridor, they came to steps leading upward. They climbed the stairs to a closed door, where Arinot hesitated. "I hate this part," Sulana heard him murmur, and he handed the lantern to Ebnik before he opened the door.

The doorway opened up into one of the hallways of the main castle, so as Arinot stepped over the threshold, an illuminator came on a little farther down the hall. Arinot clapped his hands to his ears and whimpered before charging down the hallway toward a door at the far end. He pressed his shoulder into his right ear to free that hand, quickly opened and stepped through the door.

Ebnik and Sulana hurried down the hall after him. Arinot stared balefully at them with his hands still over his ears as they joined him. Sulana slammed the door closed, and Arinot lowered his hands and let go of the breath he'd been holding once the hallway illuminator extinguished itself.

Sulana had never considered the illuminators a menace. To her, they had always been a welcome convenience. Seeing Arinot's distress made her sorry they couldn't disable or remove the illuminator in the hallway that connected to the tower, but she supposed it didn't make much sense to inconvenience everyone for the sake of one man whose existence was a secret.

They stood on a landing inside the castle tower. Steps spiraled both upward and downward from the landing. The treads connected from the outside wall to a central stone column, with cool air cascading steadily down the stairwell into the depths of the castle. Muted natural light seeped down from above.

The tower was actually part of the castle's heating system, which used vaetric heaters to warm the outside air that flowed down the tower stairwell. The warmed air rose up through the rooms and halls of the castle's interior through ventilation shafts between each level.

Arinot shivered and started up the stairs. "Let's get out of this beastly draft."

Everyone was panting by the time they reached the top landing. Ebnik rested his hand against the wall and hung his head while he caught his breath. "Those stairs get longer every year," he grumbled between breaths.

Above them, large slots in the exterior wall admitted a steady flow of fresh mountain air. She could see the underside of the pointed tower roof that protected the openings from weather.

Arinot smiled, gave Ebnik an affectionate pat on the back, and then opened the door that led out to the tower's maintenance walkway.

As a child, Sulana had loved coming up here. The tower rose high above the Archives castle and the hillside into which the castle was built. From the walkway that encircled the top of the tower, one could see for multiple days' travel in almost every direction. Only one nearby mountain peak obscured the view to the southwest, but that peak was itself a magnificent vision of rocky slopes and stunted trees. In every other direction, the tree-spiked landscape rose up to snow-capped peaks and fell down into bright green valleys.

Ebnik followed them out onto the walkway, and everyone simultaneously took a deep breath of the fresh morning air.

Arinot looked eagerly around at the view and went right up to the waist-high wall that protected observers on the walkway. "Beautiful. I don't get up here often enough," he said with a wistful expression.

"What do we do now?" Sulana asked.

"We let Arinot adjust to the noise level, and then we find out what our brethren are up to out there in the world," Ebnik said.

"What are we listening for?" Arinot asked.

"I'd rather not say just yet. Let's see what you can tell me first," Ebnik answered.

Arinot gave one curt nod and started walking slowly around the tower walkway. Sulana followed him a couple of paces behind, enjoying the view and leaning over to look down at the Archives personnel moving around on the ground far below. She could hear the breeze whisper through the treetops and caught snatches of conversation. The clouds were high and thin in the sky, which was a welcome relief from the fog of clouds that frequently cloaked the mountain.

Arinot winced and stepped back toward the wall of the tower a few times during his walk. Sulana guessed that someone nearby must have used vaetra, which had to be expected in a place populated by sorcerers.

After he completed one full circuit, Arinot moved more slowly around the tower a second time, stopping occasionally to close his eyes and turn his head this way and that. He finally backtracked to a position that faced toward the south.

"There's something going on over there that I haven't heard before." He finally stated, pointing south. He turned and nodded his head toward the north. "There's also unusual activity going on toward the north, but it isn't consistent. This," he said, nodding south, "is very consistent. And it's layered."

Sulana frowned. Layering was a term sorcerers and Sensitives used when they picked up multiple colors or sounds, indicating multiple vaetric manifestations happening at the same time. If Arinot was hearing continuous layers of manifestation, that meant someone was consuming a lot of vaetra. Sulana was unaware of any Archives-related activity that would explain it.

"Can you tell how far?" Sulana asked.

"Not exactly. It can be hard to tell the difference between something strong that's farther away and something weak that's closer, but the way it's being diffused by the mountains between here and there, I'd say it's down by Teardrop Lake somewhere. Probably on the near shore."

Ebnik smiled. "That's exactly what I needed to hear. Thank you, Arinot."

Sulana looked at Ebnik. "But if that's true, more may be going on in Buckwoods than we realized. For one thing, it seems likely that the sorcerer is still there, given all the manifestation noise." Ebnik nodded encouragingly. "And he's up to something significant or he has a lot of help," she continued.

"Or both," said Ebnik, completing her conclusion.

"Can you tell me what's going on?" Arinot asked carefully. He was obviously used to dealing with Archives sorcerers and their secrets.

Ebnik motioned Sulana and Arinot to precede him back into the tower. "Yes. We'll talk about it on the way down. And then I have to arrange an audience with the Council as quickly as possible."

CHAPTER 17

Meldon and I crouched behind a dense thicket of shrubbery along the edge of the forest that encircled Buckwoods. From our uncomfortable position, we observed the villagers going about their daily tasks. We'd left Meldon's horse and Patches at a grassy area along the road behind us so they wouldn't make any noise that might give us away while we checked out the village.

The village had a panoramic view of the lake. Its choppy blue-grey water stretched far and wide. Beyond the opposite shore, snowy peaks rose majestically into a cloud-streaked sky.

Two of the village women were working a large garden to our right. The younger woman was busily hoeing weeds from the area of the garden that had yet to be planted. The older woman was busy inspecting the tiny plants that were already in the ground getting their start on the growing season. She checked each plant for pests or damage and tied the weakest of them to support sticks.

The short village dock that jutted out onto the lake was empty. The fishing boats were out harvesting the lake's bounty, bringing home the fish that gave Buckwoods its living.

On the shore next to the dock was a covered fish-cleaning station. Sitting next to it was a small smokehouse, with smoke threading out of the walls and ventilation holes. A strong wind from the south whipped the thin, fish-scented smoke toward the gardeners and the two of us.

The wind was a blessing. It covered any small noises we might make and prevented the horses and mules in a nearby corral to our left from catching our scent. Tree branches and the leaves on the shrubs waved around creating a visual distraction as well.

"I don't see anything unusual. Do you Meldon?" I looked over at Meldon to find he was staring wide-eyed at the older woman working the garden. I followed his gaze, but saw nothing unusual. I could once again hear the strange noise I had heard the last time I was here. The wind seemed to have no affect on my ability to hear the humming sound.

"What is that? What is she wearing?" Meldon whispered with a shaking voice.

I took a closer look at the older gardener and could see one of the strange amulets dangling down from her neck. "Do you mean the amulet?"

"Yes. Why does it glow?" he asked, easing back away from the bush that obscured us and swallowing hard.

He seemed about to turn and run, so I grabbed his arm. "It's glowing?"

His eyes were wild and he whispered harshly over at me. "Yes! Don't you see it? It's the magic you warned me about isn't it? We need to get out of here!" He tried to pull his arm out of my grip.

"Meldon, stop!" I hissed. "Control yourself. We have a job to do, remember?" I grabbed him by the shoulders and made him look at me.

The wild look slowly left his eyes and then he looked down at the ground, his neck and face flushing red. "I'm sorry, Jaylan, I don't know what got into me." He glanced up at the working woman again and shuddered. "That amulet glowing with magic is the most terrifying thing I've ever seen."

I narrowed my eyes and stared at Meldon for a moment to see if he was really settling down. I couldn't see the glow he was talking about, but if Meldon could see the amulets glowing and they were also the source of the sound, there was no longer any doubt that sorcery was at work here. I had also just learned that Meldon was a sight Sensitive like Sulana. Did he have the potential to become a sorcerer too? I almost decided to turn around and leave right then. If Meldon couldn't control his reaction to the amulets, he could put our mission at risk. But we were here, and he seemed to be getting a grip on himself.

I let go of his arm, and he gave me a weak smile. "Avoid looking at the amulets then, if you can," I suggested. He nodded and took a deep breath. We both turned back to watch the village.

The wagon that Kefer and Peltor were supposed to be escorting to Plains End sat next to a stone ice house. However, the door of the ice house was propped wide open, which was odd. Just then, a man came out of the building carrying a woman in his arms. She was wrapped in a blanket and her head rolled against the man's shoulder as he shifted his arms under her. The wind whipped up and fluttered the blanket, exposing bare legs and feet. The man carried her over to one of the village huts across the square from the ice house.

"What do you think that was about?" I wondered aloud to Meldon. He shook his head and cleared his throat, but didn't say anything. "And where are Kefer and Peltor? Do you see them?"

Something cold and sharp touched the back of my neck.

"We're right here, Jaylan, did you miss us?" Peltor said from behind us with a sneer in his voice.

I cursed myself for not considering that the wind was good cover for everyone, not just us.

I started to turn around, but stopped when the pressure on my neck increased. Kefer's voice came from directly behind me. "Don't move, Jaylan. Stay right there on your knees for now. You know what to do. Put your right hand up behind your head and undo your sword belt with your left. Same with you, Meldon."

I heard a sharp intake of breath from Meldon. Peltor was apparently a little more forceful with his jabs.

Kefer and Peltor relieved us of our swords and our daggers and then allowed us to turn around and face them.

"What's going on here, Kefer? You and Peltor should be most of the way to Plains End by now. Borlan is furious with you both."

Kefer got a faraway look in his eyes and spoke almost absently. "Something more important came up. This village desperately needs our protection. We can't leave right now."

"Protection from what?" I asked.

"Right now, you!" Peltor responded, looking at both of us suspiciously. "What are you doing here? Why were you spying?"

"Quiet, Peltor," Kefer interrupted him. "It's not our job to question the prisoners."

My heart sank when Kefer said the word prisoners. "Why are we prisoners? What do you plan to do with us?" I asked.

Kefer shook his head. "Not my decision. We need to take you to see Lord Thoron."

"Who is Lord Thoron?" I asked.

"No more questions. Get up, turn around, and walk. We're going to the temple." Kefer motioned Meldon and I to precede him and Peltor into the village.

～

The villagers stopped what they were doing to stare at us as Kefer and Peltor marched us through the small village square toward the ice house.

Meldon stumbled as we went by one of the village huts. A woman wearing one of the amulets stood in the open doorway holding tightly to the shoulders of a small boy. "They...they're all wearing one of those glowing amulets!" Meldon exclaimed. I could hear the panic creeping back into his voice.

"Quiet!" Peltor said and rapped Meldon on the top of the head with the flat of his blade. Meldon winced and subsided, but I could hear his breathing increase. I started to worry that he'd try to run and get himself killed.

When we reached the ice house, I discovered why the door stood open. It was to let in light and air. The ice house had been converted into a workshop of some kind. A few short steps took us down to the sunken stone floor. The room was dominated by two parallel stone blocks that normally held chunks of ice to cool the fish that would be packed around the floor.

A fishy odor still tainted the air, but the room had been cleared of fish, ice, and the straw insulation that would normally accompany them. Instead, one of the stone blocks was covered with a cloth and littered with tools, chunks of glass, and several of the strange amulets we had seen the villagers wearing. The other block was bare.

A man wearing a fine blue robe protected by a canvas work apron looked up from his task. "What have we here? Visitors?"

Kefer nodded and answered him. "Yes, my Lord. We found these two men spying on the village."

The man rose from his seat, and our guards pushed us down to our knees as he stepped smoothly around the blocks to stand between them.

"Did you now? Why would you be spying on our little fishing village?" the man asked us. The quality and design of his robe indicated that he was from a Ruling Family—one of the families that the Emperor appointed to control the provinces. He wore his dark hair long and it flowed onto his shoulders. His hair was just going grey at the temples, a fact that was emphasized by the silver circlet he wore to keep it back from his face.

Since I was the leader of my little two-man expedition, it was up to me to respond. "We were sent to find Kefer and Peltor and to see what was holding up the shipment they were supposed to guard."

The man smiled down at me. "I see. Well, I'm afraid that *I'm* what's holding up the shipment. I needed the glass that was being transported, as you can see." He gestured with his hand toward his improvised workbench.

"You hijacked the shipment just to steal the glass?"

He shook his finger at me. "Now, now, don't be judgmental. My need is great and my funding is...insufficient at the moment. The ends justify the means."

"What are the ends?" I asked.

His face clouded over. "That's none of your concern. But you can help play a role."

"I'm not interested. Neither of us is interested. If you don't mind, we would prefer to be on our way." I made to get up, but Kefer laid the flat of his sword on my shoulder. I settled back down onto my knees.

The man shook his head, his voice mocking sadness. "I'm sorry, but that won't be possible right now. I need your help too badly. But please, we are forgetting our manners. I am Lord Thoron, known here in Buckwoods as the Lord of the Lake." He tilted his head toward us and gestured toward me with his hand, indicating that it was my turn to speak.

"Jaylan," I said. "I'm Jaylan Forester and my associate is Meldon Wright."

"It's a pleasure to meet you gentlemen. Now, after a short indoctrination ceremony, we can all get back to work." He turned to the workbench and picked up one of the amulets. He turned to Meldon. "Meldon, you are about to receive a great honor. You will become a Guardian of the Lake like Kefer and Peltor here."

As soon as Lord Thoron picked up the amulet, Meldon started fidgeting. I looked over at him, and his face had gone pale. His eyes were wide and his hands behind his head were tightly gripped. When Lord Thoron turned to him with the amulet in hand, he shouted, "No!" and started to get up.

As soon as Meldon put down his hands and started to rise, Peltor struck the base of Meldon's neck with the hilt of his sword. Meldon grunted and collapsed to the floor.

I shot a fierce look up at Peltor. He just grinned and pointed his sword at me. "You can be next," he said.

I narrowed my eyes at him and silently vowed I'd find a way to repay him for his heavy handedness. Peltor and I had never been particularly fond of one another and seeing his behavior when put into a position of control did nothing to improve my opinion of him.

Lord Thoron glared at Peltor. "Peltor, you *must* try to control your impulses. I need the boy conscious. Wake him at once and hold him steady."

"Yes, m'lord," Peltor mumbled. He sheathed his sword and lightly slapped Meldon to wake him. As Meldon started to come around, Peltor righted him and twisted one of his arms up behind his back. Peltor held the young man upright with his other hand on Meldon's shoulder.

"That's better." Lord Thoron set the amulet aside and reached into a pocket of his robe to remove a small crystal sphere. He held it in his hand and spoke a series of words under his breath, staring at Meldon the entire time. The sphere produced a building whine.

Meldon's eyes went wide and he started to struggle against Peltor's hold. Then he suddenly stopped struggling and relaxed. He didn't go limp; he just stopped struggling. The sphere went silent, and in turn, a low throbbing sound came from Meldon himself.

"You may release him, Peltor." Lord Thoron put the sphere away and picked up the amulet again. He walked over to Meldon. He lowered the amulet's chain over Meldon's head and arranged it around his neck. Meldon's eyes were still wide and darting, but he didn't move a muscle as the sorcerer placed his right hand over the amulet and said the word "member." The amulet immediately started to hum in tune with the other amulets in the village. Then he began to speak in a low, officious tone.

"Meldon Wright, you are about to receive a great honor. Henceforth, you are a Guardian of the Lake. You join an elite group of soldiers. Do you feel them around you?" Meldon hesitated, and then nodded. Lord Thoron placed his hand on the amulet again and said, "Protector." The amulet's hum took on a second tone. He looked into Meldon's eyes and continued. "Your job is to protect the village from outsiders. Do you understand?" Meldon nodded again. Lord Thoron pulled out his crystal sphere and spoke a few short words. The sphere squeeked, and the low humming that seemed to immobilize Meldon disappeared. "Do you see any outsiders here, Meldon?"

Meldon looked over at me. The fear had left his eyes, and he had that distant look I'd seen in Kefer on my first visit to this sorcery-cursed place. "Jaylan is an outsider," he said uncertainly.

Lord Thoron smiled. "Very good, Meldon. You may rise." Meldon got unsteadily to his feet.

It didn't take a genius to figure out what was going to happen next. I was starting to understand why sorcery was so widely reviled. Powerful and manipulative people always raised my ire, but this was manipulative power taken to a new level. Someone had to stop the Lord Thoron's of the world from preying on people who had no sorcery to defend themselves.

I would have thought the sorcerers of the Archives would want to prevent or stop what was happening here in Buckwoods. Rogue sorcerers victimizing the mundane populace would do nothing good for the Archives' reputation. Perhaps they were too insular to care. (Let the mundane take care of themselves, as it were.)

Lord Thoron was watching me and saw my face set in defiance as I completed my thought. Still holding the sphere, he wasted no time talking to me and simply repeated the incantation he'd used on Meldon. Before I could even think about attempting a desperate move to escape, a low hum filled the inside of my head.

My muscles relaxed. The sorcerer put his sphere away and took another amulet from the workbench. This one he placed over my neck.

Once again, he placed his hand over the amulet and spoke the word "member." As he did, a flood of awareness washed over me. I could sense the other people wearing amulets nearby. Their positions and movements were like dim blue lights layered upon my vision. This awareness extended through the walls of the building and out toward the edge of the village.

"Jaylan Forester, you are about to receive a great honor. Henceforth, you are a Guardian of the Lake." His words felt more personal somehow, as if he were reaching out to connect me with the other guardian lights of the village. It was like walking into a room filled with people I knew and loved.

"You join an elite group of soldiers. Do you feel them around you?" I did feel them around me, and I nodded. I saw that Lord Thoron himself was one of us. His amulet was hidden beneath his robes, but I could sense its presence as if it were in plain view.

Still touching my amulet, he said, "Protector." As he spoke the word, the people of the village appeared in my mind's eye and I understood that they performed a vital service as Guardians of the Lake.

Lord Thoron continued, "Your job is to protect the village from outsiders. Do you understand?" The village and the people needed protection, and I was proud to be able to help them. I nodded to Lord Thoron.

The corner of Lord Thoron's mouth rose into a satisfied smirk, and he removed his hand from the amulet. "Excellent." Using the sphere once again, he released me from my immobility. "You may rise and take your place among the Guardians."

I got to my feet, suddenly aware of my responsibility. I looked around the room with concern, but saw only other Guardians. I was satisfied that we were all safe for the moment.

Kefer handed me my weapons with a grin and slapped me on the shoulder. "Welcome, Jaylan. I'm glad you're with us."

Peltor handed Meldon's weapons back to him, but said nothing. His face wore the sullen look I normally associated with him. I suspected that he would have preferred for us to remain outsiders.

Lord Thoron waved us out of the ice house. "Now move along, all of you. I have a lot of work to finish today."

My suspicion of him remained, but my sense of duty overrode my concerns. "May I help, my lord?"

"You can help by guarding the village," he answered. "Only I can bear the burden of creating the sacred amulets, and I'm running out of time. I don't know what is holding up my delivery, but I intend to take advantage of this location for as long as I can."

The word "delivery" tickled my memory, but I dismissed it as unimportant to my new responsibilities.

The rest of the Guardians and I left the ice house and started to patrol the area. No one gave any orders, we simply shared the watch over the forest and the road. Kefer told me that, if outsiders appeared, we needed to send them away or bring them to Lord Thoron. As Guardians, it was our duty to keep the villagers safe.

As I started to walk around the perimeter of the village to get a feel for the terrain, something deep inside stopped me in mid-step. My stomach tightened and I had the sudden urge to run into the forest away from the village. But the soothing awareness of my fellow guardians and the pressure of my responsibilities to protect them pushed the feeling away. I took a deep, calming breath, and continued my patrol. As long as I was a Guardian of the Lake, everything would be fine.

CHAPTER 18

The next morning I awoke with my heart pounding. I sat up and the shreds of a dream fluttered away, leaving me with an image of Peltor's determined and angry face. In the dream, we had been sparring in the Raven Company basement, when I realized that he was actually trying to kill me.

I looked around to get my bearings. The thin morning light seeping through the boards of the window shutters and around the door jamb revealed the interior of a one-room hut that was simple and neat. Edanos and Sati Tragas, the village couple who had let me share their quarters, were sleeping on a narrow bed in the opposite corner of the room.

In the back of my mind, I noted the glow their amulets created and extended my awareness to locate the others in the village. Some villagers were already up and starting their day, and I sensed no trouble in their movements. Lord Thoron, the brightest light of them all, was already moving around in the direction of the ice house. I laid back on the woven mat I had been given for a bed and tried to sort out my thoughts.

My memory of the prior afternoon and evening was a watery blur. The fishermen had returned in the late afternoon with a decent catch. Everyone helped with the disposition of the fish except Peltor and me. We kept watch while Meldon and Kefer lent a hand. With the ice house repurposed, most of the fish had to be cleaned and moved into the smoke house right away. The smoke house was becoming rather full, so some poor soul would have to venture out amongst the outsiders to make a delivery soon. I shuddered at the thought.

During the course of the prior day, my sense of belonging and protectiveness had settled around me like a warm blanket. I was a Guardian of the Lake and all had been well on my watch.

But this morning, something was different. I felt a sense of detachment, as if I had two minds sharing the same body. One mind was satisfied with the state of affairs; the other was uneasy. I had the feeling I was forgetting something... something important.

The amulet felt different as well. Wearing it gave me a sense of pride, and the connection it gave me to the others provided comfort. However, I could also sense that it was taking something from me.

I let my mind relax and explored the sensation of draining energy that flowed from my inner core into the amulet. That sensation was what my second awareness found disturbing. To that other awareness, the steady hum of the amulet was poisonous. If I could figure out a way to stop the unpleasant drain, perhaps I could silence my conflicting emotions and get on with my duties.

I wasn't sure how to go about it. The situation reminded me of my experience at the healer's cabin. When I thought back on how it had felt to operate the Seeker, certain parallels came to mind. As much as I hated to admit it to myself, the amulet was obviously a working of sorcery, even if it was a revered symbol of the Guardians.

With the Seeker, I had activated it and deactivated it with a word. No, that wasn't quite right. It wasn't just the word that mattered, it was what I was thinking when I said the word. Lord Thoron had used the words "member" and "protector" to activate this amulet. What word would deactivate it? Did I even want to try deactivating it? I didn't want to lose my connection to the others.

I shifted uneasily on the mat. The sensation of being poisoned wouldn't go away. I started to feel physically ill just thinking about it. I had to try to stop the energy drain.

I thought back to my experience with the Seeker again. Sulana had told me to say "stop" and think about telling the amulet to stop seeking the ring she held. The problem here was that I wasn't sure what I needed to stop.

I quietly said, "Stop," but nothing happened. I tried the word "release." Still nothing. Sati shifted around on the bed to face me, her cloud of sleep-touseled black hair obscured her face, but she appeared to remain asleep.

I relaxed and mentally probed at that sensation of draining again. I could feel some kind of energy flow from several points in my body out into the metal chain that held the amulet. That energy must be the vaetra that Sulana had talked about. The more I focused on the flow, the worse I felt. I needed to cut that flow somehow.

Taking off the amulet would probably stop the flow, but doing that was impossible. The amulet was what made me a Guardian of the Lake. It connected me to the others. I'd become an outsider if I took it off, and I certainly didn't want that.

I closed my hand around the amulet while I thought. As I did so, I realized something. The amulet's hum actually consisted of two separate tones. Only one of the tones was the source of my unease. It was the poison. If I could stop that tone, the poison would be gone.

I spent a few more minutes holding the amulet and quietly trying different words. Nothing worked. I started to despair.

Finally, with angry determination, I mentally focused on the point where the vaetra flowed from my body into the amulet's chain and said "stop."

And it did.

The amulet stopped humming, and dizziness crashed over me like a giant wave. If I hadn't already been lying down, I'm certain I would have fallen to my knees. As the dizziness ebbed, my memories of who I really was and what I was doing here came rushing back. My hand was still clenched around the amulet, and I nearly tore it off my neck in disgust. My awareness of the others and the sense of belonging faded away.

As my mind continued to clear, I heard a gasp and a rustle of covers. Sati had sat up in bed and was staring at me. She screamed, and Edanos sat up quickly to see what was wrong.

I felt completely exposed, sitting there in the middle of a village of Guardians. I had to make a decision quickly. The amulet was the only thing keeping me safe among these people. If Lord Thoron learned I had deactivated it, I doubted things would go well for me. But activating the amulet would put me back under its spell. Would I be able to clear my mind enough deactivate it a second time? Or was this my only chance to escape it?

Sati screamed again and pointed at me. "Outsider!" she said to her husband in a shaking voice. The sound of running feet came from outside in response to the woman's screams. Edanos turned to look at me, and his eyes widened.

In spite of my fears, I mumbled the word "member" to reactivate the amulet. Nothing happened. My thoughts were chaos, and I struggled to focus them. I thought back to what Lord Thoron had said after he activated the amulet. The first step of the process had created the connection to the villagers. That was what I needed to think about. Say the word, think about the effect. I needed to restore the flow of vaetra into the amulet.

I tried again. "Member." This time, the source of vaetra within me reached toward the amulet's chain and snapped back into place. The amulet started to hum again, and my awareness of the others resumed.

Sulana's explanation of channeling suddenly made complete sense to me. The process of activating the Seeker had been only a vague sensation, but activating the amulet had given me a more distinct sense of the vaetra within me and the way it could be directed.

But I wasn't done yet. Lord Thoron had activated the amulet twice. The second command had been "protector."

I was about to continue activating the amulet when I noticed that Sati and Edanos had calmed down and were looking back and forth between each other and me. Edanos shrugged and let himself fall flat on the bed. Sati continued to peer at me, holding the covers up tight to her chest. Someone pounded on the door to the hut.

Kefer's voice called from outside. "Is everyone alright in there?"

"We're fine," I shouted back.

Sati got up and padded barefoot over to the door in her nightshirt. She opened it and stepped aside to let Kefer and another villager enter the hut. I sat up, placing my hand next to the hilt of my sword.

"What happened?" Kefer asked Sati.

She shook her head and looked over at me, pushing her hair away from her face. "When I first woke up, I looked over and thought he was an outsider."

Kefer turned and looked at me intently, his hand going to the sword at his side. After a brief moment, he relaxed. "You were mistaken. Jaylan is one of the Guardians. Can't you sense him?" Kefer turned to look at Sati with narrowed eyes.

She glanced over at me and nodded. "Yes. I must have been mistaken."

So. Only the first enchantment, the Member enchantment, was necessary to establish membership in the community. My mind was still my own. The compulsion to serve the village and reject outsiders was part of the second enchantment. I had stumbled upon a way to infiltrate the village. But to what end?

~

Kefer left the hut once he was satisfied that nothing was amiss. I quickly dressed and armed myself, wondering how I was going to use my freedom and the knowledge I'd gained.

Edanos got dressed at the same time that I did, but Sati waited for us to leave. They both kept an eye on me with sidelong glances, but seemed to accept that they had been mistaken about my moment as an outsider.

My primary responsibility was to get Meldon out of this mess. I needed to figure out how I could get him out of the village and get his amulet off him. If I took it off while we were near others, he would be recognized as an outsider immediately and anyone nearby would raise an alarm.

Steps approached the hut again as I was belting on my sword. Meldon's voice came through the door after he knocked. "May I come in? Lord Thoron is ready for Sati's Contribution Ceremony."

I looked over at Sati, and she nodded to me. "Come on in," I said. Sati looked nervous, but not afraid. I wasn't sure what a Contribution Ceremony was, but it sounded like a euphemism for something unpleasant.

Meldon entered the hut. Edanos left as Meldon came in, apparently unconcerned about what his wife might be "contributing" to Lord Thoron's activities. My blood started to boil as I thought about Lord Thoron taking advantage of these simple villagers with his sorcery. I decided to learn the truth, even if I really didn't want to know it. "I'll take her over to Lord Thoron," I volunteered.

Meldon looked at me in surprise. "Okay, sure." He looked down at my amulet, which I had not yet tucked into my tunic and cocked his head. "There's something different about your amulet," he said glancing down at his and then back at mine. "Are you okay?"

I kept my face neutral, belying the anxiety that suddenly twisted in my gut. I could hear the difference between my amulet and the others, and apparently Meldon could see that difference. My amulet emitted only one pure tone, while the others had two. I casually placed my hand over the amulet protectively, shielding it completely with the back of my hand toward Meldon.

Meldon was a sight Sensitive, like Sulana. Was Lord Thoron a Sensitive? I was pretty sure that all sorcerers had to be. When I had worked the Seeker and Meghan the healer had noted that I was a Sensitive, Sulana had said I was much more than that. I was a Channeler, as it turned out. I couldn't be sure, but it seemed that all sorcerers were Sensitives, but not all Sensitives were capable of being sorcerers.

The next question was what kind of Sensitive was Lord Thoron? Based on the few people I'd met with some form of sensitivity, the odds favored him being a sight Sensitive. I could just tuck my amulet inside my clothing, and he would not be able to see it. However, if he was a sound Sensitive, like me, he'd hear it even though it was inside my clothing. And didn't Sulana say there were other types of sensitivity?

I had to make a quick decision. I couldn't risk Lord Thoron finding me out, but activating the second spell of the amulet would restore the mind control. I had disabled the amulet once; would I be able to do it again?

I decided it was a risk I had to take. I focused my thoughts on activating the second enchantment and answered Meldon with careful wording. "I'm fine. The amulet is fine. I'm still a *protector.*" I focused my thoughts on activating the Protector enchantment as I said the trigger word. I could feel the channel to the amulet expand and feed more vaetra into the device.

The heavy sense of responsibility for the village and the wariness of outsiders spread through my mind like a fog. But this time it was different. This time, the Protector spell was less pervasive. I knew that I could let it take over and guide my actions, or I could resist its influence. I nearly sighed with relief. I dropped my hand from the amulet and smiled at Meldon.

Meldon squinted at the amulet for a moment after my hand fell away from it. "You're right. It does look fine. It was probably just the lighting in here," he said looking around the dim hut.

"So, do I take Sati over to the temple?" I asked Meldon. The Protector spell made me say the word "temple" with reverence, but my true feelings mentally added a note of sarcasm.

"Yes. Lord Thoron is waiting. Thanks, Jaylan. Lord Thoron makes me nervous."

It was noteworthy that the Protector spell didn't seem to extinguish all of our natural inclinations, since Meldon was still nervous around sorcery, just as Peltor was still a cretin. That factor might be helpful if I failed to completely conceal my newfound control while I was near Lord Thoron.

Sati immediately started walking toward the door, not bothering to change out of her sleeping shift, which made me even more suspicious about the nature of her contribution. I hurried to catch up with her.

"Are you sure you're okay with this?" I asked her as we walked toward the ice house.

"It is my duty," she said with a shrug.

I glanced over toward her husband, who was with the other fishermen. They were busy preparing to leave in the boats. "Doesn't your husband mind?"

"He does his duty."

I had no response to that, so I said nothing more the rest of the way to the ice house. We stepped down into the room, where Lord Thoron was standing and waiting between the stone blocks. He had a thick blanket draped over his left arm. He looked at me in surprise as we came in, and his right hand quickly went into the pocket that held his crystal sphere.

"Hello, Jaylan. I was expecting Meldon."

"Meldon seemed nervous, so I volunteered to bring Sati." It was hard to keep the disgust and anger out of my voice.

"I see. Yes, it turns out that Meldon is sensitive to sorcery, and he's what we call a Phobic. His reaction to sorcery is quite out of his control, I'm afraid."

He removed his hand from his pocket and waved Sati over. "Come here, my dear. You know how this works." Lord Thoron unfolded the blanket as Sati slipped her shift over her head. She wore nothing underneath but her amulet.

I had limited experience with being in the presence of a naked woman, so I was shocked into immobility to have Sati unclothed and so close to me that I could feel her body heat. I looked away in embarrassment, but not before concluding that Edanos was a lucky man.

I considered rushing Lord Thoron right then while his hands were occupied with the blanket, but I could feel the Protector spell immediately flare and dampen that train of thought. I'd have to disable the amulet in order to take action unhindered, and Lord Thoron, who seemed wary of me as it was, would know the instant I did. I almost turned to leave the ice house instead, but Lord Thoron had not dismissed me, and I couldn't abandon Sati until I was sure she wouldn't be harmed.

In spite of my horror and discomfort, I turned back to watch the rest of the ceremony and hoped for an opportunity to stop it.

Seemingly unembarrassed by her nudity, Sati laid herself down on the bare block of stone with a shiver. Goosebumps instantly rose all over her bare skin. Lord Thoron draped the thick blanket over her completely, and he patted her shoulder. "Sorry, I know the stone is cold. You'll feel better once the blanket warms."

Sati looked up at him and smiled. "Thank you, my lord."

Lord Thoron reached over to his work table and picked up a glass piece. The glass was a flattened oval, similar in appearance to the Veil Sulana had used, but the flattened bottom was set into a silvery metal base. Lord Thoron rubbed the stone between his hands to warm it a bit and slid the device under Sati's neck. Before releasing it, he mumbled a word I couldn't make out and stepped back. The device started to hum, building slowly in volume and pitch until it settled into a steady tone.

Lord Thoron looked over at me and saw the confused look on my face. This was not what I had expected to see, although I was glad it wasn't something worse.

"Don't worry," he said. "The ceremony doesn't harm her. She'll be good as new and ready to contribute again in a couple of days."

"Will you need me to contribute as well, my Lord?" The Protector spell encouraged me to ask the question. It wanted to serve however possible, and I allowed it, wanting to know the answer myself.

He laughed. "No, Jaylan. That won't be necessary. Women are able to regenerate vaetra, their magical essence, faster than men, and I have enough women here to provide all the additional power I need to create the sacred amulets."

I was relieved, but kept it out of my voice. "As you wish, my lord," I said with a small bow.

"You may return to your duties now. Come back at mid-morning to collect Sati, please. I'm afraid she'll need to be carried back to her home."

"Yes, my lord." I turned and left the ice house. My thoughts were in a whirl. Lord Thoron needed vaetra to create the amulets. More vaetra than he could provide on his own. Somehow, he drained what he needed from the women of the village. But where did it go? Did the device store it? I suspected he had set up his "temple" in the ice house for a specific reason. Was it the stone? If the stone stored vaetra, the entire ice house would serve as a giant reservoir of power.

I shook my head in frustration. I just didn't know enough about sorcery to figure out how I could sabotage his efforts and get us all out of this situation...without possibly getting myself killed in the process.

CHAPTER 19

Sulana tucked the last of her gear into her saddle bag and then mounted her horse. She looked around at everyone else to see that they were ready to go and waiting for her order to head out.

Daven grinned at her, and she smiled back at him. She knew he was excited to continue the adventure. Barek had watched her final preparations, hands folded loosely over the pommel of his saddle. If Barek had a motto, it would have to be, "Let's get on with it." Talon covered a yawn and squinted into the early morning sun, which sat just above the mountain peaks. For him, this was just another day's work.

Ebnik fidgeted in his saddle, tugging at his riding clothes and fumbling with his reins. The long robes he habitually wore were impractical for riding, so he had changed into loose-fitting pants and a long, flowing, hooded tunic for their journey.

The Archives Council had authorized their mission to Buckwoods late the previous afternoon. Ebnik presented

Arinot's findings to the Council and convinced them that the buyer for the ring was indeed a sorcerer, he was up to something significant, and the mundane population in the area was potentially in danger. The first two arguments alone might not have been enough, but the third silenced the remaining opposition.

"Sorry we have to ride," Sulana said to Ebnik.

Ebnik sighed. "The need for haste is regrettable. Horses are such smelly beasts."

"At least we don't have to go very far," she reassured him.

"Indeed. If we had to ride the entire distance to Delta, I fear it would take me days to recover."

Sulana chuckled and motioned for Talon to lead on.

Rather than heading down the trail to the valley floor, Talon led the group toward a trail that crossed over a small pass and dropped down toward one of the nearby lakes.

Sulana looked back over her shoulder as they rode away. From the outside, the castle barely hinted its size. It looked more like a giant manor house than a true castle. The three stories of the front wall were checkered by dozens of windows that let natural light into the outermost rooms of the structure. The mountain appeared to have swallowed most of the building. The brow of a ridge extended out over the top of the castle, creating a natural peaked "roof." The observation tower she had visited with Ebnik and Arinot rose just above the top of that ridge. The true scope of the castle was hidden within the ridge behind it and in the levels that extended deep into the mountain below it.

After a few minutes of riding, the trail took the riders out onto a flat and wide outcropping of rock that gave them a commanding view down the crease between the two ridges that bracketed the trail. A tree-studded ravine swooped down and away from them, and the steady sound of a nearby waterfall filled the air. Hooves clopped loudly and echoed across the broad stone overlook as their horses left the hard-packed trail.

Ebnik dismounted somewhat ungracefully and fussed with his tunic in an attempt to straighten it out. Sulana suppressed a smile.

Ebnik raised his left hand and made a fist, which he pointed toward the open edge of the overlook. On his ring finger, he wore the ruby ring Sulana's team had worked so hard to recover. The ring began to glow.

Ebnik looked over at Sulana. "We'll have to lead the horses through on foot. The portal is not large enough to admit a horse and rider." He walked forward and stopped just before the edge of the overlook. He reached out as if to grab a handle and pulled his hand back toward his body. As he did so, a vertical crease appeared in the air that widened into a doorway. The doorway had no apparent threshold; it was simply an opening.

Fascinated, Sulana dismounted and stepped forward to get a closer look. The inside surface of the door was visible and appeared solid. It partially obscured Ebnik, now that the door was fully open. She peered around inside the portal. The light coming in through the doorway revealed what appeared to be the ground floor of a tower. All but one of the angled walls held another door. The one exception was where a staircase went upward.

Sulana stepped to the side of the doorway and looked behind it. From behind, the portal was an opaque rectangle with a dark grey, swirling surface. Sulana looked back around the portal at Ebnik, who was patiently holding the door open while she explored. "What happens if you touch the back side?"

"I have no idea. I've never known anyone willing to try it and find out," he answered her with a wry smile. "It has been many years since the portals were created, and no living sorcerer retains full knowledge of their construction."

Sulana moved quickly back to the front side and cleared her throat. "As the leader of this expedition, I probably shouldn't take chances just to satisfy my curiosity," she said.

"Wise decision," he responded, with a slight bow of his head.

Sulana walked back to her horse and took up the reins. She noted that the others had also dismounted and were ready to move. Daven held the reins of both his horse and Ebnik's. Would the horses be willing to go through an opening in thin air? She was about to find out.

Sulana led her horse forward and tightened her grip on her reins, ready for resistance. When she went through the portal into the tower, she was relieved that her horse simply followed her in. As she entered, illuminators sprang to life and lit the interior. She released her horse and returned to the doorway to take the reins of Ebnik's mount from Daven.

Everyone entered the tower without incident, and Ebnik closed the door behind them. He turned to face them all. "Welcome to the Portal Keep," he intoned, raising his arms to encompass the interior of the chamber.

The tower floor was crowded with all five horses and their riders, but everyone still had room to move around. Sulana could see now that the tower was octagonal with walls made of carefully fitted stonework. Each of the eight walls, except the one with the stairway, had a door in the center. The stairs led up to a wooden walkway that went along the walls of the next level to more doors. That level had a stairway that led to yet another level above it. The center of the tower was open, so she could see that the tower rose at least four levels higher before disappearing into darkness.

Daven turned to Ebnik. "How were you able to see the doorway? I saw nothing until you held the door open."

Ebnik held up his hand and wiggled the finger that wore the ruby ring. "This Portal Key allows me to locate the Keep's portals from a distance. It also lets me see them and open them. Perhaps more importantly, it allows me to exit the Keep." He gestured toward the other doorways. Sulana realized that their surfaces were completely blank and smooth. They appeared to be made out of some kind of grey metal, and had no apparent handles or lock that would make it possible to open them.

"So, what you're saying is, stay close to the wizard or you'll never get out of here." Daven joked.

"Precisely," Ebnik said with a tight nod.

Sulana looked over at the stairs and the walkway above them. A banister ran along the inside edge for safety, and the walkway seemed plenty wide enough to accommodate a horse if necessary. She wasn't sure how excited the horses would be about going up the stairs, however.

"Are these walkways strong enough to hold a horse's weight?" She asked.

Ebnik nodded. "Yes, if we bring them up one at a time. However, that won't be necessary. We're fortunate that the portal we require is here on the ground floor. If we had needed to ascend the tower, I would have recommended we leave the horses behind, in spite of our haste."

"Where are we?" Daven asked.

Ebnik understood what Daven was really asking. "The Keep is actually far underground in a location that is known only to Council members for security reasons. The secrecy is less important now, since the original tunnel used to begin construction has long since collapsed. The portals are presently the only way to reach the Keep."

Upon hearing that they were deep underground, Barek cringed and darted his eyes around the tower interior. "When do we leave?" he grumbled.

"Right now," replied Ebnik, as he stepped over to a portal that was two doors down from the one they had entered through.

Ebnik looked up at a blank plaque that was affixed above the portal. "This is the one," he said, and anticipating the next question he added, "The Portal Key lets me read the name of the destination on the plaque."

A flat rectangle of stone was affixed to the wall to the right of the door opening. Two glass ovals were embedded into it. The one on top was blue, and the one below it green. Ebnik placed his palm over the blue oval and the door suddenly disappeared to reveal a hilltop clearing surrounded by trees.

Sulana started to move forward, but Ebnik held up his hand to stop her. "Wait. The portal isn't open yet. The blue implement lets us see through the portal before we open it."

Talon nodded and raised the corner of his mouth in a half-smile. "Sensible precaution."

"Indeed. Paranoia can make one inventive at times," Ebnik said.

Satisfied that the destination was clear of anyone who might observe their arrival, Ebnik removed his hand from the blue oval and the portal returned to its grey, opaque state. He moved his hand down to the green oval and covered it with his palm. This time, the door clicked and popped open about a hand's breadth. A fresh, cool breeze blew in through the opening, bringing the scent of dry pine needles with it.

Ebnik pushed the door open and stepped out into the clearing, holding the door open for the others. Everyone filed out of the Portal Keep, leading their horses. Ebnik's horse followed the others out of the tower on its own. After everyone was out, Ebnik released the door and pushed it closed. He appeared to be pushing in pantomime, except for the gap around the door opening that rapidly disappeared. Once closed, there was no evidence that the door had ever been there.

Everyone looked around, trying to get their bearings. "Where are we now?" asked Daven.

"A short ride west of Northshore," Ebnik answered.

"Excellent!" Sulana enthused. "That saved us about a day's travel time. Let's get going," she said, pulling herself up into her saddle.

"Off to Buckwoods?" asked Talon, moving his horse to take the lead.

"No, let's stop by Northshore first, since it's on the way. I'd like to speak to Jaylan," she replied.

"What do we need him for?" Daven asked.

"Well, he was very helpful last time. As you yourself pointed out before, his knowledge of the area could be useful," she said, raising an eyebrow at him.

Daven looked like he might object further, but stopped himself and shrugged. "You're the leader."

Ebnik looked at Sulana with concern. "Is it wise to involve someone who has no allegiance to the Archives?" he asked.

"He's worked with us before and proved to be reliable. As it turns out, he's also a sorcerer, although he won't admit it to himself. I'm hoping that he will know something about Buckwoods that would help us prepare for what might be going on there."

Ebnik nodded his acceptance, and the group rode off the hillside toward Northshore.

CHAPTER 20

I watched the fishermen push off from the dock. The clunking and splashing of oars faded as they floated off in search of the day's catch. The sun had risen above the trees, burning off the morning clouds and brightly warming the village. The surrounding forest was a contrasting wall of bright greens and deep shadows that hosted a hidden avian orchestra of tweets, chirps, and song.

It was altogether too lovely and cheerful a day for my dark state of mind.

I patrolled the forest edge listlessly and stopped by the corral to rub Patches' nose. After our capture the day before, the two Raven Company men accompanied Meldon and me while we retrieved our horses. Patches wagged his head up and down and snorted as I walked away, probably wondering why we weren't heading home. I shared his impatience.

Peltor hung around the ice house, glaring at anyone who came too close and threatened to disturb Lord Thoron's peace. The Lord himself was busily making another amulet.

The process seemed to take a lot of time, concentration, and a tremendous quantity of vaetra, so he could create at most one amulet per day. For me, it was a noisy process as well, but no one else seemed to notice the manifestation sounds that occasionally emanated from the workshop.

Kefer and Meldon helped out around the village wherever they could. Kefer tended the smoke house and Meldon helped in the garden. Jake, the wagon driver who Kefer and Peltor were supposed to be escorting, had left with the fishermen to help out on the boats.

As I patrolled, I tried to think of a way out of my predicament. My concentration was frequently interrupted by the influence of the amulet's Protector spell, which made finding a solution more elusive. The Protector enchantment stubbornly resisted any thoughts of escape or conspiracy against Lord Thoron. I was reasonably certain that I could disable the amulet and leave at any time, but I wouldn't get far on foot. I needed Patches to escape, but trying to saddle him up in full view of the village would raise questions I couldn't answer.

Besides, Meldon was stuck here too. I couldn't just leave him behind. And what about the villagers? They weren't technically my responsibility, but my conscience wouldn't let me leave them at the mercy of Lord Thoron and his insidious amulets. Lord Thoron wasn't hurting anyone physically, but his amulets mentally enslaved the villagers, and the rest of us, to do his bidding as surely as if we were shackled.

A small part of me still didn't want to escape. I was reluctant to scurry back to Borlan after failing in my task so miserably, or to face Dela after promising to be back last night. She would be worried out of her mind after Meldon's comments about magic. That anxiety would then turn to wrath after I returned home safely. Those concerns were minor in view of my current predicament, but the Protector enchantment reinforced them.

At the very least, I needed to free Meldon from Lord Thoron's grasp. Perhaps between the two of us, we could free the other two Raven Company men. The four of us together might be able to overwhelm Lord Thoron and put a stop to whatever plans he had.

If we could at least recover the delivery wagon and the driver, we could complete our mission. I hated the idea of leaving the people of Buckwoods at the mercy of a dangerous sorcerer, but if we left with the wagon, Lord Thoron might feel exposed and leave. I'd figure out a way to get word to Sulana somehow, and as Dela had said, let the magicians take care of themselves.

The first step was to figure out a way to free Meldon without alerting the others. Most of the morning went by while I considered and discarded alternatives.

Inspiration struck just before midday. I was grumbling to myself about having fish yet again for lunch, when a set of antlers above the doorway to one of the huts caught my eye. I thought of a duty that fit with my role as a Guardian of the Lake, so the Protector enchantment didn't interfere until I started thinking about how I would take advantage of the situation. But that was okay. The main thing was getting out of the village. The rest would have to be improvised anyway.

I walked over to Kefer, who was repairing the door of the smoke house. "Hey, how would you like to eat something other than fish?" I asked him.

He stopped working and looked at me with interest. "What do you have in mind?"

"I was thinking about running a patrol out onto the forest trail and looping back on the road. I might run across a deer along the way."

Kefer smiled as he considered my idea, and then he licked his lips and nodded. "I could go with you. You'll need two people to bring back anything you take down."

"I was thinking about taking Meldon along. He's a fair shot with a bow, and I'd feel better with a more experienced fighter keeping an eye on the village while we're patrolling."

Kefer frowned, but we both knew he wasn't much of a bowman. He finally nodded again. "Sounds reasonable. I'm almost done here anyway. I can keep an eye on things while you're gone."

I started to turn away, but Kefer grabbed my arm. "Be careful out there. Once you're away from the village, we won't be able to...sense you anymore, so we won't know if you run into trouble. Stay alert."

He didn't seem to suspect that I was actually counting on disappearing from his senses. I needed to get Meldon out of range before I could do anything to free him, otherwise everyone would know the instant I removed his amulet.

I patted Kefer's hand in reassurance. "Thanks for the warning. I'll be sure to pass it on to Meldon as well." He nodded and went back to work.

I walked over to Meldon and told him my idea. He was enthusiastic, as were the two women who worked the garden with him. They encouraged him to set aside his efforts at extending the garden beds and go with me. It seemed everyone was ready for a change of pace food-wise.

Meldon retrieved his bow and we headed toward the trail from which I'd had my first view of Buckwoods three days before.

Peltor saw where we were headed and jogged over to block our way. "Where do you think you're going?" he challenged.

"I thought everyone would like to eat something other than fish for a change, so Meldon and I are going to patrol the forest and hopefully bring back a deer."

He narrowed his eyes. "Does Kefer know about this plan of yours?"

Well, not exactly, I thought to myself. "Yes, he seemed rather enthusiastic about the idea. He's taking over my watch here while we're gone."

Peltor seemed satisfied with my answer, but still uncertain. "Maybe we should ask Lord Thoron first."

I doubted Lord Thoron would have any objections to the hunt. Having been here a while, I was sure he would be even more sick of fish than we were. However, he might not like the idea of his newest recruits leaving the village together. "Okay, we can ask him if you want. Are you sure he won't mind being disturbed?"

Peltor looked back over his shoulder at the ice house and grimaced. "Never mind. I don't want to get the Lord's hopes up in case you fail to bring something back. Good luck," he said sarcastically and walked back to his seat outside the ice house.

Meldon watched Peltor's receding back and then glanced over at me. "Peltor really doesn't like you, does he?"

I started walking toward the trail head. "No, he never has. And the feeling's mutual. Let's go find some venison."

CHAPTER 21

Sulana's team traveled east from the portal along an overgrown trail that dropped down to join the main road from Dunver to Northshore. It was mid-morning when they dismounted in front of the Snow Creek Inn and tied their horses to the railing. Sulana, Daven, and Ebnik entered the inn together while Talon and Barek remained with the horses.

The serving room was empty of customers. Dela was busily cleaning up, taking advantage of the lull between the breakfast and lunch crowds. As the trio entered, Dela squinted against the glare of the light coming in through the doorway to see who it was.

As soon as she spotted Sulana, she straightened from her task of wiping a table and threw the cloth she was using to the tabletop with a wet thud. She walked swiftly over to Sulana and stood in front of her with a tight face and folded arms.

"I should have known you had something to do with this," she said.

Sulana was taken aback by Dela's aggression and held up her hands. "Hold on. It's Dela, right? What are you talking about? I've been out of the area for the past couple of days."

Dela took in Ebnik's appearance with a frown. "You're a magician, aren't you?"

Ebnik winced and gave her a slight bow. "The preferred term is 'sorcerer' my dear, but yes, you are essentially correct."

Dela turned her glare back to Sulana. "What have you done with Jaylan?" she demanded.

"Jaylan isn't here?" Sulana asked. "I was hoping to get his help with another mission."

Dela stared at Sulana closely for a moment. She started to say something a couple of times but changed her mind. She finally asked, "You really don't know where he is?"

"No. Like I said, we just got back into town."

Dela rubbed her forehead and sat down on a nearby chair. "He promised he'd be back yesterday evening."

Sulana shook her head. "Dela, where did Jaylan go? And why did you think I was involved?"

Dela looked up at Sulana. "Jaylan said something about magic, and when you walked in the door with this...this... sorcerer, I thought it all started to fit. But if he's not with you, he must still be at Buckwoods."

Sulana's face went white. She leaned down and grabbed Dela's forearm, looking into her eyes intently. "Did you just say Buckwoods? Is that where Jaylan went?" Ebnik and Daven exchanged a quick glance.

Dela yanked her arm out of Sulana's grip and rubbed it. Her tone became sullen. "Yes. He and Meldon went out to Buckwoods to find out what was holding up a shipment from Delta. They were supposed to talk to the Raven Company men who were escorting the shipment and get them moving again."

Ebnik spoke up. "These men weren't expected to stop in Buckwoods?" Dela narrowed her eyes at him for a moment, and then finally shook her head. "Do you happen to know what was in this shipment?" he pressed.

Dela threw up her hands and stood. "How would I know? If you want to know about the shipment, go ask Borlan over at Raven Company. And while you're at it, tell him to find out what happened to Jaylan and Meldon. I don't have time for this." Dela walked back to pick up her cloth. She continued to wipe the table with her back to the three visitors.

Sulana turned back to Ebnik and Daven with a vacant expression. Ebnik glanced at Dela and tilted his head toward the door. Once outside, Ebnik placed a hand on Sulana's shoulder. "Could Jaylan be behind the trouble in Buckwoods? You said that he can channel."

Sulana looked up at Ebnik with raised eyebrows and snorted at the same time Daven shook his head and chuckled. "No. Jaylan knows next to nothing about sorcery, and he rejects what he does know," she answered.

"That's good." Ebnik said, releasing her shoulder. "I can see you care for him."

Sulana blinked. "What? Care for him? I...respect him. But it's nothing more than that."

Ebnik raised an eyebrow, but said nothing. Daven grimaced and looked at the ground.

Sulana looked back and forth between them. "Really? Why would you think that? I hardly know him!"

"Exactly," Daven said under his breath.

Ebnik nodded with a knowing smirk. "As you say."

Sulana rolled her eyes. "Regardless of any 'feelings' I may have for Jaylan, he and this Meldon person could be in serious danger. If they failed to return, it's possible they are being held against their will...or worse," she finished with a frown.

Ebnik shook his head at her. "Don't borrow trouble you don't have. Let's just get down to Buckwoods and find out what's happening there before we worry about what might be."

Chapter 22

Meldon and I walked down the forest path into the shadows of the trees. A rabbit bounded off the trail with a flash of white feet and disappeared far too quickly for Meldon to react. Small birds sang and flitted from branch to branch in the forest canopy above us. Sunlight penetrated the branches here and there, dappling the trail with spots of warm sun. We walked through alternating pockets of cool and warm air as we progressed down the trail.

I paid close attention to my awareness of the other Guardians of the Lake, an awareness inked into my mind by the amulet's Member enchantment. As we left the village, their impressions started to fade quickly. My breathing increased and the shadows of the forest became more sinister the farther we went from the others. I strained to listen around the crunch of our footsteps for any sound of something stalking us. I could see Meldon was having the same reaction. His knuckles were white against the grip on

234 of Daniel R. Marvello

his bow and he had nocked an arrow, but he left the string tension slack.

The moment my awareness of the others faded completely, we both came to a halt. A squirrel chattered and Meldon dropped into a crouch. It was like being in a strange room full of obstacles when the lamp goes out; your heart jumps into your throat and you can't force yourself to take another step. I had to resist a strong pang of isolation that urged me to grab Meldon's arm and turn us back toward the village.

"I think we should go back," Meldon said, echoing the very thought I was trying to resist. The aim of his bow followed his eyes as he scrutinized the length of trail in front of us.

I overcame the amulet's influence enough to think of a reason to keep going. "And let Peltor laugh at us for being too afraid to leave the village? I don't think so."

Meldon looked at me, his eyes wide. "I don't *care* what Peltor thinks. This is dangerous!"

"There's no one out here but us and hopefully a few deer. We're both armed and ready. We're the most dangerous things in these woods."

Meldon swallowed hard and straightened from his crouch. He looked around us again. "But don't you feel it? Being away from the other Guardians is just...wrong."

"Sure I feel it. But remember why we're here. We're going to return to the village with something that will make everyone happy, including Lord Thoron."

Meldon continued to scan the forest, but he had dropped his bow from the ready position and held it at his side. "Yeah, assuming we find anything."

I decided to try leveraging my higher rank at Raven Company and put a stern tone into my voice. "Well, I don't think it's asking too much for us to experience a little discomfort in order to help the village. Besides, we really should make sure nothing is going on out here that might threaten our fellow Guardians."

Meldon stared at me for a moment and blinked a couple of times, surprised by my reprimand. My appeal to his sense of responsibility, layered with a small amount of guilt, seemed to get through to him.

He took a deep breath and looked around again, but more casually this time. "Okay, you're right. I'll do my part."

I nearly sighed in relief when he continued warily down the trail.

Now I had to figure out how I would get his amulet off of him. The longer I wore my amulet, the more I was able to ignore its influence and gain mastery over my own actions, but I knew that I could not yet overcome the Protector enchantment and simply yank Meldon's amulet from his neck. On top of that, the neck chains were actually fairly strong, and I was sure it would take a pretty good tug to break the chain or the eyelet where it connected to the amulet.

I had to give Lord Thoron credit; the amulets were annoyingly well made.

We advanced down the trail, alert for game. I stayed behind Meldon so he would have a clear shot at anything we found, but I directed our progress away from the village. We took the right fork where the village trail met the trail back to the road, thus retracing the path I had taken the day I found Tam.

"You seem to know these trails pretty well," he commented at one point.

"I've been here before," I responded shortly.

He glanced curiously over his shoulder at the irritation in my voice, but didn't pursue the matter, for which I was grateful.

We reached the overlook where I had seen Tam for the first time. The location triggered a memory of Tam looking up from inspecting his foot, part man and part beast, but alive. An ache of guilt and shame overwhelmed me. My strong desire to leave the viewpoint had nothing to do with the amulet's influence. I gave Meldon a moment to appreciate the view, and then we turned around and headed back down the trail toward the road.

When we returned to the intersection with the village trail, Meldon looked down the path to the village and hesitated. I thought we might have another argument about continuing on, but when he glanced back at me and saw the look on my face, he sighed and stayed on the trail that would lead us to the road.

We eventually reached the clearing with the fire pit. As we approached, a mental image of Tam lying dead with his father's dagger in his chest made my steps falter. I started to rethink my insistence on going this way, and I was about to stop Meldon when he dropped into a crouch. He waved his free hand behind him, motioning me to get down and be quiet.

We were just a few paces back from where the trail opened up into the clearing. My view was obscured by the undergrowth, but through the branches and leaves, something moved in the clearing. I didn't need to see the whole animal to recognize the unmistakable reddish coat of a whitetail deer.

Meldon pulled back his arrow part way and shuffled forward a step for a clearer view. A stick snapped beneath his foot, and we both froze.

We were too close. The deer heard the snap and leaped out of the clearing, its white tail flashing upward. Meldon stood and pulled the arrow back the rest of the way in one smooth motion. He took aim, but then immediately released the bowstring tension and pointed the arrow at the ground. I stood up behind him.

"Did it get away?" I asked.

"No. I might have been able to take her down, but it was a pregnant doe."

I nodded my understanding. It was spring, and fawning season was very close. Most responsible hunters only took bucks this time of year, giving the herd the opportunity to raise their young until autumn.

"We still have a ways to go. We may get lucky yet," I consoled him.

He nodded and walked forward into the clearing. I followed more slowly.

We both stood looking around the clearing. I found myself holding my breath as more memories of Tam and that day came flooding back. I could see no evidence of the struggle. Even the glass from the shattered potion bottle had been cleaned up from around the fire pit. Jergen and Alain had been thorough in their cover-up.

"Good place to camp." Meldon commented.

"Yeah, it would be," I said heavily. "Let's keep moving."

We continued toward the road. I noticed small wedge-shaped divots along the trail, left behind by the running doe.

As we approached the road, Meldon dropped into a crouch again and signaled me to do the same. I was thinking we might get our deer yet when the clop of approaching horses and a man's voice floated into the trees. Outsiders? The Protector spell from my amulet flared and my hand went immediately to my sword hilt.

Meldon readied his bow again and eased forward. I followed him a pace behind. He peered carefully through the trees at the riders on the road.

He sat back and turned to me. "Five riders that I see. Looks like three guards, a woman, and an old man. One of the guards could be real trouble, and the woman is wearing armor too."

I nodded and whispered. "Take out the guard that worries you first. Do you think you'll have time for more than one shot?"

He nodded back and held up 2 fingers.

"Two shots?" I asked, and he nodded again. "Okay. Try to get the two most worrisome guards. Do any of them have range weapons?"

"Yes. One of the men has a bow, and the woman has a crossbow, but neither is ready," he whispered back.

I could hear the horses getting closer. We had no time to lose.

"After your first shot, I'm going to step around you and charge them from the side. I'll go for whichever guard remains after your second shot. Then you drop your bow and get out there to help me."

"Got it," he said.

Meldon moved forward and started to take aim. As I got into position to go around him, a woman's voice echoed across the road to me.

Sulana?

Meldon had said he saw three men and a woman, plus an old man. I didn't know who the old man might be, but I started to feel pretty sure that I knew who the three men and the woman were.

The Protector spell surged through my mind again. They were outsiders. They were armed and dangerous; a clear threat to the village. I tried to fight the spell's influence and reach for Meldon, but I could hardly make my arm move. I started to panic as I realized that I wouldn't be able to stop Meldon from taking his first shot.

With outsiders so close, I was finding it nearly impossible to overcome the amulet's influence. I had no choice. There was only one thing I could do. I grabbed my amulet and said, "Stop," in full voice, loud enough for Meldon to hear. I successfully severed my channel to the amulet at the same time.

My command startled Meldon just as he released his arrow. My heart sank as it arced away toward the riders.

My amulet went silent and disorientation hit me for a moment. As my head cleared, I heard a shout from the road, and then I realized Meldon was staring at me. He dropped his bow, pulled his dagger, and leaped toward me.

"Outsider!" he shouted in my face as I grabbed the wrist of his hand that held the dagger. He tried to strike me with his other fist and I blocked the blow with my forearm. His rush had caught me off guard, and I tripped as I took a step back from him. We both fell to the ground struggling.

Meldon was far stronger than I imagined. I had to use both hands to keep his dagger away, which gave him the opportunity to get in a punch to my face, which made my head ring and my cheek throb. During our struggle, his amulet slid out from under his tunic. The amulet swung tantalizingly in the space between us as he raged over me.

My target in sight, I took a calculated risk. I grabbed his amulet with my right hand, leaving just my left to hold back his dagger. I tried to yank the amulet free, but I had no leverage and the chain was too strong.

Meldon growled when I pulled on his amulet. He took his free hand and grabbed my neck, his fingers digging into my throat. Right away, my vision darkened and I started to see stars.

This was not at all how I imagined this confrontation would go.

If only I could tell Meldon to stop the flow of vaetra to his amulet as I had. But even if I could get the words out with his hand around my throat, I wasn't sure he was capable of controlling the flow. Sulana had said I was a Channeler. I was able to channel vaetra into the Seeker, and now I had control over my amulet as well. Was Meldon a Channeler in addition to being a Sensitive?

Several thoughts converged at once. In my mind's eye, Lord Thoron placed the vaetra-draining device under Sati's shoulder and activated it; he was able to control devices that worked on other people. I remembered starting and stopping the Seeker. I knew the sensation of controlling my channel with the amulet, which now sat impotently on my chest. Could I shut down Meldon's amulet *for* him?

I focused my thoughts and stared straight into Meldon's glaring eyes. I imagined stopping his flow of vaetra into his amulet, which I still held tightly, and I said, "Stop." But the word came out as a grunt as Meldon leaned in to put more pressure on my neck.

I could feel myself starting to lose consciousness. With the last of my fading strength, I pressed the fist that held the amulet hard into Meldon's chest. I pushed him back just enough to release some of the pressure from my neck. I focused on shutting down Meldon's channel to his amulet and tried to stop it again.

This time the word came out as a hoarse croak, but it was clear. Meldon's amulet fell silent.

Meldon's grip loosened and I quickly pushed him off me, scuttling back away from him on the ground. He sat down hard and dropped his dagger, putting both hands up to press on the sides of his head. He swayed for a moment, and then he slowly looked up at me.

We both sat there panting and staring at one another for a few moments.

"By the spirits, Jaylan. What did they do to us?"

∽

My head was still spinning, but I was so relieved to see Meldon in control of his own thoughts again that I nearly hugged him. But before I could answer his question about what had happened to us, another voice spoke from the trailhead a few paces away.

"Jaylan?" I looked up to see Sulana, lowering her crossbow as she said my name. Daven stood next to her with his bow still drawn and aimed at Meldon.

"He seems to be more capable than you let on, Sulana." The words came from the deep voice of a tall old man standing just behind Sulana. The old man was dressed in a flowing tunic and pants.

Sulana looked back and forth between Meldon and me. "So it seems. Are you alright?" she asked, eyeing my disheveled appearance.

I stood up and brushed at my clothes. I rubbed my neck, which felt raw and bruised. "I think so. My attempt to rescue Meldon didn't quite go as planned." I stopped suddenly and looked at the newcomers, noting that Talon and Barek were not among them. "Meldon's arrow didn't hit anyone did it?"

Sulana shook her head. "No, but it barely missed Barek."

Good. My warning shout as Meldon released the arrow must have spoiled his shot.

Meldon pulled the amulet's chain over his head and threw it down the trail. He looked over at Sulana and the old man, his gaze lingering on the man. He put his head down between his knees and muttered helplessly into the ground. "Great. Another sorcerer."

The man looked at Sulana with a grimace. "How does everyone know that? Do I have 'sorcerer' written on my forehead?"

Sulana laughed. "No, but you do look the part." She motioned for Daven to drop his aim, and she handed her crossbow to him. She walked past Meldon and bent to retrieve his amulet. She brushed the dirt off of it and looked it over before walking back to the old man and handing it to him. "Jaylan, this is Ebnik, a friend of mine and a wizard of the Archives. Ebnik, this is Jaylan, the man I was trying to find in Northshore."

"Good to meet you," I said, uncertain if I really meant it.

"Hello Jaylan," he said. He looked at the amulet around my neck and then back to the one in his hands. "What can you tell me about these amulets?"

Meldon looked up at Ebnik. "They're evil!"

Ebnik glanced at Meldon and raised his eyebrows, but waited for my answer.

"This is Meldon," I said. "I won't disagree with him about the amulets being evil. Once Lord Thoron activates them, they take over your mind."

"Lord Thoron?" Sulana and Ebnik said in unison.

Sulana looked at Ebnik and narrowed her eyes in thought. "Paeter Thoron?" she asked.

Ebnik snorted. "Who else? That explains a lot. Paeter always was rather good with mind control incantations. And his skills as a Smith are uncontested." He shook the amulet in emphasis.

"Smith?" I asked.

"Yes, a few of our kind are able to create vaetric implements, or 'magical devices' as some would have it, like this one. Those sorcerers are known as Smiths. Without them, Channelers like Sulana, and yourself, would have no way to create vaetric manifestations. You provide the vaetra; the implement provides the incantation."

"Like the Seeker?" I asked.

"Exactly. Seekers are also vaetric implements, enchanted with a seeking incantation." He held up the amulet. "Could you describe the effects of these amulets?"

I nodded. I was all too familiar with "the effects of these amulets."

I explained how Lord Thoron had activated the amulets with two trigger words and what had happened to my mind as each enchantment took hold. I told him about how I had finally disabled my amulet that morning, and how I had come up with a plan to release Meldon as well.

Ebnik listened carefully, asking a few questions along the way. When I completed my story, he took a deep breath and smiled. "I'm impressed you were able to accomplish all of that with no training. But then, if you'd had training, the amulet would never have been a threat to you."

"What do you mean?" I asked.

"You are just learning to channel. If you had full control over your own flow of vaetra, you could have prevented the amulet from activating. Even if you had allowed it to activate, the 'separation of awareness' you spoke of would have been present from the beginning, and you could have disabled the amulet at any time."

My cheeks grew warm as I considered the unnecessary risk my ignorance was creating.

Ebnik seemed to read my thoughts. "Don't feel bad, Jaylan. You did quite well, actually. In fact, I'm surprised you were able to disable Meldon's amulet. How did you know to do that?"

I explained how my memory of Lord Thoron draining vaetra from the village woman made me realize that he was able to control a device that worked on someone else. In retrospect, I realized that was essentially what he had done when he put the amulet on me as well.

"Besides, Meldon was about to kill me and I had nothing to lose by trying," I concluded.

I looked over at Meldon to find that he was staring at me, an incredulous look on his face. "You're one of them?" he asked. "You're a sorcerer?"

I opened my mouth to deny it, but stopped myself and shook my head. "I honestly don't know, Meldon. I have these abilities I didn't ask for. Ignoring them hasn't been working out very well so far."

Chapter 23

The five of us went out to the road and met up with Barek and Talon at the entrance to the trail. We made introductions and then settled into the business of deciding what to do next.

Barek looked around the group. "We have plenty of strength for a frontal assault. We could end this quickly."

Sulana stared at him. "Sure, and do what? Kill a bunch of innocent villagers? No. We have to do this carefully. We need to protect the villagers somehow and get Ebnik close enough to Paeter to disable him."

Ebnik chuckled. "I appreciate your confidence my dear, but I think our best bet is to surprise Paeter *before* he has a chance to mount a defense, or 'disabling' him may be a challenge even for me."

I spoke up. "Our main problem is the Raven Company men. They are well-armed and experienced fighters. On top of that, Peltor is suspicious of me and stays very close to Lord Thoron."

"When are the fishermen due back?" Sulana asked.

"They usually return in the late afternoon. Not long from now, actually. Why?"

"I think it's best if we wait until everyone who is under the influence of the amulets is present. We could have big trouble if the fishermen return home to a bunch of 'outsiders,' as you put it."

"Won't that just be more people for us to fight?" Daven asked.

Sulana looked around the group before answering. "I'm hoping we can do this without a fight. The villagers are innocents. If we fight, someone is sure to get hurt, maybe killed."

I nodded. "The timing will be critical then. We'll have to deal with Lord Thoron and the two Raven Company men without alerting the villagers, and we'll have to disable the amulet on each villager without alerting the rest of them. I'm honestly not sure we can do either of those things. As soon as you disable an amulet, the others will recognize that person as an outsider."

"May I make a suggestion?" Talon interrupted.

"Please do. We could use one of those about now," Sulana said.

"The Raven Company men are our biggest problem in a physical conflict. Since Jaylan is on good terms with one of them, perhaps he could lure that man away from the village first."

Sulana nodded. "I like that. We could disable his amulet and get him on our side, or at least out of the fight."

I thought about Talon's suggestion. It seemed reasonable. I just needed a good excuse to get Kefer out of the village. An idea came to mind immediately.

"I have an idea for getting him out of the village, but he won't willingly let me touch his amulet," I said.

Ebnik reached into the folds of his tunic and removed a crystal sphere, much like the one Lord Thoron had. He held it in the palm of his hand. "Just get him here," he said. "I'll take care of the rest."

When he saw the sphere, Meldon took a couple of steps back and stared at it. When nothing more happened, he stopped fidgeting but kept a wary distance.

"What is that?" I asked, tilting my head toward the sphere in Ebnik's hand. "Lord Thoron has one. He used it to immobilize us. Does yours do that too?"

"This is a casting orb. Unlike the amulets, it has no specific function. I can use it as a focus device to cast any incantation I wish."

I looked at Sulana. "That seems a lot simpler than carrying around individual implements. Why don't you have one?"

Sulana shrugged and shook her head. "I can't cast, I can only channel. A caster like Ebnik can speak an incantation and focus it through his casting orb to produce manifestations. Not all Channelers are able to do that. The rest of us need implements that have the incantation built into them."

"Wait...you said earlier that Lord Thoron was a Smith. Now he's apparently a Caster as well. How many types of sorcerer are there?" I asked.

Ebnik explained. "Vaetric ability appears in layers. Most of the mundane population is Insensitive; they are unable to sense vaetric manifestations in any way. Perhaps one in a hundred individuals is a Sensitive. Sensitives are able to sense vaetric manifestations, just as you are able to hear them and Sulana is able to see them. Many Sensitives, about half of them, are able to control the flow of vaetra, or channel it. You and Sulana are both Channelers. Some Channelers can only work with vaetric implements like a Seeker or Veil, which have the necessary incantation enchanted within them. Other Channelers—again about half—are Casters such as myself. Casters can speak an incantation and focus it through a casting orb like mine. The orb has no incantation within it; it is simply a focusing device for whatever incantation one casts. Finally, a certain number of Casters are Smiths like Paeter. A Smith can enchant a glass or crystal implement, creating the devices that non-casting Channelers need to work sorcery."

I pursed my lips in thought. Some of the things that had happened over the past few days were starting to make more sense. "Meldon is apparently a Sensitive too, because he can see when the amulets are active. But Lord Thoron called him something else. He said Meldon was a Phobic."

Ebnik turned to regard Meldon, who shrank back at his scrutiny. "Ah, I understand now. I'm sorry this situation is causing you such distress, Meldon."

Ebnik turned back to me. "A certain number of Sensitives have strong reactions to vaetric manifestations. Phobics, like your friend Meldon here, have a strong fear reaction. Euphorics have a joyous reaction, sometimes to the point of hallucination. Manics go berserk with anger, usually attacking the sorcerer who produces the manifestation."

Another thought occurred to me, and I turned to Daven. "That's why you kept such a close eye on me the first time

Sulana used the Seeker in my presence. You thought I might be a Manic."

Daven shrugged. "You never know."

"So, really, Meldon could be a Channeler too." I said to Ebnik. Meldon's jaw dropped and he looked absolutely horrified at the suggestion.

Ebnik nodded. "It's possible. However, we don't know of any Phobics or Manics who have been able to overcome their reaction sufficiently to pursue training in sorcery. Sorry, Meldon."

"That's fine with me," Meldon mumbled.

Barek stepped forward and leaned toward Sulana. "Can we save the sorcery lessons for later and deal with the problem at hand?"

Sulana grimaced. "I suppose you're right, although it seems that Jaylan needs to understand more about what's going on in order to help us. Okay, so we need a plan. You said you had an idea for getting Kefer out of the village?" she asked me.

"Yes. I'll tell him Meldon shot a good-sized buck just up the road from the village, and that we could use his help bringing it back. We'll need to be far enough back from the village that his amulet fades out of range before we take it from him; otherwise, Peltor may figure out that something's up. The road curves just before you get to the village, so we'll be able to get fairly close before we're seen. I'll walk down the road until I start to detect the other members of the Guard, and then I'll scratch my head as a signal. You'll need to set up the ambush well back from that point."

Sulana nodded and looked around at the group. "Is everyone ready?" We all indicated that we were, and she turned back to me. "Go ahead, Jaylan. We'll follow you."

I started walking down the road to the village. When I was about half-way there, I stopped and put my hand on my amulet. "Member," I said, and channeled vaetra into the amulet. It started to hum. "Protector," I said, and a second tone joined the first. Now that I had more practice activating and deactivating the amulet, the Protector spell had even less influence over my mind. It crashed against the door of my self control, but I was able to hold that door closed. Being able to exercise control over the spell sent a thrill of excitement through me.

I started walking again. About fifty paces from the curve in the road, the flickering awareness of the other Guardians resumed. I raised my hand and scratched my head, signaling the others. I glanced back over my shoulder and saw that they had stopped a good twenty paces behind me.

After I went around the curve in the road and got closer to the village, Kefer ran forward to intercept me, his hand on his sword. "Is everything okay? Where's Meldon?" he asked, craning his neck to look around me and down the road.

"Meldon's back with his prize." I said with an eye roll. "He got a buck and didn't want to leave it behind even for a moment. It's just down the road, and we could use your help carrying it back. It will be easier to dress it out back here in the village."

Kefer responded to my news with a grin. "That's great! Let me tell Peltor what's going on and I'll give you a hand." Kefer jogged over to Peltor, who stood as Kefer approached and listened to Kefer's enthusiastic explanation. Peltor frowned in my direction, nodded to Kefer, and sat back down.

As Kefer walked back to me, I glanced around the village. Everything seemed quiet, and I noticed that the fisherman had not yet returned. Then my eyes caught movement out on the water. The two fishing boats floated around a rocky point to the south, rowing toward the village. They'd be back soon.

Kefer was still grinning as he rejoined me and he slapped me on the back. We started walking back down the road away from the village. "The fish here is excellent, but fresh venison will be a welcome change," he said.

"I couldn't agree more. Everything quiet while we were gone?" I asked.

"Yep. Same as ever. I almost wish some outsiders would appear just to relieve the boredom."

The irony almost made me laugh, but I kept a straight face. "Not me. A little peace and quiet is welcome after what I've been through the past few days."

"Aw, you're just used to things being slow at Raven Company," he scoffed. "A little excitement would do you some good. Get the blood flowing again. Makes you feel alive."

I was going to make a flip reply, but his words unexpectedly struck home. Maybe he was right. Maybe it was time to shake things up and try something new. "You may be right," I finally said. We walked around the curve in the road, and I shook my head to dispel the distracting line of thought. I started paying careful attention to my awareness of the other Guardians.

"Of course I'm right," Kefer continued. He blustered on about being ready for some action for a few moments, and then slowly fell silent. Right as we were nearing the limit of the amulet's range, he stopped walking.

"What's wrong?" I asked.

Kefer gave me a haunted look. "It's spooky…the way the others disappear. I've never gone this far from the village before. How did you and Meldon stand the feeling of isolation?"

"We knew we had a job to do. We wanted to protect the security of the village, and we wanted to pay the villagers back for their hospitality while we've been here."

He absorbed that and took a deep breath. "I guess you're right. Still…"

"We're almost there. Meldon is just up the road."

"I don't see him," Kefer said, peering ahead.

"The deer ran into the trees before collapsing. We thought it was safer to leave both Meldon and his buck in the trees in case someone came down the road."

Right then, Meldon appeared, waved to us, and went back into the trees. Someone must have realized that Kefer was balking and thought to send Meldon out to ease his mind. But they forgot something; Meldon was no longer wearing an amulet.

Kefer drew his sword with a rasp of steel and stared at the place where Meldon had disappeared into the trees. "Outsider," he said, and started running down the road toward Meldon.

I drew my sword as well and ran after Kefer.

Kefer stopped where Meldon had left the road and peered into the trees, sword at the ready. Then he straightened and dropped his sword. With a clang, it fell to the road.

Ebnik stepped out of the trees, tucking his casting orb back into his pocket as I caught up to them. He walked up to Kefer, pulled Kefer's amulet out from under his clothing by its chain, and placed a hand on it. The amulet fell silent, although I could still hear a low sound emanating from Kefer himself.

The rest of Sulana's team emerged from their hiding spots alongside the road and walked over to where we stood. Talon removed Kefer's dagger from his belt and both Talon and Barek held Kefer's arms.

Ebnik nodded to them and pulled out his orb again. He stared at Kefer and suddenly Kefer was struggling in the grip of his captors.

"Who are you? What do you want?" Kefer demanded.

I stepped into his range of vision. "Kefer! Relax. These people are here to help."

Kefer looked at me in confusion. "Jaylan? What's going on here?"

"You've been under a spell. Lord Thoron put us all under a spell to help him make more of these amulets." I touched mine and looked at his.

He looked down at the amulet resting on his chest. "Yeah, I remember. Get that thing off me!"

I removed his amulet for him and handed it to Ebnik. It took us a while to calm Kefer down and make introductions. Any doubts about Kefer's willingness to cooperate evaporated quickly and Talon and Barek released him. He was all for going after a piece of Lord Thoron.

I looked around the group. "Where's Meldon?"

Meldon called from behind a tree a few paces into the forest. "Right here, Jaylan. Could you do something about your amulet?"

I looked down at my amulet and realized it was still active. It's influence over my mind had fallen to the point where I could practically ignore it. "Sorry, Meldon." I deactivated the amulet, and Meldon sheepishly came out of the trees.

"I'm sorry to be such a coward, Jaylan, but all this sorcery is unnerving."

"You aren't a coward, Meldon. In fact you've been incredibly brave. I'm sorry I got you into all this."

"Well, Borlan did promise adventure when I gave him my commitment," he said with a weak smile.

Kefer had watched me deactivate my amulet with alarm and then suspicion. "How are you able to do that, Jaylan? I couldn't even think for myself while I wore one of those things."

I hesitated before answering. I wasn't sure I was ready for the world to know about this new aspect of my life, but Meldon already knew, and everyone else would find out soon enough. "I've discovered that I have a little talent for sorcery. Not much, but enough to control the amulet."

He stared at me for a moment. "What's Borlan going to think about that?" he finally asked.

"Or Dela?" Meldon added.

I shook my head. "I honestly have no idea. I haven't even worked out what I think yet."

~

Now that we had Kefer on our side, we were faced with the true difficulty of getting to Lord Thoron and freeing the villagers.

"Under the cover of the amulets, getting close to Lord Thoron shouldn't be too difficult. He's usually deep into the process of creating another amulet in the afternoon, but that will be over soon," I said.

Ebnik looked thoughtful. "Tell me more about his amulet process."

I described what I had seen the prior day and that morning. How Lord Thoron drained a village woman of her vaetra in the morning and spent the afternoon constructing an amulet, drawing on the additional power he had acquired. As I spoke, Ebnik's face went white and then red.

"He drains the women to the point of unconsciousness?" he asked with measured words and a glowering stare.

"Yes. He used a device of some kind to drain her, and then one of us would have to carry her back to her hut a while later."

Ebnik and Sulana looked at each other, anger and frustration clear on their faces. "That bastard!" Sulana spit out.

"Why, what's wrong?" I asked, looking back and forth between them.

Ebnik waved his arms around as he explained. "He knows how dangerous it is to drain someone to the point of exhaustion! It can cause long term damage! He's probably shortened the life of every woman in that village by now. This is the same kind of thing that got him expelled from the Archives in the first place."

Sulana calmed herself and placed her hand on Ebnik's arm. "Paeter never did believe the claims of long-term damage. And we had no direct proof to offer him. Just legends from times past."

Ebnik took a deep breath and shook his head. "Yes, and Paeter is a short-term thinker. He always takes the quickest path to his goal."

"At least he has one redeeming quality," mumbled Barek.

Sulana glared at him, and he had the good sense to look away.

Ebnik's anger abated, and he started pacing back and forth, rubbing his chin. "I think we now know why he chose to set up shop in this particular village. That ice house is probably sitting on top of a rock shelf or underground boulder. The stone blocks sit on top of that and give him a huge vaetra well to work from. Creating implements requires a tremendous amount of vaetra, and draining the village women makes it possible to work much faster." He glanced over at me as he paced. "You said he could create an amulet per day?"

"I think so."

"He created one every day I was there," confirmed Kefer.

Ebnik shook his head. "Amazing. The man is as resourceful as he is unscrupulous."

"When you said the stone blocks are a vaetra 'well,' what did you mean?" I asked Ebnik.

"Minerals and living flesh store vaetra. We refer to anything that stores vaetra as a 'well,' and just as the name implies, vaetra can be drawn back out by an accomplished sorcerer. Paeter is using the ice house you described as a giant well. It gives him the ability to apply far more vaetra to his work than would be possible using just what he carries within himself."

Talon interrupted with a quickly raised hand. "Hold," he said quietly, and everyone fell silent. He was staring down the road toward the curve.

"What?" Sulana whispered.

"I saw movement down at the corner," he whispered back.

Alarmed, everyone turned to look down the road. I saw nothing but a few branches waving in the breeze. Is that what Talon had seen? Or was someone spying on us?

"We're wasting time here," Barek growled. "Surprise requires speed."

Sulana gave him a curt nod in agreement. "Surprise also requires a plan or both sides get surprised. But you're right. Let's get on with this."

We quickly debated and discarded a few options for approaching the village. In the end, everyone agreed that we first needed to take Lord Thoron out of the fight. Our best bet for doing that was to get Ebnik close to Lord Thoron without alerting him. I felt confident I could handle Peltor myself, but we needed to get Ebnik into the village without him being recognized as an outsider. He could wear an amulet, but Peltor would realize he was a stranger even if none of the villagers noticed. To the villagers, we had all been strangers, and none of them had cared as long as we wore an amulet.

Ebnik had a solution for that problem. "I can hide us with a Veil and follow you into the village. As long as no one has physical contact with me, they won't see me. I'll have to drop it before I try to immobilize Paeter, however."

"I can distract Peltor and prevent him from interfering when you drop the Veil," I assured him. "But bring an amulet with you so you can wear it when we leave."

Sulana gave us a tight smile. "Sounds workable. Let's do it. We can figure out how to free the villagers once we have Paeter under control."

I enabled my amulet and Ebnik cast his Veil. Interestingly, I could hear the spell operating, but I couldn't locate the source of the sound. Likewise, even though I knew Ebnik was there, I could no longer see him.

A hand gripped my arm, and suddenly Ebnik appeared at my side. I tried to focus on him, but it seemed like my eyes were crossing. His appearance wavered as if he were underwater and I was looking down at him from above the rippling surface. When he spoke, his voice sounded as if it were coming to me through a tunnel. "I'll follow about twenty paces behind you. That will give you time to distract Peltor while I get into position."

I nodded in response. He let go of me, and it was a relief when he disappeared once again.

We all headed toward the curve in the road. The others held back while I rounded the curve. Presumably, Ebnik was right behind me.

Before I got within sight of the village, I noticed something unusual about my awareness of the villagers. They were all bunched together for some reason. Also, tendrils of fog were floating down the road from the direction of the village. Fog wasn't particularly unusual this time of year, but it was unusual at this time of day with a bright sun still well above the horizon.

When I got all the way around the curve, the fog was so thick ahead of me that I couldn't see the village. However, my awareness of the villagers told me they all stood at the end of the road. My steps faltered to an uncertain stop.

I closed my eyes and searched through the impressions given off by the Guardian amulets. Nowhere could I feel the strong presence I was used to associating with Lord Thoron, but if he remained in the ice house, he could still be out of range. The villagers were so close together that it was hard to distinguish them. I couldn't tell exactly how many of them had gathered.

So much for our plan to sneak Ebnik into the village undetected.

Apparently, Talon had not been imagining things after all. Someone had alerted Lord Thoron that three of his Guardians were conversing with a group of strangers. That someone (and I was betting on Peltor) may have also been close enough to tell that we were outsiders again.

I turned on my heel and started walking back the way I came. "I assume you can hear me, Ebnik. Something's wrong. The villagers are gathered at the end of the road."

I had only taken a couple of steps when Ebnik suddenly appeared in front of me. His casting orb was still in his hand, and he looked down the road into the fog. "This is not natural fog," he observed. "Paeter must have raised it to slow us down."

I nodded in agreement and looked back over my shoulder. "He knows we're coming, and he told the villagers to stop us."

Ebnik looked pensive. "Paeter won't go quietly. He can make this very difficult, even with two sorcerers against him," he glanced at me, "or make that two-and-a-half. We may be in for a fight after all."

I snorted and said, "Barek will be thrilled. We need to warn the others." I walked around Ebnik, who nodded absently and continued to stare into the fog.

As I started walking, a light gust of wind flowed past me and down the road. I took a few more steps before Ebnik started speaking an incantation. I turned around to see what he was doing and looked up in time to see an arrow arcing through the breeze-thinned fog, aimed straight for my chest.

CHAPTER 24

I've had a few intense moments in my life where I thought to myself, "It's the end of the trail. I'm done." This was one of those moments. I had no time to defend myself and no time for regrets.

My eyes had just locked onto the arrow and that fleeting thought of finality had sparked across my mind when the arrow stopped suddenly in midair and shattered as if it had struck stone. I stood frozen for a moment trying to make sense of what my eyes had just witnessed.

"Run, Jaylan!" Ebnik shouted at me, and then he began another incantation.

I looked down the road and saw that the breeze had thinned the fog enough for us to make out the villagers faintly. They could see us as well. One of them had a bow and was nocking another arrow. I turned and ran before the archer could get off another shot, just as Ebnik cast another Veil and disappeared again.

I sprinted down the road realizing that Ebnik must have put up a vaetric shield of some kind to stop that first arrow. I already owed my life to the man, and we'd only just met.

I rounded the corner just as a second arrow thudded into a tree to my right. The archer was pretty good. Maybe I should tell him to speak to Borlan about mercenary work if he ever got tired of fishing for a living.

When I came running around the corner, the rest of the team stopped what they were doing and stared at me for a moment. They then burst into action. Swords and daggers were drawn in a chorus of hissing steel. Sulana stepped forward as I approached. "There's a bank of fog covering the village. The villagers are gathered to defend it," I panted in explanation.

Sulana looked around me and down the road. "Where's Ebnik?"

"He's still behind me somewhere," I answered.

She asked me how the villagers were armed. I told her I couldn't tell, but that there was at least one archer. I explained how Ebnik had shielded me from an arrow before disappearing again. She placed a hand on my shoulder and mumbled thanks to him for his quick thinking. Then she grimaced and warned me that an archer was too dangerous to be left standing. She told Daven to ready his bow. He nodded and his face went grim as he complied.

Right then, a shout came from behind me.

"There they are! Outsiders!" The villagers came around the curve in the road and charged.

The village archer held back and readied a shot, and Daven did the same, taking aim at the other bowman. But as the villager raised his bow to fire, his arms suddenly went slack and the partially-drawn arrow released uselessly into the ground at his feet. The bow fell from his hands and he stood with his arms at his sides. Daven aborted his shot as well and tossed his bow to the roadside before pulling his sword.

I scanned the forest edge along the road at the corner and spotted Ebnik between the trees. He stepped toward the bowman, but that was all I had time to see before the other villagers were upon us.

Our numbers were even, but our skills and equipment were not. Jake the wagon driver was armed with a short sword, and Sati's husband Edanos led the charge with a pitchfork. The rest of the villagers were armed with fish knives. I would have laughed if it weren't for the way they ran toward us. A screaming mob with weapons gripped tightly in their hands isn't amusing.

Barek stood at the leading edge of our group, and Edanos went straight for him with the pitchfork. Barek let him come, turned sideways, and drove the pitchfork into the ground with a powerful downward stroke of his sword. On the return swing of his arm, he stepped into Edanos and drove his elbow into the man's face. Barek's blow knocked the smaller man senseless. Edanos dropped the pitchfork as he fell backward, crashed to the ground, and lay still. Barek leaned over Edanos and harrumphed.

The other villagers streamed into our midst.

Sati went straight for Sulana with a feral scream. Her knife was raised high in her fist as she ran toward us, her eyes blazing with fury. Although Sati had a height and weight advantage over the smaller woman, her attack was uncontrolled and she didn't have years of training to hone her reactions. With a sweep of her forearm, Sulana knocked aside Sati's knife arm as it came down, and tripped Sati as the larger woman's momentum carried her forward. Sati hit the ground and rolled over quickly, only to find Sulana's sword tip at her throat.

Jake came after me. I easily deflected his first swing and the return stroke he aimed at my legs. We exchanged blows a few more times, getting a feel for each other. He was a better fighter than I would expect for a wagon driver, but no match for someone with my experience. Suddenly his eyes narrowed and he hesitated as he looked at my amulet. I had forgotten that the Member enchantment of my amulet was still active. I took advantage of his confusion to knock aside his sword and drive a kick hard into his chest. He went down on his back and I stepped on his sword arm, placing the tip of my sword against his sternum.

His amulet was right there in front of me, lying on top of his shirt. I reached down and grabbed it. He started to struggle as I did so, but I looked into his eyes and increased the pressure of my sword point. He glared up at me and bared his teeth, but he dropped his head back to the ground in surrender. I focused briefly on the amulet and disabled it, as I had Meldon's. It was far easier to do the second time, particularly since I wasn't struggling for every breath.

While Jake reeled with the disorientation of being released from the amulet's spells, I looked around to see if anyone else needed help.

It was over.

Ebnik had made himself visible again and was back among us, disabling the amulets of the villagers who were either unconscious or subdued by one of the members of our group. Sulana was kneeling next to Daven, who was sitting

on the road holding one of his arms against his chest with
blood seeping from a nasty cut along his forearm.

I released Jake and kneeled next to him. "Are you all
right?" He gave me a weary nod. I stood and extended a hand
to help him to his feet. He looked down at his amulet as if
seeing it for the first time. "Let's get that thing off you," I
suggested. He took off the amulet with fumbling hands and
handed it to me. I didn't know what Sulana planned to do
with the amulets, but I was certain she would not want them
loose among the mundane population.

I carried the amulet over to Sulana where she was helping
Daven clean the cut on his arm. Daven winced in pain as she
dabbed at the blood with a white kerchief that was already
stained deep red. "We need to clean and close this wound,"
she said. She looked up at me. "Could you get the tall brown
bottle and the implement case with a red dot on it from the
left side of my saddlebags? Quickly?"

I nodded and jogged over to Sulana's horse. The mare
was still a little skittish from the brief battle. She danced away
from me a couple of steps, but I calmed her with soothing
words and petted her neck. The horse settled down and let
me rummage around in Sulana's saddle bag.

The tall brown bottle was obvious, and the label identified
it as brandy. I found two implement cases, more like pouches
really, made of stiff leather with a flap buckled across the
front. I selected the one that had a prominent red dot on
the flap and jogged back to Sulana with the items she had
requested.

She took them from me with a distracted "Thanks,"
and uncorked the brandy. Looking up into Daven's face, she
asked, "You ready for this?" He nodded and gritted his teeth

in anticipation. Sulana put her thumb over the opening of the bottle to allow just a thin stream to pour out into the cut on Daven's arm. He jumped and sucked his breath in through his teeth when the liquid made first contact with the gaping wound. Golden brandy stained orange with blood flowed over his arm and dripped to the ground next to his leg. He swayed as she moved the stream down the cut. With her free hand on his shoulder, Sulana steadied him.

I went around behind Daven to help support him, but Sulana looked up sharply at me. "This isn't over. Let me work on Daven. You and Ebnik still need to deal with Paeter. He could have more nasty surprises waiting for you, so be careful." Talon walked over to us as she spoke, and took position behind Daven to lend a hand in my place.

I hesitated and then stepped back out of the way. Her orders made sense, but I didn't want to leave her side while she and Daven were so close.

I looked around and saw Ebnik walking toward me with several amulets dangling from the chains he held in one hand. He dropped them to the ground next to the implement case and observed Sulana's ministrations briefly. Then he turned to me.

"The element of surprise is lost, but we still have to deal with Paeter Thoron." His eyes scanned through the group around us and settled on Barek. Barek, who had been watching, acknowledged the wizard's look with a short nod and jogged over. "I'd like to take Barek with us."

"I'll go," said Kefer from behind me. He stepped forward, a hand on his sword hilt.

Ebnik shook his head. "I appreciate the offer, but I think it would be best if we take someone who has experience dealing with sorcerers."

Kefer looked disappointed, but nodded his head. "I guess I'm not that eager to face Lord Thoron again any time soon anyway. He and that orb of his captured me the first time without a struggle. I'm not sure how to fight someone like that. And I'd rather not have to fight Peltor after all we've been through together."

I snorted. "I won't have any problem dealing with Peltor." Kefer grimaced, probably imagining the worst. "Don't worry, I don't plan to kill him, just take him out of the fight."

Kefer nodded and said, "Try to remember that Peltor is a victim, just the same as you and I."

"I'll remember, but you know the amulet hasn't done anything to improve his attitude toward me," I said. Kefer looked at the ground and nodded again.

Ebnik took a deep breath and straightened to his full height. "Well, then...let's go see what *Lord* Thoron has in store for us."

∼

I took the lead since I knew the layout of the village and would have the easiest time navigating in the fog. Ebnik raised a Veil around all three of us. We were able to see and hear each other, but the sights and sounds of the forest blurred and dimmed. The sensation was similar to what I had experienced when Sulana had broken us through the healer's Ward. But this time I was able to observe the effects of the Veil by itself.

We debated whether or not we should deactivate my amulet. On the one hand, leaving it active would allow me to pinpoint Lord Thoron's and Peltor's positions, assuming they were still wearing theirs. If they had removed their amulets, Lord Thoron would have had to come up with a different way to control Peltor. On the other hand, deactivating my amulet would allow us to approach without them being able to pinpoint *my* position. In the end, we decided I should deactivate it until we got into the village. I could always reactivate it once we were closer.

When we rounded the corner in the road, we discovered that the fog had thinned to grey wisps. We continued down the road and stopped where the village opened up before us. The place was empty, except for a few last drifting puffs of fog. The door to the ice house was open, but I saw no sign of Peltor or Lord Thoron. I motioned for us to circle around in front of the huts to come at the ice house from the side.

Before we reached the third hut, the door opened slightly and a woman's face peered out. She glanced around the village with darting eyes. The whine of a young girl's voice came from the room behind her, and someone else shushed the girl. Thinking back on the brief battle with the villagers, I realized that two of the village women had been absent. These two women must have been left behind in the hut to keep an eye on the three village children.

The woman at the door stared hard at us, sensing our presence in spite of the Veil. Later, Ebnik told me that a Veil becomes less effective when you cover more people with it.

Barek took charge of the situation. He stepped out of the Veil, and the woman's eyes widened when he appeared right in front of her. She squeaked and started to shut the door, but before she could get it closed, he shoved his way into the hut. We heard muffled screams of "Outsider" and the sound of a brief struggle. A moment later, Barek poked his head out the door with a smirk on his face and showed us a pair of amulets dangling from his hand. He motioned us to move on, indicating he had things under control in the hut.

My vision and hearing sharpened suddenly, and I turned to see that Ebnik had dropped the Veil. I looked at him curiously, and he explained quietly. "If they are still here, and I'm beginning to doubt that, they'll have heard the racket and know where we are anyway. Go ahead and activate your amulet."

I did as he suggested...and found nothing. No one else was wearing an amulet within range of the Member spell. But that didn't mean they were really gone. "I can't sense them," I informed Ebnik.

Ebnik narrowed his eyes and tightened his grip on his casting orb as I drew my sword. He motioned me to lead on with a tilt of his head, and we continued to sneak toward the ice house.

We reached the side of the ice house and edged our way around to the front. Everything was quiet. Ebnik whispered into my ear. "I'll put a Shield on the doorway so you can step across in front of it and get a quick look inside." I nodded in agreement, and he raised his orb. He concentrated for a moment, and then a buzzing noise started near the door opening. He patted my shoulder to signal me the Shield was in place.

I moved across the front of the ice house in a crouch and paused at the doorway to glance around the interior. I was ready to dive aside if necessary.

There was no need. The ice house was empty.

I stood slowly and squinted into the dim ice house. Something was piled on the stone block that Lord Thoron had been using as a workbench, but it was covered by the blanket he had used to warm Sati during her Contribution Ceremony. Ebnik saw me straighten at the doorway and came forward. After a quick glance inside the ice house, he dispelled the Shield. After the buzzing of the Shield had stopped, I noticed a low hum emanating from within the ice house. I stepped through the door and down the short steps to pinpoint the source. Ebnik followed me in.

The sound seemed to be coming from the pile on the stone block. And the sound was growing in pitch and volume. Ebnik looked at my face and asked, "What is it?" I opened my mouth to tell him, but the sound was climbing in pitch rapidly and I decided I didn't have time for explanations. I turned and grabbed Ebnik's arm to push him out of the ice house. "Get out of here, now!" I shouted.

Ebnik had the good sense to not question my orders and we both scrambled up the steps and out through the door. Behind me, the sound was reaching deafening levels. I dove to the side and hit the ground with Ebnik following my lead.

The noise from the ice house was becoming painfully loud. I considered trying to crawl further away when a concussive force coughed out of the doorway and knocked the breath from my lungs. The shock wave was accompanied by a loud boom that shook the ground and knocked bits of thatching from the roofs of the other buildings. The top of the ice house blew off in an arcing cascade of tumbling timber lengths and drifting thatching. Thankfully, the higher stone walls at the front and rear of the building directed most of the material to the sides, away from where Ebnik and I had thrown ourselves. Chunks of glass and tatters of cloth spewed out of the ice house doorway to thud and flutter to the ground behind us. One piece of glass rolled and clunked against the bottom of my boot.

I looked over at Ebnik, who was up on one elbow looking back at the ice house. "Are you okay?" I asked him.

Ebnik stood and brushed the dirt off of his clothes. "I believe so. It seems Paeter left us a present."

Barek ran over to us as I was getting to my feet. The two village women stood at the doorway to their hut, holding back the wide-eyed children who were staring open-mouthed at the cloud of smoke and dust that floated from the roofless ice house. We reassured Barek that we were unharmed and walked over to check out the damage.I was amazed that the structure was still standing. The mortar had failed on a couple of blocks, and they had shifted out of position in the wall, but otherwise the thick stonework appeared sound. The interior was a mess of glass shards and bits of cloth. The walls were peppered with crushed pieces of glass which sparkled from the light coming in through the now open roof.

I noticed an unfamiliar acrid smell in the air and heard Ebnik sniff as well. "Nicely laid trap," he said with admiration. "I probably triggered it when I raised the Shield. It smells like he used Flash Powder. It's risky to carry around, but makes for a spectacular parting message."

Flash Powder made sense. When it was encased in a container, igniting it created an explosion. At one time, men had tried to use it to create weapons that fired a projectile, but the stuff was notoriously easy for enemy sorcerers to ignite from afar, which made it dangerous to keep nearby.

Ebnik smiled at me. "It's a good thing you are a sound Sensitive," he said. "Paeter covered the device with a cloth, so I was unable to see the manifestation, but fortunately you were still able to hear it. Otherwise, that would be us scattered around the ice house."

I shuddered at the grisly mental image. "I'll add that to the score I need to settle with Lord Thoron. We should go after him before he gets too far. Can you track him with sorcery?"

Ebnik waved his hand in dismissal. "He's long gone under a Veil by now. I'd need something of his to track him with sorcery, and although this cloth might have done the job, the explosion will have cleansed any signature residue that might have remained within it. I'm sure he had this escape planned from the moment he arrived here."

Our conversation was interrupted by cries of despair as the villagers came running down the road into the square and saw the destroyed ice house. Sulana and Talon ran over to where Barek, Ebnik, and I were standing, looking us over for injury as they approached. Daven followed at a slower pace, favoring his injured arm.

"Thank the spirits," Sulana gasped out as she approached. "I was afraid you'd all be dead when I heard the explosion."

Ebnik placed a hand on my shoulder. "We probably would be if not for Jaylan's quick thinking. He heard the manifestation before it blew up and hurried us out of there just in time."

Sulana narrowed her eyes and surveyed the damage to the ice house. "Paeter has a lot to answer for."

CHAPTER 25

The villagers crowded around the ice house, mumbling words of dismay. Edanos kicked one of the scattered glass chunks, cursing sorcery in general and Lord Thoron in particular. The rest of us got out of their way and gathered near the stable.

Sulana asked Edanos and Sati to join us. She still had questions about how the situation with Lord Thoron had come about. Edanos declined, saying he had to help the others clean up and plan the restoration of the ice house. Sati stayed with us and told us what happened.

Sati explained how Lord Thoron and another man had come to the village by boat a couple of weeks earlier. They initially claimed they were in Buckwoods to buy fish, but the second man grabbed one of the children and held a knife to the poor little boy's throat. The two men had used the threat against the child's life to coerce the villagers into accepting the amulets they had brought with them. Lord Thoron proceeded to set up shop in the ice house with the help of the villagers. The second man left the village as soon as Lord Thoron was situated, and he took the boat with him.

Jake, the wagon driver, spoke up at that point and described how he and the Raven Company men had ended up in Buckwoods. He had just finished loading his wagon at the Delta Glassworks when a stranger approached him. The man asked about his destination, and after being told, used a magic device to immobilize Jake and force one of the amulets on him. Under the influence of the amulet's spells, Jake was eager to join his fellow Guardians at Buckwoods and extremely uncomfortable being surrounded by "outsiders" in Delta.

Kefer nodded slowly, a sudden look of comprehension in his eyes. "That explains why Jake was so nervous when Peltor and I first arrived to escort him. We got into Delta a little late, and he was just about ready to leave without us. When he insisted on detouring to Buckwoods, we thought it was odd but figured the side trip had already been cleared with Borlan."

Kefer's features turned grim. "When we arrived at the village, we met Lord Thoron. He used that orb thing on me and someone clobbered Peltor from behind. Lord Thoron put amulets on us both and recruited us to help him defend the village."

Sulana turned to Ebnik. "I'll bet the second man was the one Raleb told us about. Raleb is one of the thieves who were hired to steal your Portal Key. Two weeks was plenty of time for that man to go down to Plains End, hire the thieves, and get back up to Delta to hijack the glass shipment."

"But what's this all about?" Daven asked. "You make it sound like this all fits together somehow."

Sulana compressed her lips and nodded at Daven. "I think it does. Paeter is trying to manufacture a lot of these amulets." Her hand went to her chest and raised her amulet to emphasize the point. "But it was taking too long. They probably scouted for weeks before discovering this village. Buckwoods was just what he needed. The ice house was the perfect work space, and Paeter had a ready supply of vaetra... contributors." She glanced over at Sati, who dropped her gaze to the ground and blushed at the oblique mention of her Contribution Ceremony.

Ebnik agreed with her assessment. "He could never have produced an amulet a day under normal circumstances. He needed a steady supply of vaetra and an efficient means of storing and retrieving it," he said. He looked over at the ice house. "I doubt this arrangement was meant to be permanent. It was probably a prototype. With enough people under his control, he could set up a much more elaborate facility in a more remote location."

As the conversation turned to matters of sorcery, Jake backed away from the group and walked over to his wagon. The wagon had been placed alongside the ice house, so the walls shielded it from damage. Most of the detritus from the roof had landed beyond the wagon. Jake brushed some loose pieces of thatching from the cover tarp and lifted it to see what was left of his shipment. He didn't look too disturbed by what he saw, so I guessed his cargo was not too far short of the ordered amount. The amulets were fairly small, and Lord Thoron couldn't have consumed more than a few of the raw glass blocks.

Meldon watched Jake as well, and then with a glance at me, walked over to help Jake ready the wagon. Sati stayed nearby, but her attention was mostly on the activities of the other villagers.

"What about the ring?" asked Daven, bringing my attention back to the conversation.

Sulana paced as she spoke, her eyes followed the ground but focused on nothing. "The only purpose for these amulets is to control people. Paeter is planning something, and he obviously has help. Whatever he has in mind, he needs the Portal Key so he can quickly move around the region. Maybe he needs to coordinate multiple efforts going on around the empire, or he needs to be able to move into an area with stealth. Or both."

"With a Portal Key, he could move a small force to within easy striking distance of a target. Like the Archives," Ebnik added.

Sulana stopped pacing and stared at Ebnik. "Would he be so bold? He would need a small army of sorcerers to even try taking over the Archives."

Ebnik raised an eyebrow. "He already has help from at least one other sorcerer that we know of."

"What can we do?" she asked. "He got away from us here."

Ebnik shrugged. "There's not much we *can* do right now. We'll have to alert our contacts around the empire and wait until he surfaces again."

Kefer looked over at the corral, checking the horses and mules that remained. "You can add horse thief to his list of crimes," he grumbled. "My horse and Peltor's are gone. He must have taken mine."

Sulana frowned. "I forgot about this Peltor person. Do you suppose he is still under the Protector enchantment, or did he go willingly?" She looked at me for an answer.

I considered her question for a moment. "In order to sneak out of here without anyone sensing them, they would have to disable the amulets. But I think Peltor would jump at the chance to work with someone less...lawfully-minded than Borlan. Do you agree Kefer?"

Kefer shrugged. Although none of the Raven Company members got along very well with Peltor, Kefer had been the most tolerant of Peltor's dark moods. "I suppose. He wasn't particularly happy at Raven Company, but I don't think he'd be happy anywhere. The promise of power or riches might have convinced him to join whatever cause this Lord Thoron has going."

Ebnik turned to Sati with an apologetic bow. "I'm sorry your village has received such unfortunate treatment from one of our kind. Please understand that we of the Archives actively seek to prevent such interference. Is there anything I can do to help repair some of the damage that has been done here? I could, if you wish, freeze some lake water into blocks you could use to restock your ice house."

Sati looked at Ebnik while she considered his suggestion and then shook her head. "It will be some time before the roof is repaired, and I believe my people have had enough of magic for one lifetime. Your offer is generous, but I doubt it would be well received. Thank you anyway." She walked off to help with the ice house cleanup.

Ebnik shook his head and sighed as she walked away. I knew how he felt. It was hard to undo some kinds of damage.

∿

Barek and Talon went to retrieve the horses that were still alongside the road outside the village, leaving Sulana, Daven, Ebnik and me standing near the corral.

Patches whickered for attention, and I walked over to him, reaching across the fence to rub his nose. "We'll be heading back soon, boy," I consoled him. I was relieved that Lord Thoron had chosen Kefer's horse instead of mine for his escape, although I did feel bad for Kefer.

"Is that your plan? To go back home now?" Sulana asked from behind me. She came forward to stand next to me at the corral.

I looked at her and our eyes locked. Her tone had revealed nothing about any feelings that might lie behind her question, but searching her blue eyes, I knew my answer mattered to her. I said nothing for a moment, just taking in her features, my pulse quickening under her attention.

Ebnik looked at the two of us and motioned Daven to come away with him and leave us alone for a moment. Daven turned away reluctantly and followed the old sorcerer.

I watched her closely as I answered. "I think I have to go back." Her face stiffened. "At least for a little while." Her eyes widened a bit. "I have a lot of things to wrap up if I'm going to be gone for an extended time." She looked down and a smile teased at the corners of her mouth.

"Does this mean you're going to the Archives to learn more about sorcery?" This time there was no mistaking the hope in her voice. She looked up at me expectantly.

I nodded. "I can't ignore my abilities, whatever they may be, any longer. Besides, I have a score to settle with Paeter Thoron, and I wouldn't stand a chance against him without being better able to defend myself."

Sulana reached out and touched my forearm. "You can't go after him yourself! Paeter has years of experience, and he has help as well. It will be a long time before you can expect to challenge him."

"I didn't say I'd be going after him alone," I said with a sidelong look at her.

She looked down and blushed. "No, of course not. The Archives will want to stop him from doing anything like this again," she said, gesturing toward the working villagers. "You do realize that the Archives will probably send a team out as soon as we get a lead on Paeter's whereabouts," she cautioned me. "That could happen before you are ready to join in the hunt."

"Then I'll just have to learn fast." I answered with a smile.

She rolled her eyes. "Oh, sure. It's easy. It's just taken me most of my life to get good enough to lead a team."

I held up my hands in surrender. "Sorry. I was making a joke. I have no idea what I'm getting myself into here. I'm just trying to be optimistic about the future."

She stepped forward, and suddenly our faces were only a few hand-spans apart. "Optimism. That's a good start," she said, her eyes looking steadily into mine.

My breath caught when she stepped forward. Having her so close sent chills from my head to my feet. I had to resist a strong desire to lean forward and kiss her. I smiled at her and found myself saying what my heart felt before I could think about it. "I'm optimistic about a lot of things."

She smiled back, and seemed like she might say more, but she suddenly realized where we were and looked around to locate Ebnik and Daven. They had both been watching us, but quickly looked away when she glanced over at them.

Ebnik redirected his attention down the road with a smirk, and Daven looked down at the ground with a frown.

She stepped back from me, and the tightness in my chest faded. I wanted to close the distance between us again, but knew that now was not the time to indulge the impulse. I had a lot of things I needed to deal with before I could even think about a relationship with Sulana. However, the revelation that she might share my interest in exploring that potential gave me added reason to seek training at the Archives where I might stay near her.

~

We bid the villagers farewell before taking our leave. Their responses were mixed. Some thanked us for freeing them from Lord Thoron's bizarre form of slavery. Others practically ignored us, mostly thankful that we were finally going away. All of them were more than willing to hand their amulets over to Ebnik. No one expressed any interest in keeping one as a souvenir.

By the time we had said our goodbyes, the delivery wagon was ready to move on as well. The wagon rolled up alongside me and stopped. Meldon had joined the driver on the bench seat. Kefer rode alongside on Meldon's horse.

Meldon called down to me as they stopped. "Jaylan, I'm going to help Kefer escort the delivery down to Plains End. We'll pick up another horse down there and head back to Northshore as soon as we're done. Do you think Borlan would be okay with that?"

"I'm sure those would be his orders if he were here. When I get back to Northshore, I'll fill him in on what's been happening."

Kefer spoke up. "Thanks. It would be nice if we didn't have to delay the shipment any longer by having to stop and explain on our way down. Jake thinks we have enough cargo left to satisfy the recipient even though we're a little short."

"Don't worry about it. Good luck. And may your trip be uneventful."

All three of them chuckled and the driver flipped his reins to get the draft mule moving again. Kefer and Meldon waved as the wagon rolled off in a clatter of creaking wheels and clopping hooves.

I waved back, wondering when I would see them again. By the time they returned to Northshore, I might very well be on my way to the Archives. I thought about my impending conversation with Borlan. I wondered how he would take the news of what happened here and how it affected my future plans. Then I thought about the much harder conversation I would need to have with Dela. I was certain she would be far less understanding than Borlan.

I collected Patches, leaving the village mule alone once again in the corral that had recently been rather overpopulated with other animals. Patches stood still while I saddled him up. He didn't even play any of his usual games of expanding his chest while I tightened the cinch. I think he was glad to be headed home at last.

I climbed into the saddle and settled myself in. Sulana and her team were already mounted and waiting patiently for me at the head of the road. I urged Patches into a walk and we ambled over to them. I took one last look around the village, thinking how much had changed for me in the short time I had been there. Buckwoods would forever be a place of endings and beginnings for me.

We rode out without another look back.

∼

It was nearly dusk by the time we left the village, so our group stopped overnight at a large Imperial Guard camp site between Delta and Northshore. The Imperial Guard maintained large camp sites around the empire, and traveling citizens were welcome to use them when the Guard was not.

We had passed Jake's wagon on the road, but they caught up to us and stopped at the same place. That turned out to be fortunate, because neither Meldon nor I had packed for an overnight stay when we'd left Northshore. It would have been a cold night for me, but the driver had a couple of extra blankets he was willing to share. He also had a two-man tent, so Meldon and Kefer were able to take turns keeping watch and sleeping in relative comfort.

Since we were still traveling together, I split the watch with them, taking the first shift. Meldon curled up next to the fire and promptly fell asleep.

I sat on a log near the fire and stared up at the stars thinking about the future. I looked at my hands, turning them over in the flickering light of the campfire at my back, wondering if these were the hands of a sorcerer. Were my days as a Raven Company man over forever? Would Dela hate me when I told her what I was and that I was leaving? How did one make a living as a sorcerer?

The soft crunch of leaves and needles alerted me to someone approaching the fire from the camp behind me. I stood and turned around to discover Sulana walking over from where her team was camped nearby. Over at their fire, Talon and Ebnik sat near each other and were engaged in quiet conversation.

"May I share your fire for a moment?" Sulana asked me quietly with a smile.

Her features were emphasized by the firelight reflecting off her face, making a halo of her blond hair. Shadows deepened her dimples, and reflections of the firelight danced in her eyes. I was struck by how such a strong woman could have such delicate beauty.

"Please do. I could use the conversation...and the distraction," I said.

She came over and we sat down next to each other with our backs to the fire. "You do have a lot to think about, don't you?"

"Yes, it's more than my poor mind can handle at the moment."

"Anything I can do to help?"

"I don't know. I'm concerned that I might be running away from something, rather than running toward something."

"What do you mean?"

"Well, there's Raven Company. My commitment to Borlan is almost up anyway, so leaving won't be a problem there. He'll be disappointed because he's short-handed right now, but he's used to dealing with that. Since things picked up, the last few jobs have been...harrowing. But that describes a lot of the work I've done in the past, and there's no reason to believe things will get any better if I learn sorcery."

I glanced at her, and she just nodded, letting me go on.

"Then there's the inn and Dela. From the beginning, my role was to be that of a silent partner, but then Dela's father Griz died. I couldn't just leave her and her mother on their own, so I found myself becoming increasingly involved in the running of the inn. That's a job I never wanted. At the same time, Dela decided it was all meant to be. Well, that we were meant to be together. But..."

"You don't love her." Sulana said softly.

My brow furrowed. "No, I do love her, but not like that. I don't want to *marry* her. I've known her since she was a child, and to me she still is, even though she has grown into a capable woman. I guess...I guess I love her like a sister, but it would break her heart to hear me say that."

Sulana glanced back over her shoulder at her camp site. "I think I understand. Daven and I have known each other since we were both children, and I love him like a brother. I think he wants more from me than I'm able to give."

I snorted. "You think?"

She gave me a light punch on the arm. "Hey, we're sharing serious stuff here," she protested.

"Sorry. Daven has made his feelings about *me* abundantly clear since the beginning."

She shrugged. "He's jealous."

I half-turned toward her and looked deeply into her eyes. "Does he have anything to be jealous of?" I asked her seriously.

She returned my stare, keeping a straight face, but her eyes took on a mischievous glint. "You tell me."

I took advantage of the moment to luxuriate in our closeness and her attention. That tingling sensation and tightness in my chest had returned. "I certainly hope so." I slid my hand over to cover hers.

She smiled and turned her hand over and twined her fingers into mine. "There you go being optimistic again. Where there's hope, there's possibility." She broke eye contact and looked down at the ground. "Did it help to talk about what's on your mind?"

I was silent for a moment, looking at her profile, taking in the soft curve of her neck and the firelight glowing in the hair that fell down along her back.

"I think so. Nothing will make it easy, but knowing more about the alternatives is always a good thing."

We sat on the log hand-in-hand through most of my watch. We said little more. Mostly, we just enjoyed the moment of silence and nearness to each other. Having her support eased my fears and gave me courage to face the uncertainties of the future.

Tomorrow would be the beginning of a new day, and for me, a new life.

ACKNOWLEDGEMENTS

I could not have written this book without the friends and family who helped shape my past and continue to influence my life today. I'd first like to thank my wife, who is my best friend and my #1 supporter. Thanks to my mom Suzanne for always telling me that I can do whatever I set my mind to and for encouraging me to read at an early age. Thanks to my brother Glenn and sister Monique for their enthusiastic support of my fiction-writing goals.

My critique partners and beta readers were essential in helping me refine the story and improve my writing. I owe special thanks to Cynthia Daffron, Kathy Goughenour, and Paul Sheriff for their encouragement and their critique.

I'd also like to thank Gary Gygax and Dave Arneson for filling my head with fantasy adventures, mythical creatures, and a taste for magic back in the 70's and 80's as I played Dungeons and Dragons with my friends. I had no idea back then that my creative efforts as a Dungeon Master would one day grow into a desire to write a fantasy novel.

I would be remiss to leave out a mention of Bethesda Softworks. If I hadn't gotten so deeply wrapped up in Oblivion, I never would have reached the conclusion that I needed to do something more creative with my time and imagination.

ABOUT THE AUTHOR

Daniel R. Marvello writes fantasy adventure stories from his log home on forty acres of forested land in the North Idaho panhandle. The setting for his Vaetra Chronicles book series was inspired by the scenic beauty of his surroundings. Daniel shares his home with his loving wife of 20 years and several wonderful animals. He hopes to one day own a horse like Patches.

Visit the Vaetra Chronicles Web site at:
www.Vaetra.com

Visit Daniel's blog at:
www.DanielRMarvello.com

CPSIA information can be obtained at www.ICGtesting.com
Printed in the USA
BVOW011048090212

282564BV00001B/1/P